# IN OVER HER HEAD

LAUDERDALE SERIES

BOOK 1

DEBORAH BROWN

This book is a work of fiction. Names, characters, places and incidents are either the product of the author's imagination or used fictitiously. Any resemblance to actual persons, living or dead, or to actual events or locales is entirely coincidental. The author has represented and warranted full ownership and/or legal right to publish all materials in this book.

This book may not be reproduced, transmitted, or stored in whole or in part by any means, including graphic, electronic, or mechanical without the express written permission of the author except in the case of brief quotations embodied in critical articles and reviews.

IN OVER HER HEAD
All Rights Reserved
Copyright © 2022 Deborah Brown

ISBN-13: 979-8-9859189-2-2

Cover: Natasha Brown


PRINTED IN THE UNITED STATES OF AMERICA

# IN OVER HER HEAD

# Chapter One

"Dearly beloved, we are gathered here today to–"

"Hold up, are you even a real lawyer?" I stopped short of barking, but just barely. What the heck was going on? I stared down at the dark-haired man who sat behind the desk, exuding arrogance. The lawyer—what was his name again? I looked at his nameplate: Martin Richards—hadn't wiped the smug look off his face since I'd stepped into his office.

"Don't get your shorts in a bunch, Maren North," Pops barked. "It was my idea that such a solemn occasion could use a little humor."

As if this day hadn't started out weird enough. My grandfather had called at an hour early for him and demanded my appearance at his lawyer's office. *No excuses*, he'd barked, and I'd thought that it would be a first to turn him down on *anything* he asked, as I'd never done so in the past. I attempted to get a detail or two out of him about what the meeting was about, but he brushed me off, more tight-lipped than ever.

"As you well know, Maxwell North, we're related, which would make that incest and illegal."

"You got it all turned around." Pops shook his head. "I called you here because it's my intention to split my estate between you and your father, and a few things need to be taken care of now… in particular, my private investigation business."

"Your estate? Don't know if you've heard, but wills usually aren't read until after the person's croaked. You look healthy to me, old man."

"No one lives forever."

"You're ornery enough to do just that. Are we waiting for Mom and Dad to show, assuming you could get them off their boat?" I glanced at the closed office door. "I'm thinking your son would like to know how much of your loot you left him."

"This meeting is just you and me."

"And him," I said, glancing at the lawyer's nameplate as if I didn't already know what it said. I was happy to see his lips compressed into a firm line and hoped I annoyed him as much as he did me.

"Although I'm not on death's door—yet, anyway—it was suggested to me that I get my affairs in order."

I shot Smugness a look, wondering if there was something in it for him besides legal fees.

"As you know, I've built North Investigations into a thriving company, and in the last year, it's suffered from my neglect," Pops continued. "It's my hope that you'll take it over and run it. I'm thinking the income would be helpful to offset any expenses for my care."

"You know I'd do anything for you, Pops, but have you forgotten that I'm not the least bit qualified to fill your shoes?" A voice actress was a far cry from a private investigator. In both careers, learning didn't happen overnight and required a lot of hard work.

"You're a smart woman," Pops said with more assurance than I felt. "I wouldn't expect you to do it all by yourself. I imagine you'll hire a team to help you get North back on its feet and take on any new jobs."

"Would you mind giving us a minute?" I asked Mr. Smugness.

The lawyer's tight-lipped expression was back, and he leaned forward. "There's paperwork to sign." He tapped his pricey pen on the desk.

"I'm hoping you're going to make this old man happy and go along with my idea. Any questions that come up, I'll only be a phone call away," Pops assured me.

From the smile on his face, I expected a pat on the head. "Pops—" I lowered my voice, knowing that the lawyer could still hear every word. "—have you lost your mind? I have to reiterate—not qualified."

"You've proven yourself smart as a whip, and I have every confidence in you." He motioned to Richards, who produced a folder, flipping it open.

*That makes one of us.* "I think we should hold off until we can have a long discussion, just the two of us. I'm certain we'll come up with someone eminently more qualified."

"This is the right decision, and the running of the place is something we can figure out as we go." Pops motioned for Richards to hand him the pen.

Except I already had a business and knew that "figure it out as you go" was a poor business model.

The lawyer slapped down a stack of papers, which told me this idea of Pops' had been in the works for a while and wasn't conjured up overnight. How do you say no to a man you've adored your entire life and would never purposely disappoint? The answer was very clear when I signed as directed—you wouldn't.

Once all the papers were signed, and we'd been handed copies, Pops stood. "I have a couple of things in the car for you."

"I'm assuming that if I have any questions, I can also call you?" I asked the lawyer, tight-lipped.

"Of course," he said dismissively. It was clear he wanted us out of his office.

I followed Pops out the door and into the parking lot. The law office overlooked US-1 and was a block down the street from North Investigation, with a variety of commercial businesses in between. One learned quickly, working in this area, that you needed to watch your timing or you'd end up parked in the three lanes of traffic that ran in each direction.

Pops popped the trunk on his older-model Mercedes and pulled out a small box.

I didn't have time to think about what surprises the box held because I was too busy trying to come up with a way out, despite having already signed the papers taking control of the business. Ones I hadn't read… yet. "You know I love you, but you've lost your mind."

"You told me that already." Pops chuckled. "You're wrong, girlie, and I have every confidence that you will prove it to me."

"You're throwing me into the deep end, and it's a big assumption that I won't sink." I wasn't one to suffer an attack of nerves, but they were on fire at the moment, and admonitions to myself to calm down weren't working.

"I've got faith that you won't let me down. Once you have a stiff drink, you'll agree with me." Pops headed over to my SUV, and I opened the liftgate. He set the box in the back and slammed it shut.

"We're going to your office so I can talk some sense into you?"

"This old man's headed home to put his feet up and catch a nap." At my intake of breath, Pops said, "There's nothing to worry about. The older you get, the more you look forward to closing your eyes for a few during the day." He pulled a keyring out of his pocket. "You're going to need these."

When I didn't take them, he grabbed my hand

and closed my fingers around the keys. "You're going to do fine. Stop by the office and have a look around; nothing's changed since you were there last." Taking note of my deer-in-the-headlights look, he added, "There are no appointments scheduled, but once word gets out that North Investigations is open for business again, the phones will blow up."

Just swell. "Maybe we should—"

He shook his head and leaned in for a hard hug and a kiss. "I know you're the one to get North back in the black again. If you have any questions, call me. I'm always available. And know that I love you." Kissing my cheek again, he walked back to his car. Once behind the wheel, he honked and, with a wave, shot out of the parking lot.

I stood and stared as his car turned into traffic and eventually disappeared. My mind was a complete blank, and it took me a couple of minutes to remember the box. Curiosity got the better of me, and I opened the liftgate and gave the box a slight shake before opening it. I lifted out a ledger and, after a quick scan of the box, was disappointed to see there was nothing else. Though I wasn't certain what I expected. The worn book was so old, it was hard to believe that this kind was still for sale. I thumbed through the pages, which were nothing more than lists of numbers with very few notations. I threw it back in the box in disgust and got behind the wheel.

The office was a two-minute drive down the

street. On the way to the front door, I took note of the half-dozen cars in the parking lot and the signage of companies that had leased offices for years without a change. I rode the elevator to the third floor, and when I stepped off, the first thing that caught my attention was that the entire floor was eerily quiet. If North shared the floor with anyone else, you wouldn't know it by the doors, as none sported a sign.

Unlocking the door, I poked my head inside before throwing it wide open. Okay — it needed a good cleaning. The place was thick with dust, and the dead bugs needed to be relocated. I took a quick walk around, opening all the cupboards and the storage closet, finding everything empty, then sat in Pops' chair behind his desk. In the top drawer were a couple of paper clips, and in the bottom a laptop that had been overlooked. It appeared to be older than Pops and left me wondering when he'd last spent any time here. I took it out and set the keys on top of it. The rest of the drawers were empty.

This was a bad idea, but Pops didn't want to hear that there was no way I could get the business up and running again. How? That one word had danced through my head numerous times since he told me what he was planning to do. I got up and brushed off the back of my dress, eager to get outside and back to my car, not the least bit bothered by making this a short visit.

# Chapter Two

The Coffee Bar sign up ahead caught my eye, reminding me that I was in dire need of a shot of caffeine to perk me up and clear my muddled mind. A fresh-baked muffin would also help. I jerked the wheel and entered the parking lot, squeezing into the first available spot. Lost in thought, I made my way inside, got what I wanted without having to wait, and headed back out, undecided on whether to sit inside or out, as neither held any interest.

Suddenly, someone called my name, startling me out of my funk. I turned and saw Rella Cabot—a friend from high school with whom I'd stayed in touch, however sporadically—waving me over to her table. The two women with her looked vaguely familiar, and I recognized their names when she introduced them as Harper and Avery. They were laughing and enjoying themselves, and besides not wanting to intrude, I didn't want to be a killjoy, so I declined the offer to take a seat.

"Some business issues came up, and I need to get back to my office and find an accountant to help me sift through some financial matters." I stepped back.

"Look no further," Avery said. She bent down and picked up her purse, rooted around inside, and came back with a business card in hand. "I'm not currently active in the business, but call my partner, Dixon Monroe, and he'll be able to set you up with someone highly qualified."

"I really appreciate the referral; someone who comes recommended will help lower my anxiety level on this project." I wanted to sigh over having one less thing to worry about but held it in.

"Any other recommendations you need, Dixon's a good one to ask," Harper said. "We have a network of people, and it's easy to put the word out."

"When I'm not feeling so overwhelmed, I'd like to take the three of you to lunch as a thank-you." I smiled at them. "The best part of my day has been running into you."

As soon as I got back in my car, I called the number on the card, introduced myself, and told Dixon Monroe how I'd gotten his number. Then told him about Pops ledger and that it appeared to be a nonsensical mess. To my surprise, he sounded excited by the prospect of looking over the records himself. Though he wasn't exactly local, he assured me that it was no problem, as he had a meeting with a client in the area in two days and suggested we meet then.

My first thought was to invite him to my house, but I quickly changed my mind. Before I could come up with something else, Dixon suggested a coffee place on Ft. Lauderdale Beach that I knew from the address would be, if not right on the water, close enough for a good view. I agreed, and we arranged a time.

I then called Pops to get the number of the cleaning service for the office, telling him, "They haven't done a very good job keeping the place up."

He laughed, which annoyed me. "Not to worry; it'll be taken care of today," he assured me. "Happy to hear that you jumped right in. Knew I could count on you."

Another bout of guilt surged through me as I was about to blurt out, *But I can't do it*, and instead, I said, "Do you know what other businesses are on the third floor?"

"The owner got lax when he paid off the building and hasn't kept the spaces rented. No worry about him, as he's seldom around," Pops said, blowing it off.

Finally, back home, I cruised into the driveway of my small two-bedroom house in a neighborhood that boasted houses with much larger square footage. I'd worked a deal with the previous owner, assuring her that I wouldn't be leveling the property to construct a mini-mansion. The front door opened into a wide-open space that encompassed the kitchen and living room, which was my comfort zone. On the far wall was an extra-long sliding door that opened onto the patio and dock that overlooked the New River.

The kitchen was chaos; the walls ripped back to the studs before the work was deserted by the construction company I'd hired. They'd gone out of business, though I'd heard recently that they'd opened under another name. The only appliances left were the refrigerator and microwave. Although skeptical at first, I found out that I could cook almost anything in the micro.

I walked over to the couch and set everything down. Before sitting, I pulled out a box of assorted cords I had stashed in the closet. Rummaging through it, I found a charger that would fit the old laptop and got it plugged in, setting it on the floor. I'd forgotten to mention it to Pops and wouldn't until I figured out if it held any useful information about the business.

Grabbing a cold water and making myself comfortable, I flipped through the ledger and perused one page of numbers after another. Most of it made no sense, as it was poorly organized and what explanation there was, was barely decipherable. I fully expected this Dixon fellow to take one look, laugh, and be long gone before I could blink.

Fishing my laptop out of my briefcase, the first thing I did was check my email—nothing new from my current clients, which was a relief. I knew I'd have to put some significant time into figuring out what I was doing with Pops' business at first. After that, I'd have to juggle the two jobs, as I wasn't going to give up the company I built and loved for one I didn't have an affinity for.

Laughing at myself, I looked up, "How to be a PI." Could it be that easy? Going through the strict requirements was enough to give me a headache. It wasn't like one could just show up at some official office, pay a fee, and walk out with a certificate of "Lookie what I can do." Then there was the licensing of a gun, which I didn't have, and getting a permit to carry. A self-defense class was suggested, and I thought about the one I'd taken a couple of years back and tried to remember what I'd learned. I air-boxed and imagined kicking butt, which left me laughing. Tired of looking at all I'd have to do to be legit or appear so anyway, I snapped the lid shut and set the laptop on the table, nestled back against the couch cushions, and took a nap.

## Chapter Three

Dixon had chosen the Beach Café, a small building nestled on its own piece of the beach. I'd told him that I had shoulder-length sun-bleached brown hair that would be pulled into a ponytail and would have on a hot-pink sundress. When I walked out on the patio, I was relieved to see a man immediately begin waving at me and happy that he'd scored a table at the railing with an unobstructed view of the water.

He stood, and I saw he had on shorts and a dress shirt, which surprised me since he'd said he was coming from a business meeting. It was even more surprising that he looked barely twenty, if that, and his dark hair flopping down over his eyes.

We exchanged introductions, and I sat down.

"Know what you're thinking." Dixon eyed the ledger I'd set on the table with eager interest. "Although I look like a teenager, trust me I'm not and have verifiable credentials. You've met Avery, and it's a toss-up which of us is smarter, though I'd clearly say it's me."

"I don't know Avery and Harper as well as I do

Rella, but since neither woman spoke up and said, 'Hold on a second,' you got their okay."

"As a numbers nerd, your project interests me. Mind if I have a look?" He went back to eyeing the ledger hungrily. I handed it over.

The server came and took our drink order, and I went with cold and sweet, as did Dixon.

He flipped through the pages and chuckled a couple of times. "You mind if I ask what you hope to find out from these ancient, poorly kept records?"

"Would probably help if I gave you the backstory on how I got myself into this..." I waved my hand. "...thinking fiasco is a good description." I told him about being summoned to the meeting with my Pops and knew I was giving more details than necessary but didn't want to waste his time. Dixon chuckled a couple of times. "It's my hope that I can figure out if North has any hope of resurrection." I was happy when our drinks were set down in front of us, and took a long drink of my tropical concoction.

Dixon took out his phone. "I have a few questions."

"Does this mean you're taking the job?" Knowing that it wouldn't be easy, I tried to keep my surprise from showing.

"I take on a lot of cookie-cutter clients, and when one comes along that's anything but, I'm in." Dixon smiled. "Avery would do the same, except that now that she's teamed up with her husband, the two stay busy with their clients."

I wondered doing what but wasn't going to ask, as it wasn't any of my business. Dixon fired off a few questions and typed my responses on his phone.

"I'll send you a comprehensive report, which will include a background check, and from that, you'll know the state of the corporation and what it will take to get it up and running again. I'll also include anything that I'm able to figure out from the ledger and any other facts I can ferret out. When I'm done, you'll have enough information to decide whether it's worth the expense of reopening the doors. If it turns out that you need to tell your grandfather 'Sorry…' and whatever reason you give, I know it won't be easy. I've had a few clients that didn't want to hear 'Don't pour money down a rathole.'"

"You just described my Pops' attitude to a tee," I said with a shake of my head. Dixon chuckled. "During the ambush… I mean, meeting with Pops, my mind felt muddled, as the whole time, I was trying to come up with a good reason to back out, and even two days later, I still haven't come up with a good enough reason to mute his disappointment."

"That's a tough one. If it turns out that the numbers don't add up, maybe that's the way to get through to him. You can sit your Pops down and go over it all with him. Or if you need me to do it, I'm more than happy."

"Pops has been a businessman forever, and I can't see him wanting to run in the red if he knew that was the situation. Hopefully, he'd understand." I smiled weakly and thought, *And no hurt feelings.*

"Another thing—when I'm finished with my report, you'll be able to put together a budget, and I can make recommendations for people you could hire. Since you lack experience, you might want to think about hiring someone who can show you the ropes as part of the deal. I can get you plenty of referrals from a PI firm in the same building as Avery and me. Even though they're out of Miami Beach, a few live locally and take side jobs. It would be a good way to start—hire one or two investigators, and then add more as you need them."

Dixon told me that he'd need at least ten days, after which he'd give me a call, and we'd set up another meeting. He said he'd like it to be at the North offices, as he wanted to check them out.

We both finished off our drinks and got up to leave, and he walked me to my car.

"You really should upgrade." Dixon pointed to Pops' laptop, which I'd left on the passenger seat.

Thank goodness this was a low-crime area, as I should've covered it. "I found it while snooping around the North offices." *Ssh*, I crossed my lips. He laughed. "Found a cord for it, let it charge overnight, and nothing. Couldn't get it turned on and thought I'd drop it at the repair shop down the street." I unlocked the door.

"You should have a referral for repair work since it can be a crapshoot what kind of service you'll get." Dixon picked the laptop up and eyed it. "How about I have a look and see if I can bring it back to life? If not, I've got a guy that can fix anything electronic. I'd call you with a quote before having him do anything with it, so you'd know what it would take to breathe life back into it."

"I appreciate Avery's referral—you're turning out to know everyone and their brother." I grinned at him.

"You wouldn't believe all the information I shove in my brain. It's fun to take it out and share it with someone else," Dixon assured me. "Don't worry about any of this. When I'm done, I'll be able to advise you on your next step, which won't include wasting any money."

"I look forward to our next meeting." I watched as he walked over to a two-seater Jeep—an older model that had been sanded and primed, specks of paint showing that it had once been red. I expected it to cough and grumble out of the parking lot, blowing black smoke, but it ran like a charm.

# Chapter Four

As it turned out, Dixon needed extra time, and he got no complaint from me as I was dragging my feet trying to figure out which end was up. Surprisingly, Pops hadn't bugged the heck out of me, wanting to know every five minutes if I was open for business and had clients lined up. He apparently trusted that I would come around. I made one trip to the office to ensure the cobwebs and dead roaches were gone. Remembering that the chair behind Pops' desk wasn't all that comfortable, I also took in a pillow for later.

Finally, Dixon called and said he'd finished going over the ledger. I offered again to go to his office, but he insisted he'd come to mine. My first official meeting, and he was right on time, but that didn't surprise me.

"Help yourself." I pointed to the new coffee maker before he could sit down. I'd purchased it yesterday, along with mugs, an assortment of necessary items, and a variety of pods, hopefully avoiding complaints about a yucky brew.

"The laptop is with my guy. He got bogged down but promised it would be ready in a couple of days." Dixon sat down, glancing around the office as he stirred his coffee. "I feel compelled to disclose that these are the worst-kept records I've ever seen. If you want my opinion…" He waited for my response.

Ignoring the pit in my stomach, I nodded.

"It's clear that whoever kept them, in addition to not knowing what they were doing, didn't really care. Once I realized that even with my talents, there was no way to make sense of the expenditures, since in most cases they weren't documented, I stopped."

"Millicent ran the office for what seemed like ever, but she moved out of state a couple of years ago. Pops isn't a disorganized person, but it wouldn't surprise me if he hadn't gotten around to looking at the records after she left. It's disappointing the books won't be able to tell me what kind of shape the business is in."

"There's more than one way to get information on a business, and I went ahead and did some investigating of my own. Hope you won't find that too intrusive, but I was curious." He shot me a big smile.

The door flew open, and an older, wild-haired woman waltzed into the room and twirled around before stopping and looking around.

*Mental note: next time, lock the door.* "How can I help you?" I pasted on a smile as I caught Dixon's wide-eyed expression.

"I'm looking for the owner—Maxi." The woman continued looking around, and it wasn't clear what she was expecting to find, as she hadn't paused on anything in particular.

"If you mean Maxwell North, he isn't in the office this morning. I'd be happy to help you." I caught Dixon's grin before he could hide it, which almost made me laugh.

"You must be Maren. Maxi's shared more than a few stories about you. You're all grown up now." Not waiting for a response, she turned her attention to Dixon. "And who are you?"

"This is Daniel, one of our top investigators," I cut in before Dixon could respond. The made-up name didn't faze him in the slightest. "I don't want to be rude, but we're in a meeting."

"You're not quite what I envisioned." She nodded at Dixon, then flexed her biceps. "Would've thought Maxi would hire someone more muscley. But you'll do." She hopped up on the smaller desk across the room.

"And you are?" Dixon asked.

"That would be helpful." The woman tittered and kicked her legs back and forth. "Caturday Ginseng." She waved to us.

I looked down and bit my lip before I could burst out laughing. Recovering, I raised my head and made eye contact. "What's your real name?"

"You know how many times people have asked that question? I changed it legally a year ago. It's so much more fun than Mildred." She danced around on her butt on the desktop.

*Okay.* I nodded. "How can we help you, Ms. Ginseng?"

"Please, that's so formal. Call me Caturday." Her arms flew in the air, and she waved her hands around. The woman didn't know how to sit still. "I need you to find my husband so I can make him my ex."

Good thing I'd been reading and re-reading the PI 101 book and knew that this type of job was fairly easy, as it could probably be accomplished with a background check that would hopefully lead to a current address. "We can handle that for you." I opened my phone to make a couple of notes. "Did your husband also change his name?"

"Heck, no… his name is Herbie Brogan. He made it clear he thought I was nuts for changing mine. Who cares what he thinks? Half the time, he doesn't even listen. Then he went out and found my replacement and now tangoes elsewhere. Frankly, I breathed a sigh of relief, as he had offensive habits." Caturday screwed up her nose.

"When we're able to get the address, do you have someone on standby to serve the divorce papers, or is that something you'd want us to do?" Dixon asked her.

*Good one.* I nodded at him.

Caturday leaned back and stared at the ceiling, making popping noises.

I tried to figure out what had her attention, hoping it wasn't a bug, but couldn't see anything.

"People can be so judgmental when they hear the word divorce." She straightened and wiggled, then jumped off the desk. Once she was steady, she twirled a couple of times, coming to a stop and leaning back against the edge, jutting out her hip.

"You did say ex. If not divorce, then what is it you want?" I asked.

"This is where your man will need to be on his game. Maxi assured me that there wasn't any job that couldn't be handled." Caturday eyed Dixon, her eyes narrow slits and her ditzy persona on hold, at least for the moment.

"When you spoke to *Maxi*, did you disclose all the details of the job?" I also wanted to know when *exactly* she'd spoken to Pops. "And did he, by chance, promise that he'd personally handle your case?" If so, we'd be chatting as soon as she left.

"Oh noooo." She waved her hand as though swatting away a fly. "No explicit promises, but it was implied."

"Why don't you tell us exactly what it is you need, and we'll be able to determine if we're a good fit for the job," Dixon told her, leaning forward, all ears.

"Our conversation is confidential, correct?" Her gaze flitted between us. "As in, you don't repeat one bleeping word. And no changing your minds at a later date."

"A non-disclosure agreement can be drawn up, if that would give you some reassurance." A little voice was telling, more like ordering, me to shove her butt out the door and lock it behind her.

"How about we agree that you don't screw me, and I won't serve up a smack-down on you?" Caturday fisted the air with one hand.

"We *are* going to need a few more details. If it's not something we do, then we'll refer you to someone that does," Dixon told her. I didn't know him well, but there was a clear "and hurry it up" in his tone.

"We've already established that I need you to locate my ex." She giggled.

"We got that part." His exasperation was showing. "You already told us you don't want a divorce, so what is it that you do want?"

"Once you've located Herbie, I want his residence searched for money and valuables, which will hopefully make a dent in repaying the credit card bills he ran up. I wasn't paying attention when he packed his bags, and he took cash, jewelry, and had a field day running up debt," Caturday hissed, clicking her teeth.

"Are you certain that Herbie was the one incurring the debt?" Dixon asked.

She hissed again. "This is what I told the bank when they contacted me demanding payment: 'Get off your hind ends and do some investigation,' and that if they did, they'd find that I hadn't made a single purchase. They told me that either way, I was responsible, as I should've taken his name off the account immediately, and my only recourse if he wouldn't pay was to take him to court."

She obviously didn't want to hear that.

"When I hung up, I beelined for the bank and withdrew all the money I had before they could put a hold on the accounts. Surprised me that they didn't do it immediately, but then, some people aren't the brightest bulbs." She was back to making gyrating movements.

Dixon and I exchanged a look that said we were also surprised.

"Once I got home, I contacted a lawyer about declaring bankruptcy, as I'm not about to pay back one dime of debt that I didn't run up."

"It's your intention to hire North Investigations to rob Herbie?" I couldn't believe I was even asking that.

"You can't expect *me* to do it," Caturday said in a snitty tone.

"After we recover what we can, and that's assuming Herbie's got anything lying around, then what?" Dixon asked.

It surprised me that he hadn't said, "There's the door." I was still stuck on the idea of stealing and couldn't believe my Pops would ever take such a job.

"Then you get rid of his body."

"Kill him?" I barely contained my shriek. First robbery and now murder? Had the woman lost her mind? I was now worried for Dixon's and my safety.

Dixon managed to maintain a neutral expression but did shake his head.

"The less mess the better. I realize that it'll create more paperwork if I want to marry again, but I have no intention of making that mistake a fourth time." Caturday eyed us. "You two appear to be squeamish. If that's the case, don't you think you're in the wrong business?"

Before I could tell her to get the hell out, Dixon spoke up. "What we can do is try to find Herbie, and if we're successful, then at that point, we can discuss options—ones where we don't all end up in prison."

"It's simple—you just don't leave blood and guts behind... although I doubt anyone would miss him. I know I won't." She appeared to be imagining the day Herbie took his last breath and enjoying it.

"What about the girlfriend?" The words tumbled out.

"Oh, her. She's certain to notice her meal ticket has disappeared, but maybe she'll think 'good riddance,' then move on and steal someone else's husband."

Dixon was far more on the ball than me—he asked a dozen questions about Herbie and took notes. I had no intention of taking the case but hesitated to tell her, wondering what she'd do when I made it clear that she'd never be a client. Dixon turned to me, careful to make sure Caturday couldn't see, and mouthed, *Business card.*

I opened the desk drawer, grabbed one of the

ones I'd printed off at home, and handed it over. He checked it out with amusement on his face. I scowled; it was a hokey last-minute job, but it was a card.

Dixon crossed the room to where Caturday, after a couple of dance moves, had gone back to lounging on the desk, and handed over the card. "As soon as we know anything, we'll be in touch." He held out his hand, she hooked her arm in his, and he showed her to the door.

It had barely closed behind her when I said, "We can't—"

The door flew open again.

## Chapter Five

A short, squat, middle-aged man rolled in the door in checked overalls, a bright yellow t-shirt, and a cowboy hat. "Mar here?" he barked. "Tell her Bobby Dill's here to see her."

Dixon sat down and shot me a quick smirk. I glared.

"Did you have an appointment? Mar got called out of the office unexpectedly," I lied.

"Heard you folks were looking for a PI, and here I am. Too bad you're not Mar; you're not half-bad looking."

"Not sure where you heard that we were hiring, as we're not open for business yet." And when we would be was still up in the air.

"Old man whatshisname told me." Bobby spat, and a toothpick shot out from between his lips.

I was happy that the projectile didn't end up on Dixon or me. It was lucky for us that Bobby had stayed at the door, one hand on the knob. Ready for a quick getaway, perhaps?

"Can't believe the old pooter would waste my time like this. I'm in hot demand." He thrust out his chest. "Had me some free time and thought I'd check it out." He took a card out of his pocket, took a few steps, and threw it on the desk.

I might've picked up the card if he hadn't wiped the back of his hand across his face and down his side before getting it out of his pocket.

"Tell Mar to ring me up, and we can get together. A drink or two loosens up any chick." He was clearly pleased with his impromptu plan.

"Her husband doesn't like it when she meets other men after work," I said.

"Well, poop. Could've sworn the old dude told me she was single. Oh well, have her give me a call anyway. Work's work." Bobby slammed the door with such gusto, I expected the building to sway.

"Would you mind locking the door?" I threw myself back in my chair. What the heck? Not one but two lunatics. Well, she was crazy; he was just… full of himself.

Dixon laughed all the way to the door. He stuck his head out, then locked it, and came back to sit in front of me. "Happy I didn't miss a second of this."

"I realize you didn't come here for this sideshow, but I'm so happy you were here. Can't thank you enough for interjecting with all the right questions for that Caturday woman and her outrageous demands. And that Bobby guy… just happy that you were here." There was so much to discuss, and I wasn't sure where to begin. "We'd just started talking about the financial shape of the company, and I want you to know that I always pay my bills. If you don't have your invoice on you, then email it."

"Take a breath." Dixon demonstrated. "North Investigations isn't going anywhere anytime soon and can afford plenty. Once I explain the finances to you, the budget and how to pay for things will be the least of your worries."

"I thought—"

"Just give me a chance to go over everything I was able to find out." He eyed the door as though he expected it to burst open again. "My first recommendation is to get a camera out in the hallway. When someone knocks, you can pull it up on your laptop or phone before letting anyone in. Unless you're planning to hire some burly fellow to sit at that desk." He nodded to the one Caturday had lolled over. "Can't tell you how many times I watched Avery grill clients, so I have a pretty good idea what to ask. Wait until I tell her I was on the grilling end. She'll probably call, so you need to back me up."

"What I'm going to do is scare Avery and tell her I'm snatching you away to come work here."

He laughed. "I'm all for pranking her, except I'm not certain it wouldn't come to a showdown, and I don't want anyone getting hurt. What did Caturday call it?" He laughed again.

"The whole time she talked, all I could think of was that I wanted her out. Don't you think Caturday Nip would've been better than Ginseng?"

The two of us laughed. Dixon recovered first and looked at me with a serious expression. "Ms. Ginseng needs to be stopped. My recommendation is that you need a real PI to help deal with her so it doesn't become a bigger problem. And I don't mean Cowboy Bobby. And you should know that a reputable PI will call in the cops."

Calling in the cops sounded like an excellent idea, as that woman needed to be in jail. The only question was how to do it without having a target on my back the second she got out.

"I mentioned earlier that I know PIs that take side jobs, and I have one in particular in mind," Dixon assured me. "After our initial meeting, I mentioned you to him. Once he finishes up his current gig, he'd like to meet you, and I can make the introductions. He'll know how to handle that Caturday woman before Herbal ends up dead."

"Herbie." I struggled not to roll my eyes. "The whole time she was prattling on, all I could think of was that Herbie needs to be warned, and wherever he is now, he needs to move, probably across country, and leave no forwarding."

"Agreed." Dixon nodded.

"While we're on the subject, I want to assure you that Pops isn't a killer. If I wasn't positive of that, I wouldn't be making this call." I picked up my phone, and when Pops answered, I said, "A woman showed up here today and seems to think North—and chiefly you—is in the business of murder." I put it on speaker so Dixon could hear his response and hoped it didn't come back to bite me.

"Hello to you too," Pops grouched.

"It's been a dreadful morning." I didn't want to whine, but…

"Getting your shorts in an uproar isn't going to get you anywhere. Some people come up with the worst damn ideas, and it's your job to talk them down and into doing something reasonable. This one is easy, as you start by pointing out how dreadful jail is. Before you even ask, I've never killed anyone—ever. Happy now? Who is this woman anyway?"

"Caturday Ginseng."

"What the hell kind of name is that? You made all this up to needle your Pops?" He clearly heard my long sigh. "That's a stupid name and, believe me, one I'd remember."

"Happy to hear that you're not a felonist."

"That's not a word," he grumped.

"I'll call you later. In the meantime, you behave." I blew him a kiss through the phone.

He snorted and hung up.

"Let's hope that Ms. Caturday is the last of the murder-for-hire requests." I attempted to shake off an encroaching headache. "But what to do about her?"

"First, you're going to run a background check on her, and one on Herbie, and on anyone else whose name pops up. If you don't have the program yet, I can install it for you," Dixon offered.

"Called in a favor, and a friend of a friend came through and got it downloaded last night." I'd felt quite proud of myself when I tested it out, and it worked.

He nodded his approval. "Once you get all the information together, give it to whatever PI you hire, and the two of you can go over everything and discuss a plan of action. The checks might not tell you much of anything, but at least you'll know if someone has a prior record."

Dixon had been more helpful than my how-to book. "Should've asked Pops about that Bobby guy. It didn't even flit through my mind, but with him calling Pops 'old man'… I know that a few people call him that, and it wouldn't surprise me to hear that he sicced the guy on me, thinking he was being helpful."

"Back to why I'm here. Do you want me to tell you what I think or stick to what I know?" Dixon asked.

"Who'd be stupid enough to tell you to MYOB? So far, everything you've done and suggested has been super helpful."

"As you know, I came to go over the books… seems so long ago now." He chuckled. "Even though I don't know your grandfather, it's my opinion that he's up to something. Was his reason for you stepping up to keep the business running financial? Or is it a legacy thing?"

"Pops suggested both. The latter is why I couldn't bring myself to quash his dream, although I tried; he didn't want to hear it."

"Maxwell North is a millionaire several times over. Money will never be one of his problems unless he develops a gambling issue, gets into drugs, or some such."

I gasped, shaking my head. "Pops doesn't have any vices that I'm aware of. Too busy working. If what you say is true, and I have no reason to doubt you, why is he worried?"

"North Investigations hasn't taken on any clients in at least a year, so I'm not sure why there's this sudden interest in getting it back up and running. Getting the answers would be helpful to you, but from what I've heard, he seems like a wily fellow; I wouldn't suggest the direct route. Trick it out of him." Dixon shot me a sly smile, then picked up his briefcase and removed a couple of files. "Ran a financial background check as well as a personal one, and all the information is in here." He handed them to me. "The top one is a report I ran on you. Thought you might like to know what's out there about you. To sum it up, both you and your grandfather are financially secure, though your personal net worth comes nowhere near his."

I flipped open the file and took a quick glance. "This should make for interesting reading," I said, curious to see how I rated financially.

"You have a long list of screen credits and have clearly built your own empire—are you certain you want to give that up for PI work? I ask because you appear to be overwhelmed and not eager to jump in with both feet, which is what it will take to get North going." He paused and looked at me inquiringly. Instead of responding, I nodded. I wasn't prepared to answer that yet—I wanted to hear everything he could tell me first. "If you're thinking of your grandfather, he's got an extensive investment portfolio and an impressive real estate one; in fact, he owns this building outright."

"I didn't know that. No wonder he didn't quibble when I asked about getting the office cleaned. He claimed to know the owner—I guess he does. I'm just happy that it got done, as the dust accumulation alone would've taken me days to clean up." I'd been surprised it was completed overnight but hadn't commented, as I was just grateful it was done. "Maybe it's just a matter of Pops wanting someone to follow in his footsteps. Other than that, I don't understand why he'd push so hard under the circumstances. Although, in one of our conversations, he hinted that he might not be feeling all that great... or perhaps it was just me reading something into nothing."

"Is that the kind of person you are?"

"Not usually." I shook my head. "Somehow, I need to figure out what he's up to and whether it's just about the business or something else. I agree with you about not asking directly. So that will be a challenge."

"Try not to tip your hand when fishing for answers; he might be less guarded if he doesn't think that something's up." Dixon eyed the office, then got up and walked over to the window, surveying the parking lot and street below. "This isn't the kind of business that gets walk-ins. I work in a building with a similar layout, and no one ever just shows up—they always make an appointment first." *Except, apparently, people like Caturday and Bobby.* "You could easily run the business from home with no one the wiser, which you might want to do, as being here alone might be a bit creepy. When you are here if you're not expecting a client, lock the elevator so no one can get off on this floor."

"It would be so much easier to juggle two companies from home. I don't want to give up my voice-over clients. It wouldn't be difficult to manage both jobs from my home office—I turned the second bedroom into a workspace and have plenty of room."

"Does your grandfather know how successful you are in your own right?" Dixon asked.

"We've talked about certain aspects of my job, but money… who does that?" I shook my head. "You'd think that having my house and car paid for would say something."

Dixon paired a short laugh with an eyeroll. "You'd be surprised how many people like to brag about the money they rake in or have stuffed under their mattress."

"You've given me lots to think about."

He eyed the ledger. "I'd keep that, even though in my opinion it's useless, as the figures aren't up-to-date. Another question on the list for your grandfather."

"I'm not leaving anything here at the office since I'll rarely be here."

"When I get the laptop back, do you mind if I have a look at it before returning it?"

"As long as it's understood that you share anything you find—good or bad."

"Agreed. How about we have another meeting day after tomorrow? Same time?" Dixon asked. I nodded. "In addition to going over what I find on the laptop, I'll introduce you to Floyd James. He's the PI I told you about. If you two hit it off, you can talk to him about the Caturday job, and if you don't like him—don't find him suitable, whatever—let me know and I'll get rid of him."

"If that happens, there goes your perfect streak."

"Am I your last appointment?" Dixon asked.

"You're my only appointment, and I'm eager to get out of here and get some fresh air."

"I'll walk you out." He stood and grabbed his briefcase. "Keep in mind that your first hire should be someone to show you the ropes of the business."

I shoved the few items on my desk into my purse, locked up, and we headed downstairs. "Good advice that I plan to follow."

# Chapter Six

I hadn't left my house for the last two days. I'd spent my time camped out on my deck in a chaise, looking up as the occasional boat went by. I'd had another how-to book shipped overnight, which told me I should've had Caturday sign a release before any discussion and included a form to use in the future. I ran all the background checks and didn't like what I found in Caturday's. For one thing, it was difficult to run, as it turned out that the woman had never legally changed her name. She'd lied through her teeth. I suppose you can call yourself anything you want, but you should be careful who you misrepresent yourself to.

I was on the way to the office for my appointment with Dixon and Floyd when Dixon called and apologized, saying he would be a no-show as he had a previous appointment he'd forgotten about. I tried insisting on rescheduling, but he wouldn't hear of it and told me that Floyd was already on his way.

I arrived at the office, coffee in hand, and settled behind my desk, taking my laptop and files out of my briefcase. From the top file, I pulled out a list of questions I planned to ask Floyd. Dixon recommending him was a huge plus, huge plus, as my other option—hiring someone off the street… well, the thought made me nauseous.

The door flew open, and a tall, reed-thin man swaggered in. His beady browns sweeping the office and landing on me, he sized me up with a slimy smirk. This man was a lot older and creepier than I expected Floyd to be based on what I'd heard from Dixon.

I pasted on a phony smile that, frankly, I was tired of. "I'm sorry you made the trip here, but the job's been filled." Dixon would either understand or drop me as a client.

The man's eyes narrowed. "That's what you think, sister." He stomped over and leaned across the desk.

I rolled back my chair, which squeaked with each turn of the wheels. "The truth is that I'm not cut out to run this business, and I'm closing down shop right after you leave." The first part was true.

"All the better for me." He sneered, staring at my breasts as though my sundress were see-through, which it most definitely wasn't. "Ran into Max, who passed along the information that the office was being run by his granddaughter. Figured you'd need help, so here I am."

Now I was confused. I obviously couldn't be dealing with Floyd, but if not him, then who? "We should introduce ourselves."

"Names are overrated. You closing your doors

will work well for me. You won't need to do anything except get up and hit the door, and I'll take over the business."

"You going to make an offer?" I should have been shutting him down, not dragging out this conversation, but he was doing a scary little dance, shuffling from one foot to the other and staring at me like I was prey.

"Why would I pony up a red cent when you just told me you're going out of business?"

"Because no one would agree to that?" I eased the desk drawer open, sticking my hand inside and feeling around.

"Don't be dense." He roared with laughter and sat down. "You have no choice."

I sucked in a breath as I inched the gun into my hand, then jerked it out and pointed it at him, finger on the trigger. "Get out. Before I lose my patience." I squeezed the gun harder, trying to steady my shaking hand.

He stood, sending his chair spiraling back, and ripped his shirt open, showing he had a gun holstered under his arm. Before I could react, his hand was on the butt...

*Oh damn!*

The next second, Mr. Personality went airborne and landed in a pile on the floor.

A massive man loomed over him, pointing a gun in his face. "You have one choice, and that's to pick your ass up off the floor and beat it out of here. Don't you dare even look at the woman. If you don't do as you're told, or if you're ever seen around here again, you're a dead man, and it won't be fast." He moved his aim to between the man's legs.

"Find out his name first," I squeaked.

The Goliath pressed the barrel of his gun against the man's cheek. "You heard her."

"Leo Rung," he choked.

"You've got to the count of three to clear the building."

Leo picked himself up and skidded out the door.

The other man kicked it closed and locked it. Turning back, he said, "Maren, put that gun down before you shoot yourself or me."

My hands shaking had only gotten worse throughout the altercation. I eased the gun back into the drawer.

"Floyd James." He held out a massive paw, engulfing my hand, which I'd tentatively held out. "You should keep your door locked." He took up a post at the window and stared down at the parking lot, or perhaps US-1.

*If you're Floyd James.*

"Butthead just left." He retrieved the chair, setting it back upright, and settled his massive frame across from me. "You look a little pale, despite your tan. Had I noticed that before Leo beat it out of here, he'd have been limping to his broken-down ride. Surprised it runs."

"Do you have ID? Not to be suspicious but…

Leo really scared me."

"Sorry I was running late; good thing I got here when I did." Floyd produced an ID holder from his pocket and flipped it open. Across from his driver's license was his license to carry. "Was that a prospective hire? Dixon told me about the Bobby guy. I'm assuming there haven't been any unexpected visitors between him and Leo?" I nodded. "Where did you get the gun?" He'd already reholstered his.

"On the drive over this morning, I remembered my Pops showing me a secret drawer in this desk and checked it out as soon as I got here. Found the gun, a handful of ammunition, and two hundreds."

"How about I take you to the gun range so you can get comfortable handling one?"

"A good idea since I don't want to shoot myself." Or someone else. I hoped not to have to draw a weapon on anyone ever again.

Floyd's brows shot up. "Are you still up for the interview, or would you rather reschedule for another day?"

There was a knock at the door. I stared, and whoever it was beat on it a second time. I put my finger over my lips. "Maybe whoever it is will go away," I whispered.

"Doesn't work for me." Suddenly, Floyd was out of his chair and halfway to the door, ignoring my headshake. He threw it open. "Yeah?" he growled.

The other person sounded male. I couldn't make out a word of what was being said, but Floyd thanked them and closed the door. He handed me a business card. "Told the man the position was filled, but we'd keep his number."

"Where are these people coming from?" I rubbed my temples, trying to remember if I had aspirin in my purse. "It's not like I posted a job opening on some website."

"Start by thinking about who knew you were opening the business and wanted to hire someone. Process of elimination, and you can cross mine and Dixon's names off the list, so who does that leave?" He hadn't bothered to sit, his body language saying he expected another knock.

"Pops." I groaned and closed my eyes. Did he know he was sending over cretins?

"How about we go sit in the sunshine, and you can conduct my interview there?" Floyd came around the desk and held out his hand. "Once we're out of here, and with the help of some fresh air, I'll charm my way into the job."

"If you want the job, you've got it. Kicking Leo out of here pretty much made you my hero." I shoved my files and laptop into my briefcase. "Not coming back here." I grabbed the gun and ammo and put them in the zippered pouch I'd found them in.

"Can I have the door keys?" he asked. I handed them over. Out in the hall, he locked the stairwell door, which I hadn't thought of, and once in the elevator, locked off the third floor. "Keeping these locked will cut down on unwanted traffic." He walked me over to his oversized Ford pickup. I was relieved to see it had a step and grateful that he offered me a hand.

Once behind the wheel, Floyd said, "Know this great restaurant on the Intercoastal — not much in the way of looks but great food." He roared out of the parking lot.

"Sounds like the kind of place I'd love." Happy that traffic wasn't stacked up, I leaned my head back and enjoyed the drive.

## Chapter Seven

It didn't take us long to arrive at the restaurant. I'd wondered what Floyd's idea of close by was when we got on the freeway, but he turned off almost immediately. The Riverboat was an actual old boat that I loved at first sight. I'd driven over the waterway on numerous occasions but hadn't known there were any businesses tucked underneath the overpass, thinking it was all spendy private property.

The server acknowledged Floyd with a smile and led us outside to a table overlooking the water. He held the chair for me, and we both ordered a drink.

"They know you here?" I asked.

"Discovered it a long time ago, and it's a favorite when I'm up this way."

"I hope I haven't wasted your time." I sighed.

"Business can wait until after we've had our drinks. Even if we don't end up working together, Dixon was adamant that I meet you." Floyd chuckled. "So you know, he's got us married, having kids—though I did forget to ask how many—and living out our twilight years. When he hears I got you to go to lunch, the little matchmaker will be ecstatic."

My cheeks burned. Okay, he was a babe, but still.

Floyd squeezed my hand. "Didn't mean to embarrass you. Even if you don't end up hiring me, I've got a job proposition for you. And nothing illegal like the wannabe client."

I did laugh at that one, and it felt good. "Good to hear, as I don't have any experience with illegal, so I'd be a bad hire."

We sat and laughed and talked about our lives, getting to know one another. We both had a love of seafood, and he suggested the platter, which came with enough yummy choices for eight people. I barely had enough room to sample everything. When the dishes were cleared away, Floyd ordered another drink for me, beer for himself. The seagulls were diving into the water nearby for the morsels tossed by patrons ignoring the "Do not feed" sign.

"I take it that Dixon filled you in on the backstory," I said finally, taking a long sip of my drink. Floyd nodded. "I knew very little… actually nothing about the business when I met with Pops that day. Based on the condition of the office the first time I visited, it wasn't hard to figure out that there hadn't been any clients in a while. If you factor in what I've learned, thanks to Dixon, I'd say I'd be lucky to offer you even the occasional job. I'm embarrassed I'm wasting your time, and I'd like to pay for lunch."

"Nice offer, but not happening." Floyd didn't

roll his eyes but close. I wasn't sure whether he was amused or annoyed. "I did hear that you're being railroaded into running the business and that your grandfather thought experience wasn't necessary. Not sure about his reasoning, but I agree with Dixon that he's up to something."

"If I'm being honest, I plan to throw in the towel—private investigation is definitely not for me. But first, I want to find out what Pops has up his sleeve."

"You and Dixon—he loathes a puzzle and is determined to figure out what the man's up to." Floyd chuckled.

"Thank goodness I was desperate for a shot of caffeine after the meeting I had with Pops and his lawyer and stopped at the Coffee Bar, where Rella and her friends were sitting out on the patio. Avery recommended Dixon, and I plan to show my appreciation by taking the three to lunch. Dixon's had one helpful suggestion after another, and he didn't desert me when the wannabe client showed up."

"Trust me, he loved every minute. His nose is always buried in numbers, and it was good to see him get interested in something else. Before you take down your shingle, which he'll be disappointed to hear, you still have the problem of Catnip."

"That woman." I shook my head. "Turns out that *Caturday* isn't even her real name; she made it all up. Her legal name is Mildred Bellwether. And her background check showed she's got an arrest record a mile long. The woman can't control her temper, and her ex needs protection from her. Did Dixon happen to mention that she wants him offed?"

"Nice job checking her out." Floyd smiled. "Freaked Dixon out when he read the report you forwarded on her, and he texted me to come to his office. I got the quick version, but enough to agree with you on the ex. Dixon decided to verify each of the addresses for Caturday and Herbie that were listed in the report and found that they're all no longer valid. Which saves a ton of time."

"Thinking that once I get Herbie's current address, it would be simple enough to pay the man a visit, tip him off and suggest that he get out of town."

"Not by yourself," Floyd growled. "Did you come up with any other ideas about how *we* should proceed?"

"Sarcasm isn't appreciated or helpful when talking to a newbie." I made a face at him. "The reports Dixon emailed were more thorough than my own, and the more I read, the more determined I got about warning Herbie. The last thing I want to do is lead Catnip to the man." Floyd looked amused that I'd used his nickname for the woman. "Another thing that worries me — what happens when she figures out that I have no intention of doing her dirty work?"

"That's why, when I heard this story, I called a

cop friend, Lucas Adler, and he'd like to sit down and go over all the details of the conversation you had with her. Lucas talked about posing as the PI you hired to do the job. Once he gets her on tape, he'll have enough evidence to arrest her and get a conviction."

"Thinking your friend should also talk to Dixon since he was in on the initial meeting, in case I forget something that would be important for him to know."

"I'll get this set up quickly so this Catnip woman doesn't go off half-cocked and do the job herself."

"I think that until I'm completely out of business, I'd like to go along on any jobs that you do for me. You know, should I get one."

"As my backup?" Floyd asked, definitely amused.

"Don't you think it sounds fun?" I asked and got a headshake. "Or I could venture off on my own, and if you have the time, you can critique me when I report in." The whole time I was talking, he shook his head, conveying that he thought my idea was nuts, and I wholeheartedly agreed with him but wasn't about to admit it.

"I've got just the job to start you out on." Floyd nodded to himself, the amusement in his voice showing that he liked his own idea.

"Wouldn't be very nice if on our first meeting, you threw out a proposition that involved tricking me."

"This plays off of your idea of learning on the job. A neighbor of my mom's came to the house, knowing that I'm a PI, and wants me to track down a dog."

I laughed, picturing myself chasing down a dog despite having no experience with them. I'd had a cat once but hadn't rescued another one after he died of old age.

"Anyway…" Floyd gave me a stern look. "Edna Haley runs an animal sanctuary. When she went to check on a pooch she'd homed, she found the man had moved, which put him in violation of the contract he signed."

"You need this woman's permission to move?"

Ignoring me, he said, "Edna would like the dog found and returned."

"I have a few questions before I'd be willing to start this job. You're thinking Ms. No Experience, which would include both the PI work and most animals, can handle rounding up a wayward dog?" He was enjoying himself way too much. But then, so was I.

"It dawned on me that you could sweet-talk all the information you need out of Edna, though she can be prickly."

"How so?"

"I run into the woman repeatedly, and she stares at me like I just committed a crime… or am about to, not sure which. Then there are times she pretends not to see me at all." Floyd grinned. "If you can get her to stop burning up Mom's phone, there's a plate of cookies in it for me."

*Yum.* Now he had my interest. "What kind of cookies?"

"Oh no, you don't," Floyd said in mock seriousness. "Any cookie is fine with me. What I could do is maybe negotiate a plate for you."

"I'm thinking…" I tapped my chin. "Since you'd be fluffing this case off on me and I'd be lead, that you'd be my backup, and I could tell you what to do."

"You could try." He held his hand out. "It's agreed then: I take the crazy woman and you the dog."

"I'm in." We shook, his hand swallowing up mine.

"You free this afternoon? I'm thinking that I'll introduce you to my mom, she can fill us in on what she knows, and from there, we can walk down to Edna's house."

"No time for cold feet." I blew out a breath. My first case.

# Chapter Eight

Mama Rosa, as she liked to be called, had an outgoing personality and immediately enveloped me in a hard hug. Her house smelled like freshly baked cookies, and I wanted to follow the scent but managed to stop myself. Reading my mind, Floyd winked. On the drive over, I'd found out that Rosa had raised five boys and then adopted two teenagers, who were now in their twenties and still lived with her.

She led me to the couch, and the two of us sat together, Floyd across from us.

"I wanted to avoid Edna's drama and certainly didn't want to drag Floyd into the middle of it, but I couldn't take her non-stop calling." She flashed a sheepish smile at Floyd.

"Please, Mama, you should've dumped it in my lap after the first call." He brushed his hands together. "If it happens again, with her or anyone else, I'll be your first call." He raised an eyebrow at her.

She grinned at him and nodded. "Truth is, after hearing what Edna wanted, I ended up feeling more sorry for the guy who adopted the dog. I heard from another neighbor that her contracts are quite detailed. Then found out that most are so eager to adopt, they often sign without reading, and Edna doesn't think anything about taking offenders to court. Tried to get out of her what type of violation would necessitate such drastic action, but she was tight-lipped."

"I've seen that particular look on the woman — it's one she's perfected."

"Now, Floyd," Rosa lightly admonished.

"Then there's the issue of you never saying no to anyone," he said with a smile.

"One of the first things I need to get from Edna is a copy of the contract, so I know what constitutes an infraction," I said.

Floyd tapped his temple. "Thinking the same thing."

Rosa grinned, first at Floyd and then at me. I had a good idea of what she was thinking. Did Floyd, or was he ignoring her?

"More gossip, which I try to ignore, but it bounces around the neighborhood like wildfire…" It appeared that Rosa was debating whether to share, but she quickly made up her mind and decided not to. "After several attempts to contact the man who adopted the dog, Edna was over here knocking on the door, and then the calls started. I bet if you can locate a current address and give it to her, she'll do her own confronting."

"What if she turns out to be like Catnip?" I asked Floyd.

He told his mom, "A wannabe client of

Maren's. Some people just don't do well with all the sunshine we get down here." He looked amused with himself. "What we'll do is talk to both sides and go from there."

"We?" I arched my brow.

"Ah yes, Boss Lady—I forgot. What do you suggest?"

Rosa had a huge grin on her face, turning her head back and forth between Floyd and me.

"We agreed that I get to boss Floyd around on this job," I told her.

She clapped. "You have to take pictures."

I laughed, more at her enthusiasm than Floyd's frown. "Do we talk to Edna now? Or should we make an appointment?"

"She's always home, but then, with all those dogs, you'd have to be," Rosa assured me.

"I'm surprised that your neighborhood zoning allows anyone to turn their home into an animal rescue," I said. Not to mention the neighbors' reaction—any excess barking and they'd have plenty to say.

"Don't know how many know that Edna rescues dogs, as she doesn't talk about it. Heard once that the number fluctuates, and at one time, it was ten," Rosa told us. "I know from another neighbor's experience that when the code department gets involved, they don't get off your tail until the violation is corrected. I'm fairly certain that if this particular neighbor ever found out who made the call on her violation…" She winced. "As for Edna, I witnessed her unleash on someone once, and it was quite vicious, which is why I keep my distance. Surprised that she showed up on my doorstep, but then she wanted something. My advice: when you do talk to her, don't disclose anything personal if you can help it."

"Good to know," I said.

"There's one other thing that you need to know since Edna will do her damnedest to press you on your personal life," Rosa said to Floyd, her cheeks turning pink. "I told her that you were married so she'd stop talking about fixing you up with her daughter. She's likely to think Maren is your wife."

I laughed.

"As I recall, it's always been a rule that we aren't allowed to lie to people." Floyd eyed his mom.

"*You're* not. But what was I supposed to say—your daughter's so high maintenance, no way in heck would I ever try to talk Floyd into going for coffee? That would put Edna's nose out of joint for sure."

"Whatever we say is going to race around the neighborhood. Are you ready for that?" Floyd asked. "The gossip flies around here with such speed that if you're not careful, you get whiplash."

"Edna can believe whatever she wants," I cut in, breaking the stare-down. "Better idea, Floyd and I will both be on our game and not verify things one way or the other." Neither looked convinced that tactic would work. "I know! How about introducing me as your side chick? That way, she'll be horrified but happy that her daughter never got involved. We have lots of options."

The sides of Floyd's mouth quirked.

Rosa snorted. "That would be the hottest gossip around until all my sons were old men."

"Any other tidbits you haven't shared yet?" Floyd stood. Rosa shook her head. "Let's get this over with." He extended his hand to me.

"You two do look cute together." She beamed.

"Keep talking like that, and you're going to scare Maren off before we even get out of the house."

"Love your mother," I said as we walked outside.

"I'm thinking if we were married, this is how we'd act." He hooked his arm around me. "Also, one of your wifely duties would be to beat off other women."

"Threaten to kick butt, like you did to Leo?" I air-boxed as we hit the sidewalk and headed to the corner.

"Exactly."

"There's something you should know about your wife—I alluded to it before, but in case you didn't catch it, I like dogs but have no experience. My mom was allergic, so no pets were allowed growing up. After I moved out, I rescued a cat from a McDonald's parking lot and had him for five years before he went to cat heaven. I do know to stick the back of my hand out for a sniff before getting too friendly." I demonstrated.

"If Edna has as many dogs as Mom says, once we knock, they'll be barking and leaping around, so I suggest we stay outside to talk. That way, we can keep it short. I think that we're of like mind on this, in that we don't want to sit around and talk the rest of the afternoon."

I certainly agreed.

We turned the corner, and Edna Haley's house was one block up on the next corner. It was an elongated yellow block-style home with white trim—a popular style and color choice in this neighborhood. There was an SUV in the driveway.

"We probably should've called and at least given her a heads up that we were on our way," I said, embarrassed that we were about to bang on the door with no advance notice.

"Let's hope she's really busy and gets right to the facts so that we can get out of here quickly."

"Though we already know from your mom, I'm going to ask her to tell us what happened and how she'd like to see the situation resolved. Then you demand a copy of the contract in that stern tone of yours."

"Got it, partner." He saluted.

"If you notice, at any time during the

conversation, that I'm about to skid off into the weeds, you better snatch me back."

"You do the same for me." Floyd rang the doorbell. All hell broke loose inside the house, with dogs hitting the door and barking like crazy.

I stepped closer to Floyd.

"Quiet down," a woman's voice yelled inside. The door opened, and an older woman peered through the chain. "Floyd, honey, how are you?" she said, eying me the whole time.

"We're here about the dog issue." He introduced me, only using first names.

"You two serious?" Edna asked, checking out my ringless fingers. "Guess not." She smiled.

He picked up my left hand and kissed it. "Honey, did you leave your ring on the bathroom counter again?"

My cheeks flamed. "I hoped you wouldn't notice. Promise, as soon as I get home, I'll put it back on." I looked him in the eye and made a face. He brushed my lips with his.

"Ohhh…" The disappointment was clear in Edna's voice. "I'd invite the two of you in, but the dogs don't know you. They wouldn't bite, but they'd crawl all over you."

"Why don't you get me a copy of the contract and then come outside and give us all the information you have on the person who adopted the dog, and we'll take it from there," Floyd told her.

"Hold on, I'll be right back." She disappeared

back inside the house. Several snouts appeared in the crack in the door.

"So, *hubby*," I said. Floyd grinned. "I'm wondering if Edna has the right to take back an animal she adopted out if there's no abuse going on. Something I'll put at the top of my list to research."

"Wondered the same thing—we'll know more after we read the contact."

"I get checking up on the animal after the transfer, but continuing to show up…? How long does that go on for?" Be interesting to know the answer. "After a while, I wouldn't answer the door."

The door opened all the way, and Edna squeezed her way out while several dogs tried to edge past her legs, eager to meet the visitors. She thrust some papers at Floyd. "Made a copy of both the application and the contract. If you have any questions, you can call anytime." With her focus on Floyd, she appeared to have forgotten that I was standing next to him.

"So, you know, it will be a few days before we know anything. Any longer than that, and Maren will be in touch."

"So good to see you, young man," Edna gushed at Floyd, then went back in the house.

Without a moment's hesitation, he had me off her front porch and headed down the street, his hand clasped around mine.

"Thought I did great for my first job," I said

sarcastically. "Maybe the reason Edna shuffled us off so quickly is that she was disappointed that she's not going to be roping you into her family. I feel compelled to warn you that if you don't want your fib to unravel, you better tell Rosa which story we went with, and no pointing your finger at me. Good cover about the ring."

"No worries about Mama—she'll get a good laugh out of it. She has a way of going with a story, not committing one way or the other. But I need to warn you—she hears the M-word, and she'll be calling with questions about what you'd like for the big day."

"Speaking of..." I pointed as a car backed out of the driveway. Rosa had the passenger window down and waved as it rolled by. I waved back. "Bummer. I wanted to say goodbye and sneak a cookie. Don't narc on me that I even thought of doing that."

"There's no one that doesn't like her cookies or anything else she makes." He opened his truck door and helped me inside. "What grade do I get as your helper?"

I covered my face and laughed.

After he drove me back to my car, I thanked him and said I'd had fun, then told him that I'd get on the dog case while he figured out what *we* were going to do about Catnip. He sounded quite amused when he suggested that we have a meeting to discuss our options.

# Chapter Nine

The next morning, I curled up on the couch, doodling on one of my notepads and making the occasional note on what I needed to get done, then decided my coffee needed my full attention. My brain always functioned better with a little perk-me-up. A knock at the door had me turning my head, wondering who the heck. I had friends in the area, but it had been a while since anyone had stopped by or I'd gone out. I hadn't been socializing much, as I'd been busy building my business. I set my mug down, ventured to the window next to the front door, and peered through the shutters. I immediately noticed Floyd's truck in the driveway before turning to the knocker, who was waving. I combed through my hair with my fingers, ran my hands down the front of my tent dress, and opened the door, wishing I'd slid into a pair of shoes.

"Good morning," Floyd said way too cheerfully.

I zeroed in on the dinner plate wrapped in foil he had in his hand. "Guessing you don't need more coffee." I pushed the door open and stepped back.

"Please, it's the sauce of life. So I've heard

anyway, but I happen to agree."

"Same here." I took the plate, inching up the foil as I set it on the small island on wheels I'd purchased for counter space. "A whole plate of cookies." I licked my lips. "Your mom is amazing." I snatched one up and almost gobbled it down whole.

"You going to share?"

I shook my head while staring him down. "I've got to make these last. Besides, you have an endless supply at your mom's."

Floyd stood in the large room and stared around, taking in its disordered state. His massive frame made the space seem small. "You got construction workers coming?"

"Not until I find new ones," I grumbled.

"Guessing that this wasn't a do-it-yourself job, so where the heck is everyone?"

I explained how I'd hired a company that, once they gutted the kitchen and received a sizeable payment for materials, stopped showing up and then ditched the job entirely. I suspected the money went into their pockets but couldn't prove it.

While telling him what happened, I grabbed a mug and filled it from the coffee pot I had ready to go, pointing him to the couch. The view through the wall-length slider was the best. This morning, the inlet was devoid of boat traffic.

Floyd took a drink of his coffee and sat down. "What the hell is the name of the company?"

"Know what you're thinking, big guy, and it's super sweet of you, assuming you're about to offer to go clean their clocks, but they're out of business."

"Not often, someone calls me sweet. And super at that." He gave me a big smile. "How do you deal with no kitchen?"

"Found out early on that you can do quite a bit with a microwave and a refrigerator, and I'm not talking frozen food." I pointed to the two appliances in the corner next to the window. "Turns out you can cook anything in that baby; just watch the time, or it turns the texture of shoe leather. My days of camping in my own house are about to come to an end," I assured him. "Got sidetracked by a couple of jobs that took precedence. Anyway, I'm about to get back to interviewing contractors. Hopefully, I'll find one that will listen to what I want—simple, clean lines—and the job will go fast."

Floyd mumbled under his breath. "I've got a guy that I can highly recommend. He may offer a few suggestions, but you'll have the final say, and he'll finish the job according to your specs. As for the other company, give me the information, and I'll find out what happened. Let me know how much money you're out, and I'll personally shake it out of the owner—in business or not."

"I'm picturing you holding the man up by the scruff of the neck and shaking him until the change falls out of his pockets." I chuckled at the image. Floyd made a face, and I knew I wasn't far off. "Welcome to my humble abode." I swept my hand around. "How did you know where I live? More coffee?" I asked before he could answer.

"You stay right there with your feet kicked up, and I'll get it," he said, nodding to the footrest that ran the length of the couch. He stood and went to refill his mug, looking around the kitchen before sitting next to me. "Sought out Dixon yesterday after I got back to the office and told him we got married. After he picked his jaw up off the floor, I told him I needed your address so I could take cookies to wifey."

"Just a reminder: I won't be sharing my cookies."

"If that's a threat, you're going to have to up your game." Floyd watched as a boat cruised by on its way out to open water. "Great neighborhood."

"Took some fast talking to get the previous owner to sell. Had to assure the older woman who'd lived here forever that I wouldn't mow it down and build something shinier and five times the square footage. I think I sealed the deal by throwing out ideas about what I'd do to update the current floor plan, with no changes to the outside except fresh paint and new plants. Think it was my enthusiasm that sold her, as she chose my offer from the handful of others I know she got."

"It may be smaller than your neighbors', but

you've done a good job making sure the exterior fits into the rest of the neighborhood and doesn't stand out like the one at the other end of the block."

"I've heard a few grumbles about the hot-pink house. It wouldn't surprise me if they went out of town someday and came back to a new paint job." I chuckled. "So you strong-armed Dixon for my address?"

"Nothing so painful." He grinned at me. "Had to go to his office to get the Catnip file anyway. Then I took it back upstairs to my office at WD Consulting and went over everything with the owners—Grey Walker and Seven Donnelley. Both ex-cops, by the way. They laughed when I told them she wanted you to commit murder for hire until they realized I wasn't joking."

"Thought the cop we were meeting was Lucas something."

"Adler. After talking to Grey and Seven, I called him and filled him in on what we've learned so far."

"Where was your partner? Couldn't she be reached?" When Floyd's cheeks pinkened, I was pleased with myself for teasing him.

"No worries, I'll get better at including you." He held up his right hand as if taking an oath. "All of us agreed that getting Herbie relocated is a priority. Then we need to get the woman on tape, or they won't hold her in jail long, and a good lawyer will get her off. With her arrest record, you'd think she'd get a serious sentence, but you never know."

"If she does get out…" I shook my head. "Thinking that Herbie should get a new identity and start over somewhere else. It's a pain, but I looked over his credit report, and he's got the assets."

"Maybe instead of it being about her money, it's about his, as her credit is a train wreck," Floyd pointed out. "Possibly thinking if he's dead, then she inherits."

"So that's why she wants him dead."

"Catnip has been arrested a couple of times on financial crimes and got prison time for embezzlement, though apparently not long enough that she thought to get her act together to avoid going back. In between jail stints, she stays busy getting married and divorced."

"She must be adept at keeping a lid on her craziness until after the I do's when there's no more need to hide her true personality." I shook my head, thinking of a friend who had a high-maintenance partner. It finally wore her out, and once she made the decision to cut ties, she couldn't get away fast enough.

"Probably not a struggle to keep a lid on it as long as everything's going her way," Floyd reasoned.

"By chance, do you have a surefire way to deal with Catnip?"

"There's no such thing." Floyd stood and

nodded at my mug.

I shook my head. "I will take a cold water though."

After filling his mug, he poked his head in the refrigerator, and I heard a laugh. He returned and sat back down, handing me the bottle.

"Herbie lives just up the coast in Pompano. I thought we could drive up and have a chat with him — let him know that if we found him, she will. Also reassure him that she won't get a forwarding from us, but that doesn't stop her from getting the information from someone else. On the way, I'll give Lucas a call and see if he wants to meet up before or after our meeting with Herbie."

"My first official case is seeing some action." I rubbed my hands together and, at the same time, let Floyd know I'd caught his smirk. "Coming or going, it would be fun to drive along the beach. Hint, hint. What about food?"

"Maybe you could whip us up something from what you have in the fridge? Probably not." He laughed. "And yes, to the drive and the food."

"Do we have an appointment with Herbie? Or are we pounding on his door?" I demonstrated with my fist in the air.

"Surprise is better. Shows him that if we can appear on his doorstep without notice, then so can Catnip." He cast a casual glance over my outfit. "Thinking we should hit the road."

"Ten minutes." I jumped up and raced to my bedroom. Thinking Floyd had on jeans and a t-shirt that stretched across his abs. I pulled the yoga pants I'd recently purchased out of my closet and paired them with a long-sleeved workout top and tennis shoes. I grabbed my purse and was back at the couch in a flash, shoving a couple of files in my bag as Floyd watched with amusement, glancing at his watch.

"You're impressive."

I noted that he had collected the mugs, rinsed them out, and unplugged the coffee pot.

He looked me over and gave me a nod of approval. "Perfect if we end up having to chase someone down."

"Look at this." I turned to the side and pulled the hidden pocket away from my leg. "In case I need to gun up?"

"I hope you keep that weapon locked up… at least until we get to the gun range." He reached out and picked up my PI 101 book with a smirk.

"Don't make fun of me. It's better than me thinking I know it all or that 'figure it out as I go' is viable."

He laughed, grabbed my hand, and we walked out to his truck.

## Chapter Ten

Once in the truck and inputting the address into GPS, Floyd took out his phone, called his cop friend, Lucas, and told him we were headed to Herbie Brogan's house. After a couple of laughs, he gave the man the address and hung up.

"We're going to take Dixie Highway, and on the way back, we'll cut over to the beach and have lunch. Lucas will join us, so I can introduce you to your new partner."

"What happened to him being my employee?"

"We decided that it would be better for Lucas to pose as your partner when you set up a meeting with the Catnip woman under the guise of having information for her. In the meantime, I've got a couple of bogus addresses you can pass along to her to keep her busy looking for Herbie."

"If I get her to talk about murdering someone, will she be arrested on the spot?" I asked, trying to ignore the knot in my stomach.

"I suggested that Lucas arrest you both so she doesn't know she was set up."

I groaned.

"The two of you will be separated when you get to the station, and you'll be allowed to leave."

I kept an eye on the road, wanting to know exactly where we were going, though I had no intention of coming back here by myself. "I thought we'd check out the previous address for the dog dude, since I couldn't get a forwarding; maybe someone knows where he moved to. If we have time, we can check it out on the way back. I read the contract, and Edna doesn't ever relinquish control. In the fine print at the bottom, it states that if the terms aren't met, she can sue. I plan to run a check later and see how many cases she's filed and the outcomes."

"It's one thing if you've read the contract and know what you're getting into from the beginning, but we both know there are those that don't. Wonder how many have read the contract, not liked what they saw, and walked away. It's one thing to make sure the animal has a good home and another to be invasive."

"If Edna's had to resort to court action, let's hope it was for a damn good reason and not because she was losing control."

"She'd need a court order to remove a pet from someone's home, and if she tried to circumvent the system, she'd find herself looking at charges."

An hour later, Floyd turned into a quiet neighborhood in Pompano. The street was a mixture of apartment buildings and condos. He parked in a visitor space in front of a white four-story building with assigned parking in the front.

I checked out the front of the building, noting

the call box. "You think Herbie's going to let us in?"

"Not if he's smart."

The two of us got out. Before taking a step, Floyd checked out the property. He then grabbed my hand, and we headed to the security door. As expected, it was locked. He pulled a tool out of his pocket and quickly opened the door.

"Lockpick?" I asked. He nodded. "They're easy to buy online, but I couldn't find where anyone offered a how-to class."

"Another thing I can teach you." He hit the button for the elevator, which opened immediately, and punched the button for the second floor.

"Just because I'm here to learn from the master doesn't mean I have to be completely ineffective. You need me to do anything, raise your eyebrows like you are now, and I'll step forward and say something inane."

Right before we got to the door, Floyd pulled me to his side, hooked his arm around my shoulders, and knocked. "This way, we don't look like we're selling something." He nodded to the peephole in the door—judging by how the light changed, someone was looking out at us.

Herbie Brogan opened the door and stuck his disheveled head out, eyeing us. "What's up?"

Floyd introduced us and showed Mr. Brogan his PI license. "We're here about Mildred Bellwether."

"If you don't have divorce papers—" Brogan shifted his gaze to Floyd's empty hands. "—you're wasting your time, as I'm not interested in news about that woman."

"Trust me, you're going to want to hear what we have to say," Floyd said. "We wouldn't be here if it wasn't important."

I nodded.

It took him a minute, but Herbie finally said, "Make it snappy." He opened the door and ushered us inside, pointing us to the living room and indicating that we should sit on the couch. "Haven't had my third cup of coffee yet." A leggy thirty-something blonde in her underwear lounged in one of the chairs, legs over the arm. "Dollface, you mind giving us a few minutes? I'll make it up to you later."

Not acknowledging us, she blew him a kiss and wiggled out of the room.

"Whatever Mildred wants, she's not getting. The woman's crazy, and that's an understatement."

"Mildred now goes by the name Caturday Ginseng. Wanted you to know the name, in case you hear it somewhere. She contacted my associate…" Floyd glanced at me, and I pasted on a lame smile. Brogan checked me out, and Floyd cleared his throat, which snapped the man's eyes back to him. "She wants you dead." Herbie yelped, his eyes going wide. Floyd went on to relay how our initial meeting had played out and ended by expressing what I had earlier: "If we're not able to stop her, she may hire someone else to locate you. Which she may have already done." He went on to tell Herbie that the cops were involved and he should expect a call because they were gathering the evidence needed to make sure that her jail stay was a long one. "Otherwise, Mildred could come at you anytime."

"Guess there's no hoping that she's going to get over her jones. I've never known her to let go of a grievance. According to her, anything bad happens, I'm to blame." Herbie took a healthy drink of his coffee.

"She contends that you ripped her off for quite a bit of money," I said. He snorted. I wasn't surprised—I'd questioned the story after looking at their financial background checks.

"What a bunch of horse…" Herbie ground his teeth. "Had two friends—well, more hers than mine—contact me, claiming that she stole from them and asking me to make good on their losses. I asked for proof and not only didn't hear from them again, but they changed their numbers. Shortly after that, my house in Ft. Lauderdale was broken into not once but twice. Cops said it's unusual for the same house to get hit twice in such a short span of time unless the robbers saw items they wanted but had no way to cart out the first time."

"What did they steal?" Floyd asked.

"Personal items—jewelry, coins… nothing

anyone would have to come back for. It seemed like they took whatever they could stick in their pockets. After the second time, I put my house up for sale and moved up here."

"Herbie Brogan isn't a common name; it's my suggestion that you change it and relocate," Floyd said. Herbie snorted in disbelief. "I know that's not easy, so another option is to keep your name but after you move, do everything you can to ensure your whereabouts don't become public. I'm not suggesting that you leave Florida but perhaps the other coast…"

"If you and Mildred have mutual friends, I wouldn't give them a forwarding," I suggested. "Or you can get a burner phone and a maildrop in another location and give that out, letting only those you trust know your actual location."

"Huge mistake, marrying that woman." Herbie sighed out his exasperation. "Appreciate your coming here to tell me all this and not just let it play out, as some would've done." The man looked at me. "I've got some advice for you. Mildred never forgets a slight, and if you don't get the job done, she'll want to get even. There was a time or two I had to talk her down. It got old. It'll be worse if she finds out you're working behind her back to bring her down."

"I didn't want anything to do with the job from the start. Another employee was there at the time, and it was his suggestion that we learn more about the case before telling her to take a hike." I had to wonder what she would've done if I'd kicked her out on the spot. From what I'd heard from Herbie, she wouldn't have kept me waiting long for an answer.

"Appreciate you doing that. If you hadn't, I might be dead by now." The look Herbie cast at me said, *and you too*, as though he was reading my mind.

"Here's my card." Floyd produced one from his pocket, and the two men exchanged numbers. "I'll keep you updated."

Herbie was definitely shell-shocked as we headed out the door. "Thank you for coming," he mumbled.

Once back in the truck, I said, "Wonder what he'll do."

Floyd whipped out his phone and sent a text. "My guess is that he's wrestling with disbelief. He knows that Catnip's capable of everything we said, and yet he has to wonder if she'd go that far. Should've asked if the two had a prenup and the only way to get money out of the guy was for him to be dead."

"I'm not looking forward to meeting with Catnip."

"We need to hurry up and introduce Lucas as your partner, and then he can break the news — let her know that there's someone new to deal with," Floyd said. "I'll give Herbie a day or two to digest everything he learned today, then call and find out what he plans to do, stressing that Catnip can't be held off forever."

"Feeling queasy, so we can skip the beach." I just wanted to go home and kick my feet up.

"Maybe a little food would help. Soup, in particular, is good for stomach issues." He reached out and patted my hand. "If not, I'll need to reschedule with Lucas."

"You morphed into your mom there for a minute." I smiled at him. "What I really need is a cookie." I'd never had any dealings with the police, so meeting Lucas should be interesting.

"Food first," he said, mimicking his mom, which had me laughing. "If you're worried about meeting Lucas, don't be; he's a great guy. Then, if you're feeling up to it, we'll check out dog dude's old address."

## Chapter Eleven

Floyd picked another fun restaurant; this one had been built on stilts sunk into the sand with a view of the pier in the distance. A man with blue eyes, brown hair tousled, and cheeks covered in scruff nodded as we approached the table on the patio. Floyd pulled out a chair for me and then made introductions.

Lucas Adler was a hottie, though Floyd had him beat in the looks department… hands down.

The server came and took our drink order, and Floyd recommended the hamburgers. By unspoken agreement, the three of us tabled all talk of work and just got to know one another. It was clear that the two men were friends, as they asked about each other's families and easily traded jokes.

Once the dishes were cleared away and our iced teas refilled, Lucas's attention turned to me. "Heard you're in the PI business." His lips quirked.

I closed my eyes and shook my head. "Only because I didn't put my foot down harder with my Pops." The two men laughed.

"Looking forward to meeting the man," Floyd said with a grin.

My cheeks pinkened as I envisioned how that conversation would go, especially if the M-word got bandied about. I gave Lucas the short version of my meeting with Caturday and assured him that the last thing I wanted to do was cross any legal lines.

"So how did Herbie Brogan take the news that his ex wants him offed?" Lucas asked.

After telling him all about the meeting with Herbie, Floyd said, "I came away with a few questions as to Catnip's motives."

Lucas glanced at me, *Who?* on his face.

"Floyd likes to call Mildred, aka Caturday Ginseng, Catnip. Kind of like it myself." I laughed along with Lucas.

"I'll remember that since I'll be pushing Floyd aside and partnering up with you."

"Just so we're clear, I'm happy to do anything you tell me to do, as long as it's within reason," I said.

"If only everyone I've partnered with was so accommodating."

"Anything happens to Maren, I'll kick your ass," Floyd growled.

Lucas assessed the two of us and nodded. "Got it."

"After talking to Herbie, I'm thinking Catnip's story of him stealing from her is bogus and guessing that she thinks it'll give her cover when he disappears," Floyd said.

"How did Herbie take your advice to skip

town?" Lucas asked.

"Shell-shocked. I'll give him some time, then get back in touch in case he needs a reminder that it's in his best interest, at least until Catnip's in jail."

"When I get back to the office, I'll give him a call and let him know that law enforcement is on the case. Tell me about this Catnip woman," Lucas directed at me.

I went into detail about how I'd met Caturday. Also told him that Dixon had been there and was surprised to learn that he not only already knew Dixon but had talked to him. I wondered why he was grilling me about it then.

"I'll need you to set up a meeting with this woman at your office," Lucas said.

I took out my phone and called her, putting it on speaker. After ringing several times, it went to voicemail.

"Leave a message," Lucas whispered. Which I did. Once I hung up, he said, "Send a text, and if she doesn't respond, try calling again before we leave."

"Surprises me that she's not answering since she was so impatient for the information." I laid my phone on the table.

"Considering her record, maybe she's being careful," Lucas said. "Like to think she changed her mind, but chances are she hasn't, since she was bold enough to ask someone she didn't know to commit a felony. If you don't hear from her, it's possible she's found someone else to do the job."

Floyd then told him about the dog case.

"It's not unusual for these rescue places to have very specific contracts. It doesn't happen often, but I've heard of a couple of cases where the animals have been taken away, but always for a good reason," Lucas told us. "Hopefully, this woman can settle without going to court, as it's a waste of time and money."

"Floyd forgot to tell you that we swapped cases; I got the dog, and he got the lunatic woman," I told Lucas. Both guys laughed.

Since I knew we were winding up the lunch, I called Caturday again, and this time, it went straight to voicemail.

"Interesting." Lucas hmmed. "Should she get back to you, arrange a time for us to get together and give me a call. We'll get this taken care of."

"When you arrest Catnip, also put Maren in cuffs. But not tight." Floyd shot him a stern look.

Lucas nodded as though it was a given. "I'm assuming you'll be waiting at the station to give her a ride home?" he asked, a trace of humor in his tone.

"Hopefully, I won't be held long." I tried not to worry over how that would go down.

"You won't be," Lucas assured me.

## Chapter Twelve

Back in the truck and before he entered the address in GPS, Floyd asked, "You up for a visit to Dog Dude's neighbors?"

"Your habit of nicknaming people is going to backfire on you when you slip and call them that instead of their real name."

"Better than Dickhead," Floyd said with a straight face.

I tried to bite back the laugh, but it escaped. "Try explaining that one."

"If you get stuck in an uncomfortable moment, mumble something that makes no sense. They'll think you've lost your mind and forget what they were mad about."

I laughed again. "Might as well see what DD's old neighbors can tell us."

"I'm rubbing off on you already." Floyd looked pleased.

It didn't take us long to get back to the heart of Ft. Lauderdale. Floyd turned onto a street that was one two-story apartment building after another that all looked alike except for the color. I double-checked the file to remind myself that the man's name was Mike York, as getting it wrong wouldn't be conducive to asking questions about the man, and I knew I wouldn't be good at the mumbling business.

Floyd found street parking, and we got out. "Just so we're clear, you're running the show. If anyone gives you any trouble, they can deal with me. I'm not averse to breaking a nose or two."

I shook my head, noting that he was amused with himself. "Doesn't blood fly everywhere when you do that?"

"It can get messy. But no worries—I'll be standing in front of you, so any splatter will hit me," Floyd said, thoroughly amused. He came to a stop in front of a door marked 106. "If a new person has moved in already, it's highly doubtful they'll know who we're talking about."

I stepped up and knocked anyway. There was no answer, and I didn't hear any sound of movement from within.

Two doors down, a woman came out of her apartment, and we turned our attention to her just as she hawked spit into the bushes. "Mike moved, and it hasn't been rented yet," she yelled in a gravely tone.

"Would you happen to know where he moved to?" I closed the space between us but stayed back in case she needed to spit again.

"What's in it for me?" She pulled a Coors out of the pocket of her pink bathrobe, popped the top, and slugged a good amount down, then licked her lips.

Ignoring her question, I said, "I'm here about the dog."

"What's with that damn dog?" She finished off the beer and tossed the can, which landed close to where she'd spit. "Back to my original question."

Noting the glimmer in her eyes, I knew she wasn't about to be helpful unless there was something in it for her. "Why don't you tell me what it is you want?" I asked.

The woman rubbed her fingers together, a big smile on her face, and gave her hips a shake. "Cash if you didn't get it."

"Let's be clear—I'm not paying for prattle." Did I just morph into my grandmother? She loved that word. And she never wanted to hear that she didn't always use it correctly. "Do you have anything worth selling?"

"I'm the one who had a ringside seat for the drama. Didn't see either of you around." She craned her neck and looked at Floyd with an appreciative eye. "If you have anything to do with the other broad that showed up, then you already know—no cash, no info."

Since I wasn't sure where the bidding started in these situations, I asked, "How much?" Wrong question, based on the nudge I got from Floyd.

"A Jackson will buy me a twenty-pack." She pulled another beer out of her other pocket and saluted, then held out her palm.

Cheaper to drink than smoke, that's for sure. "If you're not full of it, I'll toss in a tip." The how-to book said to carry petty cash but nothing about how much to pay for info. I pulled two twenties out of my pocket and handed her one, keeping the other in her line of sight as motivation. "If you turn out to be full of it, I'll chase you down and get my Jackson back."

The threat must have been believable, as she shoved it between two buttons on her robe. I looked to see if it fell to the ground, and though her bra obviously offered poor support, it did hold money. "Mike was a good neighbor, always willing to carry something heavy, unlike most around here, and you didn't even have to ask—if he saw you out, he leant his muscle." After taking a couple of sips of beer, she was back to guzzling. "Lost his job, downsized or something, and had to move. Time was running out, and with no prospects, he began to panic about what to do about Frito."

"Frito is the dog?"

"Uh, yeah," she said, like I wasn't the brightest bulb. "He ended up talking to Petunia about Frito moving in with her. She jumped at the chance to have the dog live with her after he reassured her that he wouldn't take it back unless she needed him to."

"Sounds like everyone walked away happy, including Frito," Floyd said.

I gave him a side-eye: *My case, remember?* He grinned.

"You'd think." The woman snorted. "But some

people are never flipping happy unless they're stirring… well, you get the picture."

"Is this where the other woman you mentioned comes in?" I asked.

"You've used up your first twenty." She eyed the other one between my fingers.

"This is how much useful info you've given me." I made a zero with my fingers. "You want this one? Pony up something good."

"What would your grandmother think of you badgering an old woman?"

"She's probably cheering from her grave." Her audacity reminded me of Pops.

She gave me a shocked look. "Ms. La-de-da has been around a couple of times and didn't want to hear that Mike moved—figured we were lying. You'd think that with everyone saying the same thing, she'd get it. She made a complete ass of herself, ranting on about the dog and how she had to know where it was. The only thing that did was make her look cray-cray. After that, the call went out when she was spotted lurking around, and everyone stayed in their apartments until she left." The woman took a long suck on an invisible cigarette. "If you track her ass down for a sit-down, you better not be telling her you talked to me."

"Since you haven't introduced yourself, there is a slim chance of that." Though a description would probably lead Edna right to her door. I was surprised she didn't throw back at me that I hadn't given my name, or Floyd's, either. He'd stood behind me the whole time and been little help, just laughing at everything.

"Earning my additional twenty here…" She kept her eye on it like she thought it would vanish. "The last time the woman showed up, she had some man in tow, papers in his hand. Knew that had court trouble written all over it and stayed behind my blinds."

"And then what?"

"You better not even be thinking of gypping me." She glared at me through rheumy eyes.

"Don't you worry. If I were to attempt such a thing, big guy here would step up, wouldn't you?" I glanced up at him and winked.

"Promise that I won't take my eyes off that twenty until it lands in your hand," Floyd assured her.

The woman gave him a thorough once-over, obviously liking what she saw, but then, she already knew that from the first couple of times she checked him out. "That woman didn't want to believe Mike moved. She didn't have to take anyone's word for it—all she had to do was look in the window. Saw the man she brought with her doing that, and maybe that's why she hasn't been back."

Even if I hadn't known that Mike moved, I wouldn't have done that. The drapes were cracked, but I wasn't pressing my face against the glass.

"I do know that she asked a couple of the neighbors about Frito, claiming it was her dog and that it was stolen, then changed her story." She snorted. "Heard that and warned Tunia not to be bringing Frito this way."

"Tunia?" Floyd questioned.

"Petunia." *Duh* in her tone.

"Let's rewind to when the woman showed up with the man and the court papers," I said.

"Turns out she was looking to drag Mike's butt to court." The second beer can followed the first one into the dirt.

I eyed her pockets, expecting her to produce another one. Not yet.

"Her story was that Mike didn't show proof of neutering and also that it was a no-no to find the dog another home without approval. Not sure who spilled about Frito getting new digs but hope they didn't spit up an address." She was back to puffing on her invisible cigarette. "Must've heard me mumble 'can't get blood out of a turnip,' as she turned her glare on me. Then announced to those standing around that she wanted the dog back and a judgment so she could collect if he ever did earn a dime."

*What the hell?* I raised my eyebrows at Floyd. The one thing I hadn't asked Edna was how Mike had broken the contract—rookie mistake. His smirk told me he knew what I was thinking, but no way to confirm it.

"Maybe it's as simple as getting Frito neutered,

if he hasn't been already, and Tunia approved for ownership," I said.

Floyd raised his brows, clearly communicating, *Simple?* and shook his head.

"Sounds simple, don't it?" The woman snorted. "Before you go pitching what you think is a hot idea, there's a glitch. Tunia can't be approved, as she's too old. Broad has an age requirement, and seniors don't make the cut. Guess she thinks we could punch out at any time."

"What's your take—if she gets the dog back, will she drop the lawsuit?" I asked.

She shrugged. "You want to make a hypothetical wager?" Not waiting for my answer, she went on. "There's not a chance in you-know-where. Not giving you Tunia's address, so don't ask. You take that dog, and you'll break her heart. If that's your plan, I'll spread the word, and no one will give you the time of day." She glared. "I've earned my forty, hint, hint. You got any more questions; I live right over there." She pointed over her shoulder. "Cash is king. Not sure what else you'd bring, but not interested."

I turned to Floyd. "Do you have a card on you?"

He handed me one. "You need to get your own."

"Why, when I can use yours?" I'd made my own, and they looked it, but he didn't need to know that. I handed the card and cash to the woman. "If La-de-dah comes back around, there's another Jackson in it for you if you call this number. If the big guy doesn't answer, just leave a message. I do feel bad, though, contributing to your beer dependency."

"My doc wanted me to give up the beer and cigs, and I had to remind him I'm not living forever, so we compromised on me giving up the cigs, and I got a promise that I could go out with a beer in my hand." She turned with a wave.

"A pleasure doing business, Ms. No Name," I said to the woman's back and heard her hoarse laugh before the door closed.

As we headed back to the truck, I noticed a ripple in several sets of drapes. Floyd reached for my hand.

I jerked it back. "Oh no, you don't. Happy you enjoyed yourself, laughing it up behind my back. Don't think that you being all sweet, or whatever you're doing, gets you out of foisting this job off on me when smart money says you knew La-la had more surprises up her sleeve than I could dream up." But I did take his hand as I climbed up into the truck.

"I enjoyed watching you hold your own with Miss No-name," Floyd said, getting behind the wheel and hitting the dashboard, still looking like he was enjoying himself way too much. "Didn't figure this case would be so messy, but Edna does have a reputation for wanting her own way. You have to agree that the foisting was good on my part."

"Oh no, I don't."

"Hold up a sec. I couldn't have dealt with the woman. You held your own, where I'd have run out of patience and been out of there, her yelling after me that I was a gypper. You ended up getting more details about the adoption than we had before."

"You know darn well that a wink and a smile, and she'd have invited you in for a cuddle." The face he made had me laughing. "The only reason I'm not tossing this case back at you is that I still need your help with Catnip. I'm not happy being even as involved as I am on that one."

"Got an idea that will redeem me."

"Can't wait to hear it."

"Sarcasm isn't attractive."

"The only people who say that are the ones on the receiving end."

Floyd bit his lip, and I knew he was trying to keep from laughing. "Are we agreed that Edna's the woman hunting down Mike?" He didn't wait for an answer. "I say we work a deal with Edna that makes everyone happy."

"After everything we just heard? You're dreaming. Unless you plan to divorce me and marry her offspring." I whipped out my phone and clicked away.

"That's not happening. And what are you doing?"

"Making notes on our visit if, for some reason, I have to come back, even though I can't think of a single reason that I'd need to. That said, I don't want to forget where our new friend lives or to bring twenties. We know Tunia is short for Petunia. How many women with such an unusual name could be living in the area? Bet not many. My plan—which I'm not saying is better than yours, but maybe it is—is to pay Tunia and Frito a visit and make sure the pooch has a good home before moving forward."

"Don't want to squash your enthusiasm, but don't be surprised if, despite my earlier optimism, you aren't able to make everyone happy."

# Chapter Thirteen

Over the next couple of days, Floyd and I were each off doing our own thing. He had a high-profile client come to town in need of personal protection, and I hung out close to home, finishing up a job for a client. In between, I called Caturday, and either she was deliberately letting it go to voicemail, or she'd turned off her phone.

I went to work, researching and gathering all the information I needed to close the dog case. I'd found Tunia, whose full name turned out to be Petunia Hart. Thanks to a neighbor, and a little lie, I was also able to locate Mike York, Frito's original owner, and get a phone number. He'd moved to North Carolina to be near his sister and, through her husband, had gotten hired on as a garage mechanic for a truck-racing team. Mike had just started his dream job, which kept him on the road, moving between racetracks. He was happy that Frito had Tunia and hoped it stayed that way, as he knew she loved the dog. He lamented that they could get screwed over, saying, "Frito couldn't have a better home."

"Edna came highly recommended, and not one word about all the drama that could follow if you didn't fulfill every term of the contract," Mike grumbled. "My bad—I only skimmed the paperwork—but I wanted Frito, so it wouldn't have made a difference. Now I'd read the contract before even looking at an animal."

"It appears Edna's complaints are that you didn't get permission to rehome Frito and the issue of neutering." I'd called her and asked directly, and after some evasiveness, she answered.

"I had the vet email Frito's file to Edna and can also send it to you." Mike got my address, and the file showed up not long after we ended the call. It clearly showed the date of the neutering and that the record of it had been sent to Edna.

"My goal is to come up with an agreement that makes everyone happy," I'd told Mike. Having met Edna, I knew I'd have to do some fast thinking to get that accomplished. "I've got a couple of suggestions for you: change your phone number and don't give out your address to anyone that would pass it along."

"Going to the phone store to take care of the number today," Mike assured me. He wanted to be kept updated, which I assured him I would… also that he could call me anytime.

My research had also shown that with anything short of a court order, Edna would be in legal hot water if she removed Frito from Tunia's home. Problem was, it wouldn't be that hard for her to get one based on Mike breaking the contract. I hadn't shared that part with Mike—why exacerbate the situation?—and also hadn't heard anything to suggest that Edna had located Tunia. No getting around that Mike had violated the contract by rehoming Frito, so for the dog to stay where he was at, it would require Edna to relent. I groaned.

\* \* \*

I was annoyed that Pops had been ignoring my calls, after his offers to help with anything I needed, and decided it was ambush time. I left the house early the next morning to pay him a little visit, knowing that if I timed it right, he'd be on his second or third cup of coffee and devouring the news.

The first stop on the way was to hit up the local bakery. I wanted one of everything but settled on a half-dozen cupcakes. Not breakfasty, but fun, and I knew it would take his attention off the fact that I'd barged in unannounced.

I wished I'd honed the lockpicking skills Floyd had taught me, but Pops wouldn't know to be impressed anyway, since I had a key. One of these days, I'd have to try that out on him just to see his reaction. I barged through the door without knocking, bakery box in hand.

"Good way to get shot," Pops griped after getting out of his chair to see who'd invaded his home.

"With what?" I eyed him. "Kind of hard without a weapon."

He appeared flustered, his cheeks red at being caught in just pajama pants. He skated past me and straight to his bedroom.

I grabbed a roll of paper towels and put it and the box on the coffee table, then eyed his mug, which was almost empty, and put water in the microwave for his instant brew. For myself, I'd stopped on the way and picked up an extra-large cup, knowing I'd need a caffeine jolt to hold my own with the man.

Pops was soon back in a pair of sweatpants and a t-shirt. He plopped down and eyed the box, then flipped open the lid and helped himself, about devouring the first cupcake in one bite. "You could've called." He licked his lips.

"How do I say this nicely? You're full of it. You know that I've called several times—even if you didn't listen to the messages, my number would've popped up on the screen. There *was* the one time you picked up—my guess having not checked to see who was calling—then gave a lame excuse: 'Have to go, on the way out the door.' To where exactly?" I eyed him, daring him to make up some convoluted story.

"Hmm…" He shoved another cupcake in his mouth, this time savoring it a little longer than the previous one.

"You go ahead and wolf all those down, then plan on a nap because you'll have a stomachache.

Until then, there's nothing to stop me from monopolizing the conversation." I didn't waste a raised eyebrow, as he wasn't looking at me. "Have something to share that I thought you'd like to know—I've hired a *licensed* PI. Not sure where you found the losers you sent, but if you have any more, please stop."

"Knew you were looking for someone and was trying to be helpful. With the right person, you could easily build back the business. But if you're not going to keep regular hours, then my efforts are for naught."

Just great! So Pops had someone keeping tabs. I was doubtful he'd make the trip himself. "Maybe it would be helpful if you could explain why you're trying to resurrect a business that's been closed for over a year. I believe I asked you that question before and didn't get an answer. Don't tell me it's because you're under contract to pay out the lease, as you own the building free and clear." I waved off his sputter. "Here's some advice I won't charge you for, since it's another thing I've mentioned before—" More than once. "—put someone in charge who actually knows the business, not someone who doesn't have a clue. You're not stupid, so I'm thinking if you were serious about bringing North back to its previous glory, you'd hire someone with cred."

"You quitting?"

"That's all you got out of what I just said?" I shook my head. "Not just yet, but send over another slug or murder-for-hire case, and I'm out." I didn't know for sure that he'd sent Catnip, but we were about to find out.

"You must've misunderstood."

"Which issue?" I snorted so loud it felt like I might've blown out my nostrils, and from the look on Pops' face, he thought the same thing. "You better be listening, old man, because I'm warning you—I'm going to find out what you're up to, and then heaven help you." At his raised eyebrows, I added, "I won't beat the hell out of you, but you might wish that was all I had in mind."

"Drama Queen. It's from all that acting you do. Here's *my* free advice, which comes from sucking air a lot longer than you: you might want to calm down if you want to attract the right sorts of people."

"What are you talking about?"

"Business," Pops snapped. "Tone down the snippiness, and the phone will be ringing in no time." He cut me off before I could say anything. "It's going to anyway, as I ran into an old client the other day—Ware Dowell—and told him that North is open for business and my granddaughters behind the wheel."

"The attorney that used to run ads on TV in the middle of the night—slimy as all get out and reputation to match? What kind of business did he throw your way, when his clients are the dregs? Did Dowell pay up, or did you have to shake it out of him?" Surprised his clients could even pay.

"In all businesses, you have to toss in a freebie or two to show you're up to snuff."

"Call your seedy lawyer friend back and tell him no free anything. He tries to skate on the bill, and I've got a guy that will leave him face down in the dirt, lucky to suck in a breath."

"You need to cut back on the coffee," Pops growled into his mug.

"You need me to boil you some more water?" He was right about me—I'd had enough but wasn't admitting it.

"I'm thinking on it."

"If you'd let me buy you a coffee pot, you could keep it full."

"Just one more thing I won't use," he grumbled.

"Have you talked to Mom and Dad and filled them in on what you're up to?" Nice subject change, I thought, patting myself mentally, but I needed to know, as it was time for my weekly call, and I didn't want to be as evasive as I was the last time I talked to them.

"You need to keep what we're doing under wraps a little while longer, until we know—"

I cut in, exasperated. "In the meantime, I screw up your business and... what? Or is this really a cover for something else?"

"Calm your shorts. Have a cupcake." Pops pointed, as though I hadn't been the one to set the box down. "While you're stuffing your face, tell me about this new hire."

The man was an ace at avoiding questions he didn't want to answer or didn't have an answer for and wouldn't admit to it in either case. "How about I introduce the two of you, and you can make up your own mind? Assuming he passes his probationary period." I couldn't wait to tease Floyd about that one. My phone rang with a message alert, and I took it out—Floyd. Seemed like the man knew I was thinking about him. *Brogan's car was vandalized, and he's going to visit friends*, Floyd's text read. I groaned and looked up at Pops. "You know anything about a Caturday Ginseng?"

"What the hell kind of name is that?" He thought for a minute. "Not one of my referrals. If she's a new client, find out what she wants and make sure she can pay."

Agreed on the name, but I wasn't in the mood to tell him. "How about Mildred Bellwether? Kept calling you Maxi; does that ring a bell?"

Pops leaned back, stared at the ceiling, then looked back at me. "No one's ever called me that. Dated a Mildred back when, but it's been a while. Why?"

"She showed up at the office, wanting to hire North to murder her ex and dispose of the body."

Pops laughed. "Good one. Remember thinking at the time you called about that, that you were up to something, and I still do." When I just glared at him, he asked, "How did you leave it with her?"

"Told her I'd get on it and get back to her."

He laughed again. "You're so full of it."

"Runs in the family. I've got an appointment." I grabbed the mugs and bakery box and took them into the kitchen. "Try not to wolf down the rest of the cupcakes, lest you puke and erase the fond memory of our get-together." I came back and stood over him. "I'd appreciate you not avoiding my calls; might be something important. What if I need backup, you're a no-show, and something happens? Then you'd be consumed with guilt."

"But when I don't answer, you come over with bakery goods—win for me," he said, amused with himself.

"I need to stop rewarding your bad behavior." I leaned down to kiss his cheek.

"Promise me that you'll give the business your best effort before deciding whether to ditch it or not?" He stood, hooked his arm around me, and walked me to my car, holding open the door and pulling me in for one last hug.

"How about I behave, and you do the same?" I slid behind the wheel.

"You can't snatch all the fun away from an old man."

Maybe it was as simple as Pops wanting to leave the business to someone to continue on in his footsteps, I thought as I headed home.

## Chapter Fourteen

On the drive home, I thought about the text message I'd gotten from Floyd and had more than a few questions about what happened to Herbie. Wasn't sure who to ask, as Floyd probably didn't know himself. At the next light, I used the hands-free system to call Caturday for the umpteenth time, and much to my surprise, she actually answered. I identified myself and managed to keep from grouching, *Why haven't you returned my calls?* "I have some information for you about Herbie Brogan. You name the time, and we can meet at the office."

She stammered which was a new side to her, as she'd been direct when she came to my office.

"There's been some headway," I said, filling the silence. "I also want to introduce you to the new PI on the case."

"You've been so slow to come up with anything," she mumbled. "I'm not at home and would need to check my calendar before committing to a date, as I have appointments scheduled—just can't remember the exact days."

Her lack of enthusiasm came through loud and clear and left me wondering if she'd hired someone else. "Why don't you give me a call as soon as you know? That's if you want to move forward on your case."

"Yes, yes. I'll certainly call you." She hung up.

I couldn't help but hope that she'd come to her senses and changed her mind. If she did show up, in addition to everything else, I wanted to ask how she knew my Pops. She hadn't said how it was that she turned up at the office.

Once I was home with my feet up, I texted Floyd, hoping we could catch up later. I finished downing an ice-cold water just as my parents sent me a Zoom link. It was fun to see their smiling faces, and the blue-green water in the background. My dad, a self-described workaholic who'd put in long hours as an engineer for NASA, had decided once he retired to make the most of every day. The first thing my parents did was buy a boat to go cruise the Caribbean, and they showed no signs of getting bored of soaking up the sun.

I blew them kisses and then swore them to secrecy, having them both hold up their right hands and ignoring their eyerolls.

"Your father…" I eyed my own, then went on to tell them both about what Pops had signed me up for and also that I lacked the stones to shut him down.

The two turned to one another and burst out laughing.

"Thanks for the support." But I quickly lost my snark and laughed.

"You can bet my old man is up to something." Dad narrowed his eyes, lost in thought for a minute, as though trying to figure out what it was.

"Agreed on that one," Mom chimed in. "I'm betting it has nothing to do with you running North and everything to do with finding you a husband."

I was certain that even without Zoom, my groan could be heard by anyone walking on the dock where they had their boat anchored.

"Pops has mentioned a time or two that 'Maren needs to grab herself a husband,'" Dad said, mimicking his father with a chuckle. "Despite my admonitions that it would happen in good time and to leave it alone, it sounds like he moved ahead with some cockamamie plan."

"If that's his plan… you should've seen the first three applicants he sent over." I described the two I'd actually seen, and when I got to the part about pulling a gun on one, Mom's eyes bugged out, and Dad grumbled under his breath. "No worries about having to visit me in jail, as I didn't shoot him. I did bring the gun home and locked it away so no one else would find it."

"Proud of you for holding your own," Mom said.

"You need to be adamant with Pops—no more referrals. "Have you gotten any real clients?" Dad asked skeptically.

"We've had that discussion, but I'll be

reminding him." I told them about the Caturday case, reserving the illegal details for after it was over and done with. They both laughed about her AKA.

"That's not a name I recognize," Dad mused. "Mildred sounds vaguely familiar; maybe she's an old client of Pops', and that's where I heard the name."

No need to share just now that I'd already asked, and Pops claimed ignorance, but I'd definitely be bringing it up again. I then told them about Frito.

"Who's this Floyd person you've mentioned a couple of times now?" Mother fluttered her eyelashes.

"Don't tell Dad," I said, even though he was right there and could hear every word. "He's well over six feet of hotness, and he came recommended. But you know it's not professional, mixing business with hokey pokey."

"If this Floyd gets any notions, he and I will be having a chat before he shows up at your door for a visit." Dad flexed his muscles. "Got it?"

"He already paid me a visit and was a perfect gentleman."

I'd barely finished reassuring Dad when Mother asked, "Recommended by whom?"

"You remember Rella Cabot? Well, I ran into her and…" I told them how she'd introduced me to Dixon, who introduced me to Floyd, who introduced me to his mother, who made the best cookies. Mother oohed over that.

"You let this Floyd character know that he better continue to be a gentleman."

Mom swatted Dad's arm.

We continued to talk for at least an hour, catching up on everything going on. Finally, all caught up, I blew them kisses and waved, and we hung up.

I'd barely set my phone down when it rang again, Floyd's name on the screen. He suggested that we get together in the morning to check out Herbie's place and talk to a couple of the neighbors. I had yet to hear any details about what had happened to his car but knew Floyd only had a few minutes.

"I'll meet you at the office," I offered.

"I'll pick you up," he growled.

I hung up, smiling at the phone.

# Chapter Fifteen

Floyd arrived right on time the next morning, and I smiled at the coffees he'd bought from a local drive-thru.

"Let's sit outside, since it's the perfect day for it." I led the way out to the patio, where we sat facing the water.

A boat going by caught Floyd's attention, and he watched until it was out of sight. "Interesting that right after we talk to Herbie, his car gets vandalized. Have to wonder if Caturday had someone else run a check and they found the address."

"Vandalism is a common occurrence down here, so maybe—"

"Coincidence?" Floyd snorted. "The HOA was eager to be of assistance to the police and handed over a copy of the security tapes to Lucas. They showed a black sedan pulling up to the curb, plates covered." He shook his head. "A slight individual got out from behind the wheel, concealed head-to-toe in black, a mask over their face and a drill in hand, headed straight to Herbie's car, and proceeded to inflict as much damage as they could on the exterior."

"That must've taken some time."

Floyd nodded. "All told, about half an hour. Then the person crawled underneath the car and removed the catalytic converter, which they left by the rear bumper when they approached the condo. They attempted to jimmy the security door open with a screwdriver, but no luck. Guessing they were thinking that drilling the lock might be heard by one of the residents."

"Surprised they worried about that after using the drill on the car."

Floyd shrugged. "They probably got spooked. The tapes didn't show anyone coming out to investigate, so the reason for the hasty departures unclear. On the way back to their car, they drilled through the sidewalls of all the tires, picked up the converter, and left."

"You're coming out to get in your car, probably in hurry what do you notice first, four flat tires or the exterior damage?" I asked.

"Definitely the tires. It might take you a minute or so to see the rest. Whichever you notice first, now you're looking over your shoulder, wondering if someone's waiting for you and about to pop up."

"Herbie called the cops, I'm guessing."

"Here's something interesting—the cops asked if he had any enemies that might single out his car for that kind of damage. He stumbled and mumbled, then finally said he couldn't think of anyone. They pegged him for a liar but a scared one."

"Feel bad for Herbie." I made a face. "It's hard to believe Caturday could have inflicted the damage on his car, but I wouldn't put it past her to hire someone."

"Agreed. I happen to know that Catnip is on the suspect list. Lucas had even more questions about her, none of which I could answer, so expect a call."

"You said Herbie left town."

"And this time with very little hesitation on his part. An hour after the cops had hauled the car away, he was seen leaving through a side door with a couple of bags in tow and hopping into an Uber. After talking to Lucas, I called Herbie, and he was still rattled. He admitted that he hadn't planned to take our suggestion to relocate, but the car incident freaked him out. Asked me not to tell anyone that he went to stay with friends in the Tampa area. Assured him I could keep my mouth shut."

I took my ringing phone out of my pocket and checked the screen, then flashed it at him. "It's your friend, Catnip." I didn't have to look up to see Floyd's eyeroll. I put it on speaker and answered all official-sounding, smirking at myself. "North Investigations."

"I can meet you at your office in a half-hour," Caturday said abruptly.

Floyd shook his head.

"Just finishing up with another client. The earliest I could make it is—" I looked at Floyd, who held up two fingers. "—two hours." He nodded.

"You want my business, you'll make it one." The labored breathing that had accompanied her side of the call cut off abruptly.

I double-checked the screen, and she'd hung up. "What was that about?" I grouched.

"Catnip flexing her muscles when she doesn't have any." Floyd whipped out his phone.

I guessed that he'd called Lucas when he described the call from Caturday, which was confirmed when I heard him yell, 'What the hell?' through the phone. I zoned out for the rest of the conversation, only being able to hear half of it.

When Floyd hung up, he said, "Lucas is in Naples and can't make it back in time. He wants us to string her along, feeding her the bogus addresses, and record every word. Figures if you try to reschedule, she might shy away."

"Just so happens I got a delivery yesterday..." I got up and ran to my office, coming back with an open box. "This was a fun purchase, so no teasing me."

Floyd reached in and pulled out a couple of earpieces; from his laugh, I knew he was familiar with them. I was happy not to have to read the directions in front of him. "You went top of the line—almost invisible yet with excellent sound quality." He nodded. "I'll get us hooked up before we leave the house. You're going to get your first lesson in recording and listening devices." He grabbed my cup and pitched it into the trash can in the kitchen. "Tracked your old contractor down, and I'm having a meeting with him next week." He gave the space a closer inspection.

"Does he know you're stopping by to break his nose?"

"There's no fun in warning the man," he grumped.

"Just don't do anything to get yourself hurt or in trouble."

He grinned at me.

## Chapter Sixteen

At that time of day, the streets were less congested, and Floyd shot over to the office. I used my key to open the elevator door on the third floor, and as we stepped off, our eyes were drawn to the hole cut in the door of the office, large enough that a person could crawl through. Floyd put his hand in front of me, silently telling me to stand back, and stuck his head inside, then climbed through. A few tense minutes later, he unlocked the door and made his way down the corridor to check the doors of the other two offices and then the stairwell. "The lock was drilled off of this one," he said of the latter. "None of the others have been touched."

"You'd think someone downstairs would have heard all the noise and wondered what the heck." I surveyed the debris on the floor.

"Not necessarily, depending on how the building was constructed; there could be quite a lot of insulation." Floyd held out his hand, and I went inside with him. "Even if they had, they probably wouldn't bother coming up to check out what's happening."

I scanned every corner of the office, and it didn't look any different than the last time I was here — still not much to see. Whoever it was had gone through all the desk drawers, leaving them open. I was one step ahead there, as I'd packed up the few things Pops left behind, making certain not to miss anything, and everything was now in my home office.

Floyd had whipped out his phone, and his first call was to report the break-in. I'd have to check with Pops about filing an insurance claim for the damage to the door. He then made another call and told someone, "Got a job for you." He added what was needed and gave them the address. Floyd's jaunt down the hall had answered one of my questions — whoever did this wanted something out of North in particular. But what? Why now?

"There were never any break-ins that I heard of when Pops owned it. What do you think changed… other than the ownership?" I shuddered, thinking about what could have happened if I'd come here alone when whoever did this was still in the office.

"The good news is that the door's easy to replace." Floyd eyed what was left. "I suggest that the replacement be one that's reinforced. I noticed the first time I was here that the building needed security cameras and was surprised they hadn't already been installed. I'll get our guy out here to make recommendations for a system that covers the entire building."

"It was on my list, but because I hadn't decided

how much time I'd be spending here, I let it slide." I suddenly squealed. "Caturday's going to be here any minute."

"That's why we're going to meet her downstairs." Floyd locked up, and we headed down the hall.

I was happy to be out of the office, as the thought of someone breaking in creeped me out, and to find what? Would that question ever get answered? "What if the cops show at the same time as Caturday?"

"As soon as they come in the driveway, I'll go to meet them." Floyd gently nudged me inside the elevator. "There's a cement table and bench downstairs, both a little small, but we'll make it work. Before Catnip can complain about rock-hard seating or ask any questions, the excuse will be, 'Sorry for the inconvenience, but there's a plumbing problem upstairs.' Then you launch into some beautiful day nonsense or some-such and, in the next breath, start the meeting."

Once outside, he inclined his head toward a table nestled up against a palm tree.

"Sort of knew this was here but had forgotten, and come to think of it, never saw anyone sitting here any of the times I visited Pops. What do I say? 'Have a seat, Caturday, and we'll enjoy the heat and humidity.'" I flourished my hand as I eyed the benches, trying not to turn up my nose and point out the obvious—bird poop.

"It's still a good idea," Floyd said, having

followed my gaze. "Be right back." He ran to his truck and came back with a couple of beach towels.

I chuckled as he covered both benches. "You're like a Girl Scout, always prepared."

"This wasn't made for guys like me." He straddled the bench, and I sat next to him, the two of us facing the parking lot and US-1. He caught me struggling not to laugh and glared at me, though I noticed the quirking of the sides of his mouth.

I checked my watch for the sixth time. "Catnip's late."

"How about a wager before you call her and ask, 'Where the hell are you?' My money's on her being a no-show. I say that because, if she were smart, she'd back off her idea to kill Herbie, as too many fingers would point her way. Loser buys coffee."

"Not wagering with you, since your PI senses outweigh mine." I returned his stare-down. "But I will buy coffee and something yum to eat if you're nice." Phone in hand, I called Caturday. "Hello, Ms. Day," I sing-songed, as I listened to it ring.

"It's Ginseng." Floyd chuckled.

"Surprised you didn't call her Nip." I rolled my eyes at the phone, having gotten voicemail, and left a message reminding the woman that we had an appointment and to please call if she was running late or couldn't make it. "I find it odd that she would be a no-show on the same day that we find the office was broken into."

"If she's the one who broke in, it's not very smart of her; you'd think she'd have chosen another day."

A cop car pulled into the parking lot. Floyd stood and held out his hand to me, and the two of us met the officer getting out of his car. "Hey Hank," Floyd acknowledged, recognizing the man. He introduced me.

"You had a break-in?" he asked. I nodded.

Floyd told him what we'd found.

"Anything appear to be missing?" Hank asked me.

I shook my head. "Just the obvious damage."

The three of us foot-cruised around the building, Hank inspecting the front and back doors. "Since there's no damage to either door, I'm thinking that whoever did it was let in by someone coming or going, then waited until the building cleared out to do their damage."

We then went upstairs, and I hung back as Floyd and Hank examined all the damage, and he took notes. It didn't take long before they were back in the hall.

"Since it's clear that you're not using the office and whoever broke in didn't take anything, it's likely they won't be back," Hank told me.

"I really do enjoy working from home." I smiled. I had my reasons for not wanting to spend any time here, and this was just one more.

Back at the table outside, Hank handed me his

card. "Any questions, call anytime."

As Floyd and Hank walked back to his patrol car, I sat back down and checked out the half-dozen cars in the parking lot.

I pulled out my phone as Floyd rejoined me, called Caturday again, and flashed the screen at him. This time, it went straight to voicemail. Out of patience and about to tell her to take a hike, I took a breath and instead said, "Due to a scheduling conflict, this meeting will have to be rescheduled."

"Good one," Floyd said after I hung up.

"I want her to go away and to never hear her name again." I was trying not to whine.

"That would be too easy." He pulled out his phone, called some guy named Seven, and after a couple of jokes, asked him to send someone out to make recommendations for a security system. "I expect a discount." He hung up and met my questioning stare. "You met Avery over coffee… well, Seven's her husband and a partner at WD Consulting. She keeps him dancing, which is fun to watch. Wouldn't surprise me if the two of them come out here and do the walkaround themselves."

"Running into Rella at the coffee shop that day was unexpected but has brought such great people into my life that I'm happy I was desperate for a caffeine fix."

An over-sized pickup truck pulled into the driveway, a German Shephard hanging his head out the window on the passenger side. Floyd went to meet the driver, opening the door for the dog to take a flying leap and scratching his head. The two men stared at the building as Floyd pointed from one side to the other. As they made their way over to me, I noted a large utility box and several sheets of plywood in the truck bed.

Floyd made the introductions. "Todd Bagby, this is my boss, Maren."

"Couldn't have timed the call any better, as I was in the area. Brought what I need to get it boarded up until you decide on a new door," Todd offered with smile.

"How about you choose a door that fits in with the other two on the floor and change the stairwell locks too?" It was agreed upon, and I handed over a business card. Floyd's eyebrows went up, and I'd bet he'd be asking for one later. Knowing they were about to head inside, I said, "I'm going to wait out here in case Caturday shows."

As the two men walked away, I heard Todd say, "Caturday?" Whatever Floyd said in response, they laughed as they entered the building.

I sat back down and called Caturday again, and it went to voicemail. I once again wondered if she had anything to do with the vandalism upstairs, but dismissed it, as it didn't make sense. In light of what had happened to Herbie, it concerned me more that she hadn't bothered to cancel the appointment. Traffic had started to back up, and it was all going south. I knew the side streets well enough that when we were ready to leave, I could tell Floyd how to get around it all.

# Chapter Seventeen

Where the heck were Floyd and Todd? It was a beautiful day, but I was tired of the sun beating down on me and ready for something cold to drink. A pickup pulling into the parking lot caught my attention, and I wondered if Caturday had finally decided to show up. Due to the dark tint, it was hard to make out the driver as the truck cruised by slowly and snagged a parking space at the far end. I waited but didn't see any movement and figured they were waiting on someone. I picked up my phone and clicked across the screen, checking for any new messages and debating whether to go upstairs.

The approach of footsteps caught my attention, and I looked up to see creepy Leo Rung glaring down at me. "Not sure how I got this lucky, catching you out here, but I'm not one to squander an opportunity," he snarled.

Whatever the man wanted, I wasn't interested. I did have a few questions, starting with what he was doing back here, but the last thing I wanted to do was engage him in conversation. "Sorry for how things went before — we got off on the wrong foot," I managed to say in a pleasant enough tone. "Maxwell went ahead and hired someone."

That had Leo grinding his teeth. He plopped down across from me and leaned forward; with the small table, he was practically in my face.

"I'm expecting someone," I said, hoping he'd take the hint, and at the same time attempted to inch back on the bench, but there wasn't a lot of room.

Leo slapped his hand down on the table.

It annoyed me that I jerked back at that, but the unstable look in his eyes had me on alert.

"There's no doubt in my mind that you were the one who screwed me," he growled.

"Since Maxwell's decided not to retire, I'm sure that once the business is up and running again, he'll give you a call." Not a chance in hell of that, but I just wanted him to take all the anger he was directing my way and leave.

"You and I could've been running this joint together." His leg jumped up and down.

"I had no idea that's what you wanted." Where the heck was Floyd? I didn't dare look around. "It's a moot point anyway, as Maxwell finally figured out that I wasn't cut out to be the woman in charge and stepped back in." If only. "How about I arrange a sit-down for you and him?"

"You think I'm stupid, don't you? You're just attempting to placate me so I'll skate out of here — well, fat chance."

"You might want to consider yourself lucky, as there's been a break-in, and the reopening date will have to be postponed. It would have been extremely inconvenient if you'd cleared your schedule only for nothing to come of it."

"Where are the business records?" Leo demanded.

It took me a minute as the shock sank in. "You're the one that broke into the office?"

"Answer me," he growled.

"Maxwell took everything home," I said. He shook his head, and I wasn't sure if he believed me or not. "You're a licensed PI; surely you have a lockpick—why all the damage? Overboard, don't you think?"

"Because it was fun. I didn't damage the interior in any way, as I still plan to take over the business. When I didn't find the records, I planned for my next stop to be Maxwell's, and then, whether I found them or not, I'd have ended up at your house."

Leo wasn't going anywhere—I needed to run. I threw one leg over the side of the bench.

"I've been watching you all morning." He smirked. "You showed up here with that ass from last time. Well, isn't he going to be surprised when you disappear right under his nose?" He leaned forward, whipping a white cloth out of his pocket. "I didn't want to do it this way, but you're leaving me no choice." He lunged across the table.

Guessing his intent, I leaped away before he could press it over my mouth, avoiding his outstretched hand. I fell backward and landed in the dirt and gravel. Leo moved faster than I'd have given him credit for and was instantly standing over me, glaring. Without a second thought, I began to kick and scream. My shoe made contact with his shin, and he winced and yelped, but it only served to infuriate him more.

Leo hurled himself across my body and shoved the cloth against my face. Slowly, I lost the energy to fight and started to feel dizzy. He kept the cloth pressed over my mouth and nose as he tugged me to my feet. My attempts to fight were met with chuckles.

"You're not getting away, not ever, so give it up. You won't like what I'll do to you to get you to fall in line, and trust me, you will." He dragged me over to the truck, whipped the door open, and pushed me into the passenger side, pulling the seatbelt so tight I couldn't move an inch.

I fought the dizziness, hoping a pedestrian would see and intervene even though I hadn't seen anyone the whole time I'd been sitting outside. Better yet, I wanted Floyd to show back up and kick Leo into the next state. Here I was, by myself with this nutjob, and who knew where he was taking me or if I'd ever see my family again.

"You're mine now," I heard before I passed out.

# Chapter Eighteen

I groaned as I came to, blinking, and took in my surroundings. I felt woozy and disoriented but recognized that I was in the hospital and wondered how I got there. The sun coming through the window let me know it was daytime, but which day? I attempted to roll over and bumped into the large mass of another person curled up next to me, a massive leg thrown over mine, keeping me from moving an inch. I looked over my shoulder.

Floyd grinned at me, giving me a peck on the check. "Don't ever scare me like that again," he said gruffly.

"I'm in the hospital, right?" He nodded as I plucked at my gown. I noticed he had on jeans and a t-shirt. "Uhm... you're in bed with me. Isn't that illegal or something?"

"The night nurse was about to boot me when I told her you'd sleep better with me holding you. She smiled and said, 'I won't tell. If you need anything, press the button,' and she was gone. You don't have to worry; I was a complete gentleman. Mostly anyway," he added at my raised eyebrow. "You've been here overnight, and now that you're awake and alert, you'll be released."

"The last I remember…" Fear rippled through me, and Floyd tightened his hold. "Where's Leo?" I shuddered.

"You don't have to worry about that piece of filth. He's in jail. I doubt a jury will acquit him, so that's where he'll stay for a damn long time," Floyd said with certainty.

"I was less than thrilled to see him approach me, and that was without knowing how far he was willing to go. He said he wanted the business and was the one who broke in, looking for the records." I snuggled closer to Floyd.

"Todd and I came out of the building to let you know that the door and locks would be replaced in a couple of hours and caught sight of butthead manhandling you into his truck."

"That's the last thing I remember, and his final threat was that he'd never let me go. Was he able to get me alone?"

"Damn near. I took off running and chased that damn truck toward the exit. Good thing Todd was there, as he jumped into his truck and didn't hesitate to ram the driver's side, keeping him from getting out on the highway."

Thank goodness. I didn't know what Leo had planned for me, but I bet I wouldn't have seen my old life again. I coughed, and Floyd reached over me, grabbed a cup off the tray, and held the straw to my lips. I took a long drink. "The police show up?"

"Not before I had to thwart his plans to make a run for it. Blocked by Todd's truck, Leo climbed over you and was half out the passenger door when I helped him the rest of the way. Todd had to pull me off him, after which I cuffed him and left him face down in the dirt for the police to haul away."

I reached for his hand and kissed his bruised knuckles.

"When you wouldn't wake up, Todd had to stop me from killing Leo and held butthead in place with his foot until the cops got there. They found a vial of the sedative he used and sent it along with the paramedics. The doc assured me that you'd sleep it off and be fine, and here you are—wide awake."

The door flew open, and in came a nurse with a big smile for the two of us. "How are you feeling?"

Floyd slid off the side of the bed and stood.

I assured her I felt fine and answered all her questions as she took my vitals and made notes on my chart.

"When will I be released?" I asked.

"Dr. Trevor's making rounds now and should be in shortly. Wouldn't surprise me if he releases you today." She smiled again and sailed out of the room.

"What are the chances Leo will get out?"

"Unfortunately, he'll probably make bail, which is why I asked Dixon to put an alert on him, so we'll know if and when it happens." Floyd dragged a chair up next to the bed and sat down.

The doctor came in less than five minutes later, a couple of interns in tow, checked me over, and let me know he'd be signing my release. "It was a common sedative, and you shouldn't have any aftereffects. Any issues, have your husband call your Primary Care."

Once the door closed on the trio, I turned to Floyd.

"I lied." He held up his hands. "If I hadn't said we were married, I'd have been tossed."

"I appreciate your holding my hand and that I didn't wake up alone." I smiled at him.

He leaned down and brushed my lips with a kiss.

It didn't take long for the nurse to come back with my discharge papers.

## Chapter Nineteen

Floyd had driven me home and stayed overnight, for which I was grateful. He'd cuddled with me on the couch and, when I fell asleep during the movie he'd chosen almost as soon as it came on, carried me to bed. I was disappointed that he wasn't there when I woke up, but he showed up shortly afterward with freshly baked apple muffins.

I suggested that we check out the repairs at North, but he didn't want to hear a word about me venturing from the house. He had a job and said he would be back in a couple of hours, and I'd better be home, or he was tracking me down. After he left, I went into my office, put aside everything that had to do with the investigation, and spent the morning dealing with issues for my voice clients. It didn't take long to clear up a few issues and make them all happy.

I moved to the living room, cracked open the patio doors, letting the breeze in, and sacked out on the couch for a nap. A pounding on the front door jerked me awake. Even though I hadn't heard anything about Leo being released, I was afraid to answer. Then I heard Pops calling my name and hustled over to stop the banging. I threw the door open, and he barreled inside, along with twenty pounds of black fur that cut him off and almost sent him tumbling to the floor before he managed to catch himself.

"What the hell?" Pops demanded. "When did you get that thing?"

"No-name comes by every once in a while, and sleeps out on the patio. Now that you've let him in, he probably thinks he lives here and whoever he does belong to will be upset if I feed him and he never goes home." I walked over and opened the sliders all the way, expecting him to go out and jump up on in his usual place on the chaise, but he didn't budge, camped out at the refrigerator with an expectant look on his face.

"He's hungry." Pops enveloped me in a hug, then pushed me back for a once-over. "Why did I have to hear that you'd been attacked in the parking lot from one of my tenants?" The grumpiness was back in his tone.

I raised my eyebrows and stared. "So now you admit to owning the building."

"This visit is all about you; nothing to do with me. Are you okay?" He twirled me around.

"If I barf, I'm aiming for your shoes." How had I not noticed in the past that he was so good at being evasive?

He snorted and stomped into the kitchen. "What the hell happened in here? A DIY, and you got bored?" He scanned the room with a scowl, which only grew when his gaze landed on the appliances in the corner. "You must have something you can feed this damn thing. You can't let it go hungry." Pops picked up the cat, who yowled instantly: *Put me down*.

"In case you didn't get the message, he only likes to be petted and not boosted into the air. Good way to get vomit on your shirt."

Pops headed my warning and immediately put the cat down. He scrounged up a dish and filled it with water, then looked in the fridge and shook his head. The cat lapped up the water. "No need for you to be on a diet." He hooked his arm around me and walked me over to the couch. "Now, what the hell happened? And don't skimp on details," he ordered as he sat down next to me.

"Leo Rung happened." I started with the first meeting and the lengths he was willing to go to get the business. "Were you aware that he was unstable when you sent him my way? And that's being nice. Did you know he was willing to do *anything* to get what he wanted—criminal or not?"

Pops brushed his hand through his grey shag and sighed. "I'll admit that I was the one who sent him your way. Didn't know him all that well, but he provided a couple references that checked out, with not one word that he was a nutjob."

"While you were doing what sounds like an intensive interview, did you happen to mention that I was single and hard up for a man?" I didn't bother to reign in my snark.

"Well..." Pops' cheeks turned pink. "Don't

remember exactly how the conversation went. But I would've never said anything like that."

"Please... please stop." I was annoyed with his vacant stare, recognizing it as him busily coming up with some new irritating idea. "My dating life is off limits as of now." I knew he heard me, but that didn't mean anything. "Believe I told you this already—I've hired a guy to take on any investigation job that stumbles through the door, starting with the Caturday case."

"Still a stupid name." Pops snorted. "Thought about the Mildred woman. That was such a short-lived relationship that I don't see how it could be the same woman, as she surely wouldn't have remembered about North. Wasn't interested in a relationship after your grandmother, and no one sparked my interest anyway. I was a one- or two-date guy." The cat, done looking for food I didn't have, jumped in the chair across from us and stretched out.

"Don't know what's up with this cat, but I know he's hungry and needs to go home. When you leave, take him with you. Drive around the neighborhood and figure out who he belongs to. Maybe you'll get lucky, and someone will be out yelling, 'Here, Kitty.'"

"At least you didn't lose your sense of humor during your tussle with Leo."

Translation: I'd be the one walking door-to-door, trying to find the owner.

"I apologize for the whole Leo fiasco. You've

got to know I wouldn't sic a weirdo on you. Good news, though. Called the jail on the way over here, and a friend that works there told me he hasn't made bail, and it's set high enough he probably won't. My friend also promised to call if that changed."

*Really happy about that.* "What I'd like is a promise from you—no more meddling."

"I'll… uhm… try. You know, old man… old habits." He did appear humbled. "How about a good reason why you didn't call right after it happened? I'd have come to the hospital in a flash."

"Took a while for the drugs to wear off, and then I was getting released and didn't want you to worry. Planned to come over with cookies and spring it on you." I smiled at him, but his frown didn't lessen.

"Cookies? No reason you can't come through on that one, now that my taste buds are perked and ready."

"You're on." I gave Pops a sideways hug. "Speaking of treats, time for a muffin." I got up, made a fresh pot of coffee, and turned the bag upside down on a plate. Motioning Pops over, I noticed that the cat had split and looked out to the patio, but he was nowhere to be seen.

## Chapter Twenty

Several hours later, after spending the afternoon doing investigation work, Floyd called and asked what I wanted for dinner. Since the cat was back and now camped outside the door, one eye on my every movement, I asked for cat food, which had him laughing but didn't prompt questions for some reason.

I grabbed my phone and snapped a couple of pictures of the feline, and the two of us walked the block, the cat never venturing far from my side. A woman halfway down was able to tell me where he lived. I rang the doorbell several times and didn't get an answer, so I went back to my house, the cat still at my side, scribbled a note, and went back to tape it on the door while he napped at my place, apparently exhausted from our previous excursion.

When Floyd arrived, brown bags in hand, one held taco dinners and the other a can of cat food. I held it up and looked at him.

"How was I supposed to know you got a new roommate?" He shrugged. "You were light on details."

Out of the last bag came a six-pack of beers and one of the margaritas. I held up a can of the latter.

"Have you taste-tested one of these before?"

He shook his head. "If your freezer works, might try it over ice."

I thought that was a good idea but wasn't going to tell him. I got myself a glass, poured the contents of the can over ice, and took a sip. "Not bad." I grabbed a plate, emptied the cat food, and set it down for the cat waiting at my feet.

We took the food containers and went outside to the patio table, where Floyd and I devoured everything. I recognized the restaurant, and they lived up to their reputation for great food. Once I'd cleared all the trash away, I handed him another beer, and we moved to a chaise and sat side by side.

"Did you adopt the cat or snatch it off the street? If the latter, you were supposed to be resting."

"He lives down the street…" I told him about Pops' visit and how the previously aloof cat had made himself at home.

Floyd chuckled.

"Found an address for Catnip," I told him. "Thought, if you have time tomorrow, that we'd check it out." Or I'd go by myself, which I wasn't throwing out as an option.

"Tomorrow is all yours. I'm guessing Catnip still hasn't called back. Wonder what her game is."

"If she does call, I'm curious to hear what kind of story she'll come up with for ducking my calls.

Wouldn't surprise me if she didn't acknowledge the issue at all."

"What's your plan? We get to this address, and then what? Knock under the pretense of making a welfare check?" Floyd stopped short of a snort.

"You have the best ideas."

"Just remember you thought it was a good idea when she flips out." He laughed. "Even though we now know it wasn't Catnip who broke into the office, I still wouldn't turn my back on her. She spends days burning up your phone, wanting so badly to locate her ex, and now where is she?"

"I did wonder if she somehow figured out we were trying to set her up to get arrested, but how could she? There's only three of us that know, and none of us are talking."

"Guessing the reason she hasn't called back is because she's hired someone else, and they came through," Floyd said. "If she were smart, she wouldn't have mentioned murder right off. Either that or Herbie's got more enemies than he wants to talk about. When I questioned him, he came across as straightforward in his responses, and I didn't pick up any hint that he was lying."

We sat outside until it got dark and the stars popped into the sky. Finally, Floyd stood and pulled me up from chaise.

"I'll be back in the morning and plan to take you to breakfast at Ruth's. It's a nearby café that's known for its good food."

I knew it received rave reviews but hadn't been

there. "I have a better idea."

He smirked.

"Spend the night here again, and we'll watch another movie. I can't promise I won't fall asleep, but I'll try."

"You're right; it's a great idea."

\* \* \*

On the way out the door the next morning, I caught sight of the cat sacked out next to the slider and went to open the door for him. He leaped up on one of the chaises and watched as a couple of seagulls cruised past. Since Leo was still a threat, I closed the slider, leaving the cat outside, and made sure it was locked.

Floyd was right about Ruth's, and we both devoured our breakfast. I made a mental note to tell Pops, as he would love the casual atmosphere.

Back in the truck, I handed Floyd an earpiece with a microphone — that way, if we got separated, we'd still be able to hear everything. He held it in his palm and smirked. "We're breaking in your new purchase."

"You have to agree that not only is it fun, but it's also useful."

"I should've mentioned it before, but I've got a box of fun stuff behind the seat." He motioned to a storage box behind him.

I eyed it. "If it goes missing, you'll know who took it."

"If you could organize everything, that would be helpful." He chuckled. "Always say I'm going to get to it and never do."

Floyd turned onto US-1 and followed it north for several miles. According to the information I found yesterday, Caturday lived inland on the outskirts of Ft. Lauderdale. Eventually, he turned into a maze of quiet neighborhood streets. All the houses basically looked the same — single-story block-style on manicured lawns. Most had one or two cars in the driveway. He parked in front of a beige version with brown trim.

"Didn't she drive a sedan of some sort?" I nodded at the small silver SUV in the driveway. "Friendly reminder: it's Caturday and not Catnip." I squinted at him. "Rolling your eyes isn't very nice, considering that the tip was helpful."

"Got it." Floyd bit back a laugh and stared over the steering wheel, eying the house. "Okay, sweets. *Catnip* opens the door, she's going to know we hunted her down. Be prepared for a reaction, and don't be surprised if it's not civilized."

I turned to him with a sad expression and swiped at non-existent tears. "We were so worried when you were a no-show." *How was that?* I smiled. A shake of his head was all I got. "Testing." I tapped my earpiece. "Can you hear me?"

"What did you say?" Floyd and I both laughed

as we got out. He whipped out his phone as we walked up the brick-paved driveway, snapping a picture of the license plate of the car and checking out the interior as we walked past. He slowed and eyed the empty boat trailer on the side lawn, then took another picture.

A forty-something man answered my knock, and I stumbled, not knowing who to say we were looking for. "Stopped by to check on Caturday and see how she's doing."

"You have the wrong house." He had the door half-shut when I stopped it with my hand. He glared until I dropped it back to my side.

"You might know her as Mildred Bellwether."

"The previous owner. We closed on this house and moved in two weeks ago." His mouth had tightened into a hard line, and anyone looking at him could guess that negotiations hadn't been pleasant.

Floyd, who'd stepped up to my side, asked, "Do you by chance have a forwarding?"

"Sorry, can't help you." He'd had enough of any pleasantries, and Floyd barely managed to thank him before he got the door shut.

Back in the truck, I noticed that the man was standing in the living room window, not taking his eyes off us. "That was a big waste of time." I heaved a sigh.

"Was Mildred the only one on the title?" Floyd asked as he wound through the streets, finally finding the exit back to the main road.

"Herbie and Mildred were both on title as joint owners. Wouldn't they have had to show up together at the closing?" I winced at how ugly that situation could've gotten.

"The closing company can accommodate separate times for all the parties. And if necessary, it can be done by mail." Floyd scrolled down the screen on his phone and then pushed a button on the steering wheel. The sound of a ringing phone came through the speakers. "The fact that something is none of my business doesn't stop me from asking questions." When a man answered, he said, "Hey Herbie, Floyd here. How you doing?"

The answer was long-winded, as we heard all about his nervousness and nausea. He finally chuckled. "You didn't call to listen to my aches and pains. What's up?"

"My partner and I—" Floyd winked at me. "— stopped by the house you lived in with Mildred, not knowing that you'd sold it."

"How the hell did she do that?" Herbie's yell reverberated through the phone. He managed to calm down slightly and said, "Probably whoever you talked to was lying, covering for her for some reason. I'm telling you now, I didn't sign off on anything. There's no way it happened."

"I'll tell you what the man told us: he closed on the property two weeks ago. If you didn't sign off, then you need to get your lawyer to check it out."

"Damn it," Herbie yelled, then lapsed into

silence aside from his heavy breathing.

"Anything I can do, call me anytime," Floyd assured him.

"Thanks," Herbie mumbled and hung up.

"That woman's got some…" I shook my head rather than say it. "… as well as a hate-on for the man. I didn't feel that the guy back at Catnip's was lying. What about you?" Floyd shook his head. "How easy would it be to pull off a fraudulent sale?"

"Real estate fraud is a problem, which is why closing companies are extra vigilant, as they find themselves on the hook. Their insurance company will investigate to the nth degree, which will take time and run up lawyer fees on both sides. But if it can be proven that Catnip defrauded Herbie… Be interesting to know who she got to pose as him and where they got the identification," Floyd mused. "Insurance won't settle for less than prison time."

I stared at him, shaking my head. "I've had enough of Caturday/Mildred, and I'm officially closing the case. As my partner, you can be the one to tell your friend Lucas." I made a sad face. "Blame me and tell him, 'Sorry, Maren wussed out.' I'm blocking her number."

"Lucas already knows you're no wuss. Hold off on blocking the number, but if Catnip does call back, don't answer; be interesting to see if she leaves a message. I'll talk it over with Lucas, and we'll figure out the next step. The one who needs to watch his back is Herbie. I forgot to ask if he's still out of town." Floyd suddenly grinned at me. I squinted, trying to figure out what he was up to, and didn't have to wait long. "You ready to go meet with Dog woman?"

I groaned.

## Chapter Twenty-One

"You know, these forays about town are turning out to be a huge waste of your time." I was surprised he hadn't already said, *Call me when you actually get work.*

"Hardly." Floyd gave me a quick glance, grinning. "Good luck getting rid of me."

I turned to the window so he couldn't see my pinkened cheeks and big smile. I'd thought we were headed to Edna's house and was surprised when Floyd parked in the driveway of his mom's house. "Thinking you must have a plan."

"I arranged for my mom to invite Edna over so we can sit down and come to a resolution for Frito."

"This is way too much drama over a dog that has a good home. But since this is your case —"

"Oh no, you don't," Floyd huffed. "We traded cases fair and square."

"Except you have an advantage here, since you're the one she wants doing the naked dance with her daughter. Although I think she really wants you for herself."

"Good thing I didn't just eat." He puffed out his cheeks.

Even though I turned away, I knew he could

see my shoulders shake. I struggled to wipe all expression from my face before turning back. "I'm going to tell your mom you've been mean to me, just to watch how you explain that I made it all up."

Floyd scrunched up his nose. "You just turned into one of my brothers."

Rosa already had the door open and waved for us to get out. "Edna's on her way. Hope you've got good news."

"You didn't tell her?" I said, loud enough for her to hear, and winked at her.

"Thought we'd have some time before Edna got here," Floyd played along, not about to be bested.

"Guess not." I nodded at the car that had just pulled up and parked. My phone rang, and I stepped aside as the other three exchanged greetings. "Who is it?" I asked, taking a couple more steps so I wouldn't be tempted to listen to both conversations.

"Ware Dowell," the man said, as though I should know.

*Oh yes, seedy attorney.*

He continued without any acknowledgment from me. "Got your number from Max. Assured me that you could handle any jobs thrown your way. Thought I'd run by your office, and we could discuss what I need to be done. I—"

"That won't be possible," I cut him off. "A pipe broke, and the office isn't useable. It would be better if you found someone else." *Was all PI work like this, or was Pops a really bad judge of character?*

"Nonsense. Max and I are friends, and he recommended you highly, so we can meet someplace local—your call."

"I'll have to call you back, as I'm headed into another meeting."

"Don't drag your feet getting back to me. I'm someone who can make your career." Dowell hung up before I could tell him again to find someone else. One quality he had in common with Pops: neither wanted to hear no. Turning, I bumped into Floyd's chest. "Were you listening in?" I peered around his shoulder and saw that the two women had gone inside.

"Do we have secrets, hon?" His eyes twinkled. "Phone call appears to have irritated you."

I ignored his question. "Weasel attorney friend of Pops', who recommended me. He's got a job for me but got off the phone before getting any details."

"That's why I'll be coming along. If he doesn't take no for an answer the first time, he will the second." Floyd cracked his knuckles.

"You certainly know how to charm a girl." I winked.

He looped his arm around my shoulders and held up my hand. "You forgot your ring again."

I groaned. "Does your mom know that we went with the married story?"

"She knows. Edna got hot on the phone before

we cleared the block and demanded answers. Mom's a champion and played along. Then called and asked me to stop by, literally backed me into a corner, and demanded an explanation."

"Man, I miss all the good stuff. The big guy backed into a corner, put there by a slight woman." I couldn't quite picture Rosa pulling it off and wished I'd seen it.

"Happy you're so amused."

Rosa met us at the door and grabbed my left hand, sliding a gold band on my ring finger. "You need to stop leaving it on the counter." She winked.

I could barely make eye contact with the woman, but Floyd only chuckled. Rosa led us into the living room, where Edna was seated… and watching us, eagle-eyed. Floyd and I sat on the couch with the two women across from us. Rosa offered something to drink, and we all turned her down.

"My partner and I have an update for you," Floyd started off agreeably, looping his arm around me. Edna's eyes narrowed to slits. "Everything happened at once for Mike York. It began when he lost his job, then had to rehome the dog he loved and move to avoid eviction. We understand that one of the issues that concerned you was the neutering, and after a call to the vet, they were more than willing to email you a copy of the report, which I understand was done."

"Very happy that it was taken care of, since it

was clearly stipulated in the contract." However, Edna didn't look happy but calculating. "Now, about Frito—" She wrinkled her nose, apparently not approving of the name. "—and his whereabouts."

"Mike hadn't read the fine print of the contract before he signed," I said. "He approached a friend that he knew already loved Frito, knowing the dog would be well taken care of. Uppermost in his mind was that Frito be in a loving home."

"That is my decision to make," Edna snapped. "Sounds to me like you know where the dog can be found. Hand over the address, and I'll go and pick him up."

"In order for you to do that, you'll need an order signed by a judge," Floyd informed her. We both knew that this wasn't new news, as she'd been to court before, according to the record I'd pulled.

Edna remained militant. "I can get one."

"Do you really want to go to the expense of hiring a lawyer to pursue this?" Floyd asked.

Edna's mouth turned to a thin line, and rather than answer, she asked, "Do I need to remind you that you work for me? And that we had an agreement?" she insisted as she met Floyd's determined stare. "It's clear to me that you were the wrong person to hire. It won't take me long to find someone more competent." She stood.

"Why don't you sit back down while we come to an agreement that'll make everyone happy?" I barely managed to sound friendly and knew that the chances of making such a deal were slim, but we had to try. "Frito's been neutered and has a good home, so what exactly do you want?"

"I only have your word for it, for whatever *that's* worth, as I don't even know you. Besides, I hired Floyd, not you, and that's turning out to be a big disappointment," Edna snapped. "I didn't hire you to stick your nose in and make judgments. All these decisions are mine to make. When I get Frito back, I'll find him a really good home."

I felt Floyd stiffen and patted his thigh: *Got this*. "You're going to spend however much time and money it takes to track down Mike? Because he's who you'll have to take to court. You must realize that it won't be cheap."

"Good thing my husband left me a sizeable estate with no restrictions so I can do what I want," Edna sneered.

I'd had enough of her and struggled to remain pleasant. "Why not be happy for Frito? You're in a snit because your royal edicts were ignored and not taking into consideration that it wasn't done on purpose." So much for nice.

Edna's face filled with fury as she turned on Floyd. "You could've done a whole heck of a lot better than her." Her nose in the air, she jumped to her feet.

"Everyone needs to calm down," interjected Rosa, who up until then had been taking it all in.

"Something cold to drink would hit the spot."

"I've had enough," Edna sputtered. "Don't think for one second I'll ever come back here."

I jumped up and stepped in front of her, face-to-face. "You sit your ass back down, and I'll tell you how this is going to go."

Edna stepped back as though she feared me, and slowly, she sat back down.

Floyd looked on, wide-eyed.

Rosa smirked.

I turned on Edna but stayed back. "You taking Frito from the current owner would be nothing more than meanness on your part. I'd totally understand if the dog were being mistreated, but I visited him myself, and he's damn spoiled. I'm not going to stand by and let you break the owner's heart." *If you had one of your own, you'd be thinking straighter,* I thought but kept to myself.

"It's not your decision. And besides, there's not a damn thing you can do about it."

If looks could kill, I'd be laid out on the floor. However, I noted that Edna didn't stand this time, so my glare must be working. "If I hear that you've made one single attempt to get Frito back—and don't think I won't know, as I'll be staying in touch with Mike York and the current owner—if I have the slightest inkling that you're creeping around, I'll bring the city code department down on you for the multiple violations that you're committing running the rescue out of your house. They don't need a court order to remove the dogs, and good luck getting them back."

Rosa's and Floyd's eyes flitted back and forth. I had to wonder if they were silently betting on the outcome.

"You'd do that to poor, defenseless animals?" Edna sniffed.

If the woman wanted people to believe her distress was real, she needed to hide the meanness in her eyes. "I'd see it as my civic duty, not only looking out for the rest of the neighborhood but the defenseless animals, which can't possibly be cared for properly in such crowded surroundings. Can't have someone breaking laws now, can we?"

"You're pure evil," Edna sputtered.

"First I'm hearing of it. That aside, do we have an agreement? Before you answer, you'll only get one attempt to make an end-run around me to get Frito, and after that, you're out of business." I jerked my thumb over my shoulder.

"You…" Edna spit as she jumped to her feet.

She was halfway to the door when I said, "You leave here without giving me a yes or no, and you won't like my reaction."

"Fine, the dog can stay. Happy now?" Edna jerked open the door and turned to Floyd. "Young man, you need to get a divorce, and don't drag your feet about it." She gave the door a slam that shook the house.

Rosa hopped up and threw her arms around

me. "You were impressive. I feel compelled to apologize for getting the two of you in such a mess."

She smiled at her son, who said, "You were pretty damn hot."

Rosa cooed at his admission.

"And by the way, you didn't tell me you visited Tunia," Floyd growled.

I'd stayed fixated on the 'hot' part, but apparently Floyd had already forgotten, as he was irked at the oversight.

"We've been busy, *dear*, and I didn't want to pile more on your plate." The truth was, I forgot. I thought my explanation sounded good but couldn't decipher Floyd's stare.

"You're perfect for each other," Rosa gushed. "I'd thought you were a little too soft for my son, as he needs someone who can hold their own, but watching you take on Edna wiped out any reservations I had." She threw her arms around me for another hug and, this time, a kiss on the cheek. "Welcome to the family."

"Calm down," I said, though her expression indicated no chance of that happening. "I feel compelled to remind you that this is pretend. We haven't even… you know… dated. Sort of, maybe." The grin on Floyd's face was irritating.

"But who slept with you in the hospital?" he asked.

"Which you lied to convince them to let you do."

"The what?" Rosa stepped back and plopped down.

Floyd told her about Leo and the kidnapping attempt.

"My dear, are you okay?" Rosa asked.

"It could've been way worse. Your son glossed over the fact that he saved me from…" I shivered. "I hate to think what that man had planned."

"Back to the dating, so I don't get a 'mom' lecture later." Floyd was definitely enjoying himself. "What about the times we've been out to eat? Lunch at the beach right on the water ring a bell?"

"Loved that restaurant." I smiled at him. "The ones you've picked out have had great food."

Rosa's grin almost split her face. "Change of subject before you two have what might be construed as your first lover's quarrel…" She wiggled her brows. "Why not just tell Edna about this Tunia woman having Frito?"

"Edna has an age requirement for adoption, and Tunia's too old," I said, my exasperation with the woman back. "Another thing… if that woman whispers one bad thing about you or your family, you can tell her to shut it or you'll sic me on her."

"You're a keeper." She raised her eyebrows at Floyd. *Hint, hint.* "Would you like a cookie?"

"She hasn't had lunch," Floyd snapped.

"Neither have you," I snapped back, hands on my hips. I turned to Rosa and said, "I'd love one," barely stopping myself from licking my lips. "Has anyone ever turned down anything you made?"

Rosa linked one arm through mine and the other through Floyd's. "Come along, you two love birds, and I'll get you fed. One of the perks in this family is a full stomach."

I leaned over and kissed her cheek.

## Chapter Twenty-Two

"Anything else you failed to mention?" Floyd asked after we'd gotten in the truck. "I'll decide if it's important or not. And if I think you're holding out, I'll shake the info out of you."

"Sounds fun." I rubbed my stomach. "Lunch at your mom's was amazing. And cookies." I patted the bag next to me.

"You changing the subject?"

My phone rang, saving me from having to answer. I glanced at the screen, and the number looked vaguely familiar. Wondering where I recognized it from, I answered.

"Are we getting together today, or are you jerking me around?" Dowell, the sleezy attorney, grouched. "Need I remind you that Max said you'd help me out?"

"When and where do you want to meet?" An excuse eluded me, and the next best thing would be changing my number, but for now...

"Now would be good. You know Stout's?"

I'd driven past the coffee shack a couple of times, and from what I could remember, it had minimal outside seating, as most who frequented the place used the drive-thru lane. "I'm on my way." I hung up. "I'm going to need my car."

"What was that all about?" Floyd gunned the engine.

"Being bossy isn't an attractive quality." He snorted, so I guessed he didn't agree. "That was Ware Dowell again—Pops' attorney friend. He decided he wanted my talents for a job after Pops talked up my non-existent credentials."

"I'm not one to let my *wife* go gallivanting around when I have no clue what's going on."

"Kind of happy about that."

"Tell me where we're headed, and you can fill me in on the way."

The directions were easy, as it was just off US-1.

"You were impressive with Edna. Had it been me, I would've backed off and tried to come up with a 'happy for all' ending, even though it was clear it would never happen."

"I think it's easier for a woman to call out another one on the way she's acting, especially when she's not friends with your mom. As for Ware, it's okay if you don't want to come along; I'd totally understand your not wanting to be dragged around everywhere. Is this what you signed up for? No, because we haven't ironed out all the details of our working relationship," I answered for him.

"Or our personal relationship."

"We need to kiss more." I winced, kicking myself for blurting that out.

"There's something we agree on, and I plan to rectify that."

*Soon, I hope.*

"Since Leo, I don't want to let you out of my sight. Now, if you carried a gun and I thought you'd use it…"

"Can't imagine pulling the trigger, but then, I suppose you don't know what you'll do until you're in a life-or-death situation." I didn't want to find out.

Floyd reached over and grabbed my hand. "Tell me about Tunia."

"It was a last-minute whim, and you were on a bodyguarding job. It was a brief visit once I completed a background check on her and tracked down and talked to Mike. If Edna had known I didn't spend hours checking out the woman, she'd have gone even more ballistic than she did."

*It was late morning, and I'd done a few errands and was headed home when I realized I wasn't far from Tunia's neighborhood. I pulled over, double-checked the address, and entered it into the GPS.*

*It was a quiet neighborhood. I knocked on Tunia's door and was surprised at first not to hear barking, but then not at all when she answered the door with Frito in her arms. He leaned towards me, wanting to lick hello, but his interest in me waned quickly.*

*"I'm a friend of Mike York's." We'd had a friendly conversation, but friends was a stretch. "I have a few questions about Frito."*

*"Mike told me that you called." Tunia hugged the*

*little dog even tighter, invited me in, and offered me a seat.* "I can't believe that woman wants Frito back. I talked to my neighbor two houses down — he's a lawyer and told me to call the police if she shows up or I see anyone lurking around."

"That was good advice. I want to be clear that I'm not here for any nefarious reason. It's my hope that I can get Edna to agree to do what's best for Frito, and that looks like you." *While I talked, he'd climbed out of her arms, curled up in her lap, and gone to sleep.*

*Tunia stroked the dog's head, looking about to cry.* "I don't want to lose my baby."

"You're not going to," *I promised, hoping I could keep it.* "I've heard lots of great things about you and wanted to meet you for myself." *I smiled.*

"Come look around." *Tunia stood, Frito in her arms, and gave me a mini tour of the house, showing off the fancy dog bed and toys, and then took me over to the sliders to show me the big yard.* "Frito rarely goes out just to play; he likes the long walks we go on twice a day. He's got several friends along the way that he likes to catch up with."

"I don't want you to worry, but you do need to stay alert until this situation is settled. Edna doesn't know who Frito's living with, and I have no intention of giving her that information. But it's always possible Edna could find out another way. Your neighbor gave you good advice, and you shouldn't hesitate if you see someone who looks out of place."

"That's good advice in general." *Tunia smiled.*

*I nodded. I pulled a card out of my pocket.* "If you have any questions, call anytime. I'll also let you know *when this is settled." I left, swearing to myself that I wasn't going to have any part in separating the two.*

"I knew that, if necessary, I'd stand up to Edna but didn't plan on it being as contentious as it was," I told Floyd.

"Edna needed someone to tell her that what she was doing wasn't right, and she didn't have a good reason why Frito couldn't stay right where he was. I think that what irked her the most was that it all happened without her say-so. The good news is you've got Mom's approval and can be assured that if she gets wind of Edna planning a snatch-and-grab or something similarly nefarious step, our phones will be ringing."

We made good time, as the traffic cooperated all the way to Stout's. Floyd parked in the dirt lot, and we got out and wandered over to the lone man sitting on a cement bench at a faded brown steel table.

"Mr. Dowell?" I asked as we approached. His suit was cheap, and his black hair looked like it had been touched up with shoe polish.

"Maren?" he asked. I nodded, and he waved for me to have a seat, staring at Floyd—*Who are you?*—who sat down next to me, ignoring the unspoken question. Dowell handed me a manila envelope. "I need this served. Tried a couple of times myself, and no luck. Got a court hearing that I need to attend this afternoon. Whatever you do, don't dump it. Not that I'm against that method of service, but if he shows up in court and can prove to the judge that he was elsewhere, it'll make for a sticky situation. Trust me, I know."

"What kind of papers?" I asked.

"Paternity lawsuit." Dowell stared at my hand, then pointed at the ring. "I was led to believe you were available, or is the ring a ruse to keep the ass-wipes at bay?"

"She's mine." Floyd threw his arm around me and tugged me to his side.

"Where did you hear that I was available?" I had a good idea but wanted to hear him say it.

"It's been a while since I talked to Max, and at the time, you were just getting ready to take over North." Dowell had yet to acknowledge Floyd directly. "Consider this job a rush, and give me a jingle as soon as it's done." He stood and stared at me. "Max owes me, and this job would clear off a couple of tick marks." He made his way across the dirt and gravel to an old white Mercedes.

"Want something to drink?" Floyd asked after the car had left the parking lot.

"I'll take something cold." I stood and brushed off the back of my jeans. "Between a conversation I had with my parents and this one, I'm more convinced than ever that I know what Pops is up to." This had always been about finding me a husband.

# Chapter Twenty-Three

Floyd cruised through a drive-thru, grabbed us a couple of cold drinks, and pulled into the only empty parking space. "Let's see those papers." He wiggled his fingers.

I handed them over and turned my attention to my iced tea, pleased to see that they weren't stingy with the ice. I took a long drink. "Let's see if I've got this right—I knock on the door, get whoever it is to fess up to their identity, hand off the papers, and then skate out, all while the person's trying to figure out what's going on. Or do I owe them an explanation?"

"They can figure it out for themselves." Floyd flipped through the pages. "This says that a DNA test is wanted from one Rodney Jackson. He apparently had sex with Crystal Balk, who wants to prove that he's the daddy of her kid. My pro-opinion, which I'm sure you're expecting, is that this being served means he hasn't been cooperative." He handed back the envelope and entered the address into the GPS.

Just swell. "What happens if Rodney knows there are legal papers out there with his name on them and never answers the door?"

"Then a stakeout would be required, but only if

the client wants to pay up, as the hours needed for that could easily end up being more than they're willing to pay."

"If you do camp out in front of someone's house hoping to get lucky, don't you have to worry about getting your butt kicked?" I narrowed my eyes at him. "Happy you think this is funny."

"I'll admit that seeing this through a newbie's eyes is amusing." Floyd pulled me close and laid on a long kiss that left me starry-eyed. "I've served a handful of papers, and I wouldn't do it as a regular gig, as it comes with its own set of problems, mostly dealing with irate people. Wonder why Dowell isn't using a licensed process server. My guess, from the way he pitched the job, is because he's too cheap, which could come back to bite him. States vary in how many papers you're allowed to serve without a license, and it could be none, so you need to check into that."

"You'd think Dowell would know if it's legal for me to do or not, and if it's not, then why call me?"

Floyd rubbed his fingers together.

"How did my Pops get mixed up with the likes of him? Dowell said that this job would cover something that Pops owed, whatever the heck that is. You can bet I'm going to find out."

"Dowell's probably used to cutting corners, legal and otherwise; you do it often enough, and you don't think about it. But get caught serving papers illegally, and you could be banned from getting a server's license." Floyd made a shocked expression, but humor-filled his eyes.

"I can't be taking up your time when we both know that there is no business and that if Pops wants North to stay open for business, he needs to do it himself, or find someone else, as it's not going to be me."

"Then what? Our business relationship is kaput?"

"I'm certain that you weren't expecting the jobs would go this way." I know I didn't expect it. But if asked what I did expect, I wouldn't have had an answer.

"It's been much more fun than I thought it would be. Since we've got some time now, we might as well make an attempt at Rodney's house. We might get lucky, and if not, we'll at least see what we're in for. You've got about five minutes to update me on what you think your Pops is up to before we arrive at our destination."

"Got my weekly call from my parents… swore them to secrecy. Barely got out the story of what Pops had been up to before they burst out laughing. If we hadn't been zooming, I'd have been tempted to pour another drink. I couldn't help thinking it was about Pops insinuating himself into my personal life but kept discounting the thoughts when they popped up since I didn't have any proof. But my parents were positive it was his way of finding me a husband."

Floyd burst out laughing. When he sobered, he said, "Then why did he send subhuman men? Why send anyone at all? And wouldn't the personal approach, as in him making the introductions, be better than sneaking around?"

"That's mean, but yes, the men were… not my type. It's hard to imagine they're anyone's type. Especially Leo. And that's putting it mildly. If you count Dowell, based on what he said, that makes four. More and more when I talk to Pops, I realize how shifty he can be — he's certainly perfected the art of not answering questions."

"If you don't want to tell him 'knock it off,' I will."

"I've tried talking to him about not meddling, but he doesn't listen. What I need to do is grow a pair and tell him this business isn't happening, not with me at the wheel. Soften it up with how much I love him and always have and hope that he backs down. But first, I'm dishing up a little payback. I'm planning to set him up with someone — do as you suggested and introduce them over lunch or dinner. Surprise." I threw up my hands.

"My guess is that you've got someone all picked out. Does this paragon know she's being set up?" He shot me a suspicious look.

"Thinking your mom would be perfect."

After a look of surprise, Floyd burst out laughing. "Mom's never going to go along with your plan. First off, she won't approve of you getting even. Another thing: if you somehow tricked both of them and your Pops wasn't a perfect gentleman, I'd have to rearrange his face." He turned off the highway and cruised into a quiet neighborhood and up in front of a brick single-story, an older model Mercedes parked in the circular drive.

We got out, and a man walking two terriers who was about to pass us did a double-take when his eyes landed on me. "So good to see that you're checking on your grandfather. Been worried about Rod, as I haven't seen him out and about lately."

Instead of correcting him, I pasted on a smile and hid the envelope behind my back. "I'll tell Rod to come over and say hello." The dogs jerked on their leashes, and with a wave, the man was off.

"Here. One of us is legal to do this job, and it's not me." I attempted to pass off the envelope to Floyd, but he kept his hands clasped behind his back. I could feel his smirk, though I wasn't looking at him as I went up the two steps to the door. "If Rodney is as old as Pops, this is going to be awkward." I rang the doorbell and was relieved to hear no movement — nothing. All was quiet. Pressing my luck, I rang it again and the same thing. "How about some ice cream? My treat." My mouth dropped open when Floyd stepped into the planter. "What are you doing?"

Instead of answering, he tilted his head to peek

through the slanted shutters. The living room, I presumed. He knocked on the window.

"That's really obnoxious." I stepped back off the porch.

"Ring the bell again," Floyd said as he shifted around, trying to get a better view.

I didn't want to but did as he asked.

"Again," he called out, then stepped back up on the porch without crushing a single plant. "Dude's asleep on the couch; didn't move an inch. Maybe he's hard of hearing. Or…" He stepped back and stared at the house, then walked out to the sidewalk and checked it out from one end to the other.

"Or what?" Did I want to know? I watched as he found a path that ran along the side of the six-foot privacy hedge and disappeared. *Oh no, you don't.* I was hot on his tennis shoes.

Floyd came to an abrupt halt and turned to me. "You stay here." He stepped onto a grass strip in the backyard that ran along one side of the pool. Rodney had a variety of patio furniture to make himself comfortable and enjoy the view, as he lived on one of the many canals throughout the area.

"Fat chance," I said to his back and followed, adding, as though he didn't know, "We're trespassing."

"Got a bad feeling about this." He walked over to the sliding glass doors and peered inside, then once again knocked. Not getting an answer, he tried the door. It was unlocked, and he pushed it open and stepped inside.

We just ventured into illegal. Thus far, I hadn't done what I was told and had no intention of changing that. An appalling smell smacked me in the face. I turned away, afraid I was going to be sick. After turning to suck in some fresh air, I turned back, peered into the house, and caught sight of a bloated body on the couch. My feet felt glued to the bricks as I stared wide-eyed. Then I screamed and ran, ending up at the edge of the pool.

Floyd was in clear view as he walked around the couch, not touching the body, before coming back outside. He closed the door and pulled out his phone. "Based on the condition of the body, I'm guessing he's been dead about a week. I didn't see any signs of foul play, but that's for the coroner to decide." He called 911 and reported the dead man, then grabbed my hand and led me back around to the front.

"Are we going to be arrested?" I asked, fearful of the answer but needing to know.

"We didn't kill the man, and when the police question us, we'll tell the truth." He opened the truck door for me.

I got in and leaned my head back against the seat. "Do you think that's Mr. Jackson?"

"No way of telling. That will be another thing for the coroner to figure out."

Minutes later, two Ft. Lauderdale cop cars

pulled up to the house and parked. Floyd met them at the end of the driveway, and the three men talked. He then led them around to the back of the house.

It took a while before they were back. One of the cops went to his car, and the other came over with Floyd, who introduced us. Turned out the two men went to the same high school and played on the football team together. Then Floyd gave him a nod and walked away. He didn't go far, but I couldn't help feeling abandoned.

"I have a few questions," Officer Mike said, dragging my attention back to him.

"My first dead body, and it smelled really bad." I swiped at the tears on my cheeks.

"You never get used to it," he sympathized, then asked me what happened.

I probably gave him more information than necessary, starting with Pops' antics, then getting a call from Dowell and meeting him at Stout's.

Officer Mike shook his head. "Looks like a dump, but Mrs. Stout makes the best baked goods, and they're gone early." When I finished, he said, "Dowell's a cretin. You might factor that in before accepting another job."

I nodded, thinking for the umpteenth time that I wasn't cut out for PI work and reminding myself that I hadn't done anything to get out of it.

"Do you have a contact number for anyone in the family?" he asked.

I shook my head but wasn't sure if he noticed,

as a white van pulled up just then, "Coroner" was stenciled on the side and back. A guy got out carrying a bag and disappeared through the now-open front door.

The cop's attention turned back to me, and he took my contact information. "I'll be in touch if I have any questions." He then made his way over to Floyd, who was standing next to the boat trailer. They talked a minute; then Floyd came back to the truck and climbed behind the wheel.

"What do I tell Dowell?" I asked.

"Tell him that when you got to the house, a body was being taken out, and that's all you know. He's such a hot shot, or so he thinks… Both my friend and the other cop thought he was a piece of—. Well, he can figure out if it was Rodney or not through his connections, if he has any. I could easily find out, but I'm not using my connections for that man."

"Will you follow up and let me know what happens?"

"Maybe." He grabbed my hand and squeezed, then pulled out of the neighborhood.

"Not a no, so that's good." We were headed south, and I hoped that meant home. I pulled out my phone and called Dowell and was relieved when it went to voicemail, and I could leave a message. I hoped he wouldn't call back, but he probably would, since he'd want his papers back. "If Rodney's dead, what happens with the paternity case?"

Floyd chuckled humorlessly. "Dowell will have to hustle to court to get an order for a paternity test on the corpse. If that's denied, there's always the possibility that surviving family members might want to know if they're related to the child. But I'm not sure whether a court would force them to do a DNA test if they didn't." He eyed me, and the humor was back in his eyes. "Any more papers to serve? Cases that need our immediate attention?"

*Thank goodness, no.* "I need a drink."

## Chapter Twenty-Four

"How about we go to dinner? You choose the restaurant." Seeing the traffic backed up, Floyd went the opposite way, knowing a shortcut of his own, and we were soon headed toward my house.

"Or I could cook, and we could sit out on the patio with our feet up."

Floyd gave me a sideways squint. "What can you whip up in the microwave?"

"Frozen pizza." I struggled not to laugh when he mimed getting sick. "You know, you sound more like a cat hocking up a mouthful of fur."

"I suggest that we compromise on take-out."

"Sounds good. If you were more open-minded, you might find you like what I can conjure up."

"Uh huh."

I didn't pay attention to where Floyd was headed until he stopped in front of the house where the cat lived.

"The note you taped to the door is gone." He pointed.

"A little surprised I didn't get a call. I'm going to hop out and see if anyone's home."

"Not without me." He pulled over and parked, and the two of us got out.

I knocked on the door while he hung back. No

answer, and I wasn't peeking in the windows, not after the last time. Retracing my steps, I found Floyd chatting it up with the neighbor woman, who was busy flirting.

Floyd motioned me over. "The owners of the cat have moved."

"A couple of months ago, they packed up and left Gato behind," the woman said. "I've seen him around a few times, but he's not very friendly. I called animal control, and they did come out, but nothing came of it, and I haven't seen him since."

"Maybe the new people…" I nodded toward the house.

"Oh no. They don't like animals of any kind. Claim to be allergic." She wrinkled her nose.

"Since he's curled up on my patio and I'm feeding him, guess he's mine now," I said.

"Isn't that stealing?" Her nose went up.

"Gato ran inside when I opened the front door and made himself at home, so I'm thinking he made up his own mind. If anyone has any objections, they can fight me for him." I bit back a laugh, as it was clear she found me annoying. Oh well. "I live in the smallest house on the block."

"Oh, that one." Her smile looked like it hurt. Her eyes went straight back to Floyd. "Any more questions, you know where to find me."

"Nice meeting you." He grabbed my hand, and we walked back to the truck.

"You have an admirer," I said as he held the door open.

"She's married," he said, getting in. "And if she weren't—not my type."

I groaned. "I need cat food."

A couple of turns later, he stopped at a convenience store and hopped out. Since he left the engine running, I assumed I was to stay put. Minutes later, he was back with a bag in his hand that he dropped in the back seat.

I craned my head to look over the seat. "Me and the cat thank you."

"Got enough dry and wet food for a week. Since it's unclear how long Gato's been on his own, I suggest that you take him to the vet. I can give you the name of ours; she's great with animals."

"You sure you won't let me cook for you… show my appreciation?" I asked as he turned into my driveway.

He whipped out his phone. "What's your favorite?"

"Tacos." I looked at him expectantly. "I know you're a beer drinker, and I just happen to have a local craft brand in the refrigerator."

Floyd placed an order that sounded like he'd chosen one of everything on the menu. It couldn't be the first time he'd used that restaurant, as he relayed his order like he had a menu in front of him.

Once inside the house, I went over and opened the sliders. Gato craned his neck in my direction. "Hey dude, ready for dinner?" He leaped off the chaise and went straight to the kitchen. I wasn't sure if he was hungry or just tired of being outside. "Is there a way to rig this door so Gato can come and go?"

"There's a special panel you can get. About the rest of your repairs, I've got a friend that's going to call. His mom needed surgery, and he flew up to Tampa to be with her, but she's about to be released, so he'll be back in a day or two. Just know that if you two don't see eye to eye on the project, I'll find you someone else."

I filled a bowl for inside water, then grabbed a can of cat food and another dish. He started eating as soon as I set it down. I joined Floyd on the couch. "You're a handy guy."

And then he kissed me. Long and oh-so-sweet.

Enjoying it immensely, I didn't want it to end. When it did, I smiled and got one back.

"Thinking this makes us official." He kissed me again. "This weekend, we're doing something fun—nothing that smacks of trouble."

"You mean no more dead bodies."

"That's the last thing I wanted you to see or smell."

"If you hadn't found Mr. Jackson, who knows how long it would have been before someone else did." I shuddered. "Is it possible to get that smell out of the house?"

"It would take a professional." Floyd put his arm around me and pulled me up against him. "Enough about that. When the food gets here,

we'll take it outside."
  "And talk about my clients."
  "No business talk."

# Chapter Twenty-Five

We had a couple of days of peace, and then Floyd got a call that one of his regular clients was flying into Miami International and needed his personal protection skills for the next three days.

Not long after he left, my phone rang, and it was Todd Bagby, Floyd's contractor friend. Since he was in the area, I told him to come on over. It wasn't long before he was knocking on the door. Well over six feet, he wore a big smile and, in some ways, reminded me of Floyd.

I motioned Todd inside and pointed to the torn-up side of the room. He asked me what happened, and I told him the last contractor bailed. When I mentioned the name, he groaned.

"Sorry to hear you were taken advantage of by that company. Unfortunately, you aren't the only one."

I answered all Todd's questions while he took notes and snapped pictures with his iPad.

"Your ideas are great—clean and simple—and I see no problem about giving you what you want. There's no problem with you staying here, as I'll tarp off the construction zone from the rest of the house." He took a few more measurements. "How about I come back tomorrow with samples?"

"I have some from the previous job." I led the way to the garage and was happy to hear that there wouldn't be a problem matching them.

He quoted me a price and said he'd send a contract by email for me to peruse. "My team can start right away, and I estimate the job will take about two weeks." I agreed to everything, as I couldn't wait to get the job back on track.

Todd was as good as his word, his workers showing up the next morning. I worked in my sound studio for the next couple of days, putting on earphones to drown out the hammering. I'd renovated one of the bedrooms into the perfect office space. Several files on my desk taunted me, a reminder that I had jobs I needed to finish up before my clients started looking elsewhere. I hadn't missed a deadline in the past and wasn't going to start now.

I'd left my phone off that whole time — the first time since I took over Pops' business — and was reluctant to turn it back on. I couldn't keep ignoring my friends and clients just because I didn't want to deal with PI business, so I went online and ordered a phone for the business, then braced myself and turned mine back on. As I anticipated, there were several "Call me" messages from Dowell. While I was contemplating calling him back, my phone rang, and it was him. Oh joy.

"Where in the hell have you been?" he growled when I answered.

I ignored his question. "What can I do for you?"

"I need you to go back to Jackson's house and figure out whether he was the dead person or it was someone else. He wouldn't be the first person to fake his own death."

If that wasn't Rodney Jackson, then who was it? I didn't even want to think of him dying from anything other than natural causes. "Don't you have police connections you can contact?"

He sputtered and changed the subject. "I know business is slow for you and can get you more papers to serve. Here's the thing—you need to get your license on the off-chance that one of the services is contested and you get hauled into court."

I shook my head the whole time he talked.

Not noticing my silence, he continued. "Got another job for you."

I'd have thought my groan could be heard down the block but guess not. Since I had zero interest in any more work from the man, I wasn't sure why I asked, "What kind of job?"

"It's pretty damn easy." Dowell's tone clearly implied even a simpleton could get it done. "You'll pick up two boxes and take one to the UPS facility in Plantation and the other to FedEx in Miami."

I shook my head, not believing what I'd just

heard. You'd have to be completely stupid or hard up for cash not to know that what he was asking reeked of illegal. For one thing, he was too cheap to pay someone to run all over town (unless he was expecting another freebie?). Not to mention that there were plenty of drop-offs for both companies locally. Why not use one of them? And oh yes, do it himself? I didn't ask because I didn't want to know anything more.

He prattled on about how easy the job would be.

I'd asked myself several times what it would take for me to end this charade, and it turned out to be this annoying lawyer and his dubious job. "I'm no longer involved with North Investigations. You should contact your friend Maxwell; I'm sure he can get your jobs assigned to someone else."

"Hold on a second —"

"Thank you for your business." I hung up.

To my surprise, he didn't call right back. I blocked his number, then made a note on my calendar not to answer any calls from unknown numbers and circled it several times.

I then composed my last business email for North — not that there'd been more than a couple while I was *in* business — Dear Dixon... I went on to tell him that I was closing up shop and couldn't thank him enough for all he'd done, signing off with the hope that we'd stay in touch. I knew he'd be upset at losing the chance to figure out Pops' ledger, but I didn't think we'd ever get that out of him at this point. I planned to tell Floyd of my decision in person. I was going to miss running around with him and hoped that the end of our business relationship didn't mean the end of more kisses and getting to know one another better.

Then I put my headphones on, feeling like life was back on track, and spent the rest of the day doing what I loved—producing a commercial for a client.

Hours later, I leaned back in my chair, removed my headphones... and realized that someone was pounding on the front door. Not very friendly for someone selling something, which was rare in this neighborhood anyway.

Whoever was banging clearly wasn't going to take the hint from my not-answering and get lost. I went into the dining room and peeked through the blinds, and a pair of eyes stared back at me. I screamed loud enough to bring the house down and jumped back.

"Maren," roared a male voice I recognized as Floyd's.

I stomped over to the door and threw it open. "You about gave me heart failure."

"You'd have known I was on my way if you answered your damn phone." He slipped past me, grabbing my hand and kicking the door shut, and in a blink, we were sitting on the couch. He swooped in for a long kiss that left me smiling, then looked over my head at the clear plastic separating us from the kitchen. "Todd got started — good."

"It's great news. Soon the partial war zone look will be gone." I told Floyd about how easily Todd and I had come to an agreement.

"Went to see the other guy a couple of times, and he ducked me. It was unfortunate as I planned to see how much of a refund I could shake out of him. I did get from the perky receptionist that business was slow."

"Got this mental image of you hauling him up by the scruff of his neck and looping him around until he vomits." I demonstrated, holding my hand in the air.

"If I thought that was about to happen, I'd drop him on his ass so fast…"

I laughed. "How was the job?"

"Pietro is exhausting. Happy this trip was a short one. He jets in, goes from one meeting to another, and in between, finds time to chase women. He's upfront and tells them it's a one-off, but a few don't want to believe him. It's embarrassing when he runs into one of his previous conquests and can't remember their name. A couple of them have physically attacked him, which amuses me, but I *am* hired to protect his ass and do my best to separate them before the woman can do lasting damage. Can't have his pretty face mucked up. He's a pain in the butt and requests me every time."

"Where's Pietro now?"

"In his private plane headed back home to Italy. It's his philosophy to work hard and play even harder."

"Happy you're back and don't appear scuffed up." I ran my finger down his arm.

"I go out on the town for a few days and you… what? Shut down North? Should I be checking my phone for an email I maybe missed about my services no longer being needed?"

"You talked to Dixon." I blew out a sigh. "That was quick. Hope he's not upset with me. I should've called him… I guess it's not too late — I'll invite him to lunch."

"What about me?"

I had to keep myself from laughing at his screwed-up nose and the *What*? on his face. "Fess up — haven't I proven myself to be a sucky backup? I'm just not cut out for this. And Dowell and his latest request was the last straw."

"Another one?" he barked.

"Hold your… well, something." I told him about the phone call.

"Here's my update… It's confirmed that it was Jackson who died… according to the coroner, from a heart attack. Surprised Dowell couldn't get that information without asking you. Or maybe that was just the lead-in to asking you to ship something illegal." Floyd was shaking his head, fuming. "Dropping packages at different locations is what criminals do when they don't want to get caught shipping whatever's in the box. They also know that if it comes to the attention of the cops, the security tapes can be checked and will show who dropped the boxes off. So they use a third party, such as yourself, which could land you in a lot of legal trouble and result in your sitting in jail while it's sorted out. Then, if they still don't believe your plea of ignorance, they charge you anyway."

*Good thing I have some sense.* "I thought you'd be relieved that I was no longer dragging my feet about making a decision. I did plan to tell you face to face."

"We'll just have to have a different kind of fun—no dead or crazy people allowed," he said, and we bumped knuckles. "Have you told Pops sayonara? And if so, I hope you're going to tell me that you called him out on his scamming."

"Pops called not long after my good-bye chat with Dowell, but I didn't take the call and instead sent a text that I was on a deadline for a project and would call as soon I finished." I'd have to get him on the phone later, or he'd be marching over here.

"Or you could turn the tables, set up a lunch date, and Mom and I will meet you at the restaurant."

"Rosa agreed?" I asked, wide-eyed.

"We'll surprise her too." Floyd was clearly amused with his idea. "She's burned up my phone, one message after another, about how cute the two of us look together. And that, from all my smiles of late, I should have a woman in my life. And if not you, then she has friends." He bared his teeth.

I laughed.

"Then I remembered your idea and thought, why not meddle in her love life and see how she likes it?"

"Are you prepared for this to backfire?" I mimicked an explosion sound. "Pops and Rosa lock eyes and fall head over heels and into lustful activity? And just because you rolled your eyes, I've decided it's an excellent idea." I jumped up.

He grabbed the back of my shirt and tugged me back down. "Where do you think you're going?"

"I'll be right back." I leaned in and gave him a quick kiss. Back on my feet, I ran to my office and retrieved my phone, which I waved at him as I came back and sat down. Before Floyd could ask what I was up to, the call had connected. "So much to tell you. When can you do lunch?" I asked Pops. "You choose the restaurant, and I'll pick up the check."

"Or cruise the drive-thru, grab hamburgers, and bring them back here to eat," Pops suggested with a hint of amusement.

I mouthed *Tomorrow?* to Floyd, and he nodded. "Tomorrow work for you?" I asked Pops. We agreed on the time and place. I hung up and turned to Floyd. "Your turn."

As he reached for his phone, Gato jumped up

on the footrest and stretched out, taking up the entire length. "What happened to his foot?" Floyd eyed the bandage.

"That would be paw." I laughed at the face he made at me. "Noticed he had a limp, and off to the vet we went. Loved her, by the way. The best part is she'd seen Gato in the past. She wasn't happy about how he came to live with me but relieved that he had a home. She thought he'd caught his paw in barbed wire. She cleaned it up, and we go back at the end of the week."

Floyd eyed the closed slider. "Gato's an indoor cat now?"

"Until he's healed. After that, I'm hoping he won't miss roaming the streets and will want to stay inside. He hasn't howled at the door, so that's good."

"Another thing you failed to update me on."

"Maybe I should make a list the next time you go out of town, but hopefully, it'll be drama-free."

"In my experience, when you say that, all you-know-what breaks loose." Floyd turned his attention to his phone.

"There's a chance that this little payback might end in our deaths," I said before the call connected.

Rosa vetoed lunch out and offered to cook. Floyd overruled her. They agreed that he'd pick her up and ended the call. "What restaurant did your Pops choose?" he asked, tossing his phone back down.

"His favorite—the Swamp Shack. Not much to look at, but the food's great."

"Sounds good. Then what?"

"If you're expecting more of a plan, I don't have one, so I say we play it as it happens."

"You got any more updates for me?" Floyd asked. I shook my head. "If Dowell calls you again, let me know, and I'll take care of him." His grin was hair-raising. "Got an update of my own. Lucas wasn't happy that we tried to pay a visit to Catnip. He reminded me that it's law enforcement that needs to get the goods on her. I asked if he was at least happy he didn't have to chase her down at a bad address. He begrudgingly agreed that he was, then asked if we got a forwarding, to pass it along."

"This gives me a stomachache to say, but I'm thinking Lucas is going to need me to get her out in the open."

"You're not confronting anyone without me by your side."

"It might be a moot point, as I'm thinking we might get our butts handed to us by my Pops or your mom."

Floyd chuckled. "But think of the fun."

"They moved the micro into the living room before starting work on the kitchen, so I can still cook for you. Soup? Or that frozen pizza you turned your nose up at?"

Floyd made a face, which had me biting back a laugh. "How about we hit the drive-thru for that

hamburger you ixnayed for your Pops?"
  "You're on."

# Chapter Twenty-Six

It took some work to talk Pops into letting me drive—he had a long-held opinion that there was no one better behind the wheel than him. We arrived right on time at the Swamp Shack, a tiki-style restaurant on stilts that overlooked an intercoastal waterway. If you wanted to drive your boat in, they had a dock in the front with easy access to the inside.

On the drive over, I told him about finding the body and that it was just more proof that I wasn't cut out to assume control of the business. "But of course, none of this is actually about the business. Funny how I can't find anyone willing to bet against the idea that this has more to do with you getting to mess around in my personal life than you wanting to resurrect your business."

Pops clutched his shirt dramatically "You never get used to dead body stink," he said, ignoring the fact that we'd moved past that topic.

Once we were both out of the SUV, I checked him out again. We both had on tropical attire, me in a spaghetti-strap sundress and sandals, and him in shorts, a pressed shirt, and a pair of boat shoes that still had some life in them.

The Swamp Shack had been around a long time

but had maintained its popular status. The tables were filling up as we stopped at the bar and placed our drink order, then followed the hostess out to the covered patio, where she seated us. We had a view of the water or could watch the rerun of a dirt bike race on the big screen just feet away.

Our drinks were delivered, and we toasted.

"In case you didn't know, your lawyer friend is as shady as all get-out." I told him about the latest job offer.

"When I talked to him, he was looking for someone to serve papers and nothing else." Pops grunted. "Thought it would get you out and about and meeting people."

"Here's your legal papers, and once you're done dealing with whatever, want to date?" I rolled my eyes. "You were hoping I'd meet some nice gentleman that's being sued into oblivion? Or maybe one wanted by the law? We'd even have a lot in common once I got arrested for serving papers without a license."

"You're so dramatic. I meant the lawyers and professional people."

"Yeah, Dowell's such a catch."

"Okay, scratch that idea." Pops scrunched up his eyebrows and stared over my shoulder.

I turned and saw that Floyd and Rosa had appeared at the end of the table, drinks in hand. Floyd pulled out the chair next to Pops for Rosa and sat next to me.

I introduced everyone, and the men shook

hands. "Wanted you to meet Floyd. I hired him, since he's a *licensed* PI, to handle any jobs that came in, and he offered to show me the ropes." I was surprised to see that Pops actually looked embarrassed. "If you're wanting to keep the business open, he's the person to talk to."

"Everything has a way of working out," he said, but wouldn't meet my eyes.

Rosa filled the awkward moment with stories of Floyd growing up and what a brat he was. Not to be outdone, Pops shared a couple of stories that showed I was a close second.

After what felt like an eternity, the server came to take our order. Rosa and Pops grabbed their menus. "Can you give us a minute?" Floyd asked.

"Just wave when you're ready." The server was off to the next table.

The two looked at us questioningly. "I'm ready to order," Rosa said. Pops nodded.

"Being on the receiving end of you two wanting to be up in the middle of our personal lives…" Floyd paused at Rosa's hiss and then said to me, "Forgot to tell you—Mom wanted to fix me up with June Bug."

*June who?*

"I was adamant that she better cancel the date, as I'd be a no-show. Shot a few questions at her on the way over, and all I got were waffly responses, which meant she ignored my wishes. Telling you now: I'm not going; the chick isn't normal."

I couldn't help myself and laughed, which

earned me admonishing glares from Rosa and Pops. "On the 'normal' scale, knowing it includes Leo and Dowell, where does your friend June fit in?"

Pops grumbled under his breath.

"We'll discuss family matters in private," Rosa said in a stern tone.

"What better place to air dirty laundry than in public, where hopefully we'll all stay on our best behavior? My Pops tried to match me up with a couple of criminals." I eyed Pops. "You want to tell your mom about the body we found?" I asked Floyd.

"No, he won't be doing that," Pops spit. "It's done and over; stop fixating on it."

I saluted, which he didn't find amusing. "Then, without further drama, how about I tell you two why we're really here?" I looked at Floyd, who had a "go ahead" smirk on his face. "Floyd and I thought… maybe a little more my idea." I made a shocked face. "How much fun would it be to fix the two of you up?" I clapped as though it was the best idea ever. Their open mouths said otherwise.

"We're old enough to manage our own lives." Pop snorted, then winked at Rosa.

"Good to know that there's an age where one can decide for oneself. What is it?" Floyd asked.

"Don't you sass me," Pops snapped back.

"Hold on. There will be no fighting on your first date. Especially not in front of your intended." I struggled not to laugh.

"Marriage?" Rosa gasped, wide-eyed.

"Floyd and I didn't talk about the joining of our families, but wouldn't that be fun? I'd love it." I smiled around the table, then stood, took my car keys out of my pocket, and handed them to Pops. "After you two have lunch, you might want to take Rosa on a nice drive—along the water is always good—before taking her home."

"I'll get the check covered on the way out." Floyd looked at me—*Ready?*

"Wait," Rosa shouted. The dozen or so people in the restaurant turned, all eyes. "I've already got a boyfriend," she blurted.

"You what?" Floyd's head just about popped off his shoulders as he jumped up. "For how long? Who is he? Who's met him?"

Pops sat back, hands behind his head. I shot him the stink-eye and frowned, and he got the message to wipe the grin off his face.

"Honey, lower your voice." I patted Floyd's arm. "People are staring, and a couple are holding up their phones. Unless you want to be a social media star by tonight, you need to quiet down."

He plopped back down and leaned toward Rosa. "You have a boyfriend? And this is the first I'm hearing of it? You better have a good explanation."

"You've forgotten who the parent is here, and it's not you. You want an answer? Look no further than yourself and how you're acting. I knew you'd overreact, and I was right." She crossed her arms with a militant glare.

"What's his name? After I run a background check, *if* he passes, he and I will have a little sit-down."

"You most certainly will not," Rosa screeched.

"Okay, you two," I cautioned. "Think sideshow, because all eyes and cameras are on the two of you. How about a family dinner—you invite your sons and introduce your new friend?"

Rosa glared at me, clearly telegraphing, *Mind your own business.* "You think that's such a great idea after your ringside seat to how Floyd reacted? Picture this same scene times five."

I did and flinched.

"Voice of reason here." Pops waved his hand.

He'd lost his mind, but I'd tell him later.

"You two calm your shorts," he continued. "This can be worked out without an audience. As for you, young man, here's a reminder for you: your mom's over twenty-one and can decide who she wants to date."

Rosa smiled at Pops.

"Twenty-one is the cutoff." That earned me a couple of glares. "How about we all have some lunch?"

"I'm not hungry." Rosa stood and stomped out of the restaurant, Floyd hot on her heels.

"Okay lover boy, you've got my keys in your pocket, so hop after them and offer Rosa a ride home. And keep your mitts to yourself. You'll live longer."

"We're going to have a talk about this one." Pops stood and brushed my cheek with a kiss, then went after them.

"I've got more grievances than you," I said to his back; he stiffened, so I knew he'd heard me. I got up and walked over to the server, who was eying the other three leaving. "Family misunderstanding." I made sure the drinks were all paid for and handed him a big tip. Once outside, I noticed Pops holding the door of my SUV open for Rosa. The two took off, and Floyd was at my side before they got out of the parking lot. "You calm down yet?"

"Just damn barely," he gritted. "My mother's dating, and it's the first I'm hearing of it. And who? I still haven't gotten a name out of her. Trust me, one way or another, I *will* get it."

"Surely you didn't expect her to sit at home twiddling her thumbs. Rosa's an attractive package." Judging by Floyd's glare, he didn't appreciate my assessment.

"Whoever *he* is, he better not be a stooge like your Pops tried to set you up with." He blew out an irritated sigh, then managed to calm down somewhat. "How about we go back inside and have some lunch?"

"No way I'm going back in there anytime soon. But if you were to suggest tacos… I'd agree."

Floyd hooked his arm around me and walked me over to his truck, opening the door and helping me inside.

"That went well." He slid inside and beat on the steering wheel.

"I'm about to give you some good advice, so listen up. When you go see your mom later, after you've calmed down, take her favorite candy or flowers or something. And when you do meet the boyfriend, do not beat the smack out of him, even if he is a turd. It needs to be your mom's decision, and you don't want her running off just to be ornery."

Floyd and I had a quick lunch, as he was anxious to see his mom. He had a long wait, however, which probably irked him to no end, as Pops ended up taking Rosa out to lunch, where they had a good laugh over everything. As soon as Pops turned into my driveway, I corralled him and insisted he come in so I could hear the details.

"No more matchmaking." I extended my hand.

He eyed it suspiciously. "You sweet on this Floyd fellow? Rosa thinks you two would be good together."

"Today wasn't enough drama for you?"

"Just humor an old man. I'm only thinking of your happiness."

"That's such a load of b—"

"Missy," Pops said sternly, cutting me off, "that's inappropriate talk."

"It could've been another 'B' word—bologna."

Pops snorted. "How about getting back to bologna? I'd like you to take some more time before deciding to shut North down. It would make me happy if you put a little more thought into it before making up your mind." He gave me a cheesy smile. "Know that either way is fine with me."

"How about the next job I get, you come along and see your protégé in action?"

Pops grunted and stood, giving me a hug. "Feeling a little gypped, so let's make a new date for lunch. But no company."

As I walked him out, I noticed that he hadn't answered my question.

# Chapter Twenty-Seven

I got a call the next day, and the woman introduced herself as Rodney Jackson's daughter, Pam. The dead man I'd never met. I asked twice how she got my number, and she evaded the question both times. She said she wanted to meet to thank me for finding her father. I told her that wasn't necessary and debated whether to tell her that it wasn't me, but I didn't want to involve Floyd without his go-ahead. Pam had a hundred questions, and when they began to exhaust my patience, I offered the number of the police officer who'd shown up on the scene, which she already had. Finally, I told her I was getting ready to go out of town, and if she had any more questions, she should call the officer.

Later in the day, there was a knock on my door that I wasn't expecting. Hoping it was Floyd, I peered out the blinds and was disappointed to see a well-dressed man in suit pants and dress shirt, not bad-looking. He caught me peeking and waved. I needed to either get better at not getting caught or get a peephole installed in my door. I had no interest in whatever he was selling. Thankful for the chain lock, I slid it into place before opening the door.

"Ms. North." He slid a business card through the opening, introducing himself as Peter Wilson, attorney-at-law. "I have a couple of questions for you. It should only take a couple of minutes."

He didn't have any papers in his hands, so he wasn't here to serve me. Did lawyers even do their own work? "What's this about?"

"I represent the Rodney Jackson family and have a few questions."

Just great. First, the daughter and now a lawyer. No way was I inviting him inside, so I stepped outside and closed the door. It probably wasn't my worst idea but close. He didn't seem offended that I was keeping him standing in the driveway.

"The police report states that you were at Mr. Jackson's house to serve him papers, and the family wants to know what they pertained to. They don't want any surprises when it comes to settling the estate."

"Wouldn't that be part of the record?" Yes, and he would know that. Or should anyway.

"The cop who questioned you either didn't ask or didn't make a note of it, and when I contacted him, he wasn't able to tell me anything about the papers." He managed to maintain a practiced smile. "My assistant checked the local court records and couldn't find anything."

"It was a paternity case," I told Wilson, who blinked in surprise. "Ware Dowell's the attorney representing the other side." A look of distaste flitted across the man's face. "He'd be the one to answer your questions. As for the rest..." I gave him a brief account of what happened. "My condolences to the family."

"Mr. Jackson was known to have heart issues, and his heart attack took him fast, according to the coroner," Wilson told me.

I feigned ignorance. Floyd had already told me that, but I wasn't dragging him into the middle of whatever this was. Out of curiosity, I asked, "Why did Mr. Jackson's daughter call if she knew you were coming?"

"She called? When did she do that?" Wilson shook his head. "I'll have to remind her that's why she hired me." He slapped that same phony smile back on.

I didn't know if I believed him or not. Then wondered if he was really here about something other than the papers and decided I needed to stop talking. "That's really all I know. It was the only time that I was at the house, and I never went inside."

"I know my sudden appearance at your door was awkward, but I do appreciate that you were willing to answer my questions." Wilson nodded, walked back to his Mercedes, which was parked at the end of the driveway, and didn't waste time pulling away.

I stood there for a minute to make sure he didn't come back with an excuse of forgetting something. After a few minutes, I scanned the street and noted that all was quiet. I'd given the attorney enough time to get a few blocks away, and there was no sign of him, so he was clearly gone. I went inside and closed the door, leaning against it and unleashing a big sigh. First the daughter, then the lawyer. The combination had me hoping that I wouldn't somehow be dragged into this case. I didn't think I had anything to offer, but who knew if they'd agree.

I went back to my office, settled in front of my microphone, and recorded pickup lines for one of my clients. I'd just sent the file when my phone rang. My eyes fell on the note I'd made on my calendar, reminding me that if I didn't recognize the number, I wasn't going to answer. I flipped the phone over. Seeing Floyd's name, I smiled.

"Need backup on a stakeout—guess who I thought of?"

"Thinking you've lost your mind." We both laughed. "What's in it for me?"

"I've got sandwiches."

"You should've started with that. I'm in."

"Wear comfortable clothes and shoes, and in addition to food, I'll bring entertainment."

Hanging up, I raced to my bedroom and changed into black jeans and a t-shirt, hoping we wouldn't be twinsies. I shoved a couple of sodas and water into a tote bag and was ready when he pulled into the driveway.

# Chapter Twenty-Eight

Once we were on the road, I asked, "Didn't you just finish up a job?"

Floyd nodded. "Swung by the office, and one of the guys called in sick while I was there. They had him on speaker, and he sounded like death. I offered to fill in with the stipulation that if he's not back on the job tomorrow, they need to find someone else. Pretty sure he's not going to be, and they're working on it now."

"Have a few questions, which I should've asked before saying yes, but you sidetracked me with the mention of sandwiches."

"If that's all it takes…" He laughed. "By the way, my mom made them, and I know there are cookies. Hit me with your questions."

"No one in their right mind would turn down Rosa's cooking." I mentally licked my lips. "What exactly does a stakeout entail? We going to be chasing bad guys? I didn't bring Pops' gun." I shot up the dashboard with my fingers. "Probably a good thing," I said to his raised eyebrows.

"Once we have time, I'm taking you to the gun range and getting you comfortable shooting. If you're going to have it in the house, you should know how to use it."

"Agreed. I don't want to get into a situation where it's taken and used against me due to my own ignorance."

Floyd nodded his approval. "This case is for a new client, Rita Best, who met this man on a dating site, and they hit it off. After dating for about six months, she noticed small items around her house had begun to disappear. Then, one night while she was out with girlfriends, her house was robbed."

"Why do I get the impression that this is going to come back around to loverboy?"

"Loverboy was never a suspect, at least not in Rita's mind, until she was out with friends again and a woman one of her friends had invited proceeded to tell the table about how her new boyfriend had wined and dined her, then stole everything he could get his fingers on and disappeared."

"Oh no." I shook my head.

"The women then dropped the man's name — James Fisher — and all eyes turned to Rita, whose boyfriend has the same name. The announcement didn't go over well, and Rita stormed out of the restaurant, unwilling to believe that *her* Fisher was a thief."

"Makes me wonder if whoever invited the other woman knew the details of the story she was going to share. If that's the case, there goes that friendship." Which didn't sound solid to begin with — a true friend would tell you in private. "Proving Fisher's involvement might be difficult unless you beat it out of him."

Floyd chuckled, shaking his head. "Not marring these pretty hands."

"Afraid to ask what your client wants you to do."

"We're not here to do anything illegal, if that's what you're thinking," he said in a slightly admonishing tone. "After thinking about it, Rita realized just how strongly everything pointed to her boyfriend being a thief. Before she drags Fisher into civil court, however, she wants to know everything there is to know about him."

"If I were her, I'd broker a deal — give me back my stuff, and I won't have you arrested — and remind him the loot does him little good if he's behind bars."

"Rita filed a report with the cops, who investigated, but there was no proof Fisher was involved in the thefts. He fully cooperated with the authorities, even allowing them to search his house, and they found nothing to implicate him."

"Isn't it kind of risky to let the cops conduct a search, even if you're innocent? I'd want my lawyer involved before I agreed to that."

"Agreed — not something I would've done," Floyd said. "Then Rita went and talked to the woman who broke the news, got the names of a couple of other victimized women, and decided to investigate for herself. And that's how she found out Fisher has a track record of being accused and nothing coming of it. Even if she'd known that at the time she filed her police report and had shared it with the cops, it wouldn't have changed how the investigation turned out, as they couldn't find anything on him in this case. An accusation isn't evidence. Though, after reading the case file, the crimes are so similar that I'd say Fisher is a busy man."

"We're going to sit out in front of his house and… what?"

"Have you been reading your PI manual again?"

"I'll have you know that I finished it—both of them." I turned and looked out the window, ignoring his chuckle.

"My boss, Grey, isn't one to turn down a new client, though he is ethical and did take the time to point out that she might not get her questions answered. He also warned her, based on his own experience on the police force and as an investigator, that watching Fisher is unlikely to produce any evidence that could be deemed helpful in getting a conviction. She could possibly get a civil judgment, as it requires less proof, but it's still not a sure thing." Floyd turned off the main highway just as I was about to ask where we were going.

"Nice neighborhood." I checked out the quiet street and well-kept houses.

Floyd pulled up next to a truck and powered down the window.

A man who'd been scrunched behind the wheel poked his head up. "Happy to see you," he rasped.

Floyd backed up and parked behind him. One leg out the door, he said, "Be right back." He then walked over to the passenger side of the other truck and climbed in. It must have been a short conversation, as within a few minutes, he was back out and walking across the street. Two houses down, he slowed to snap pictures of the license plates of two cars sitting in the driveway of a single-story with lights showing through the shuttered windows.

The other truck driver inched away from the curb and was gone.

Floyd continued halfway down the block before turning around and coming back. Getting in the truck, he coasted up and took the other driver's spot, putting us catty-corner from the house in question. "We sit here until the lights go out or the cars leave. If Fisher is in one of them, we'll follow it."

"It's dinnertime, and I can't imagine that he's going to bed anytime soon, since it doesn't get dark for another couple of hours. I'm thinking you better bring on the entertainment you promised."

"Food first." Floyd reached in the back, pulled a picnic basket over the seat, and set it between us.

"Very sweet of your mom to do all this." I

peered into the basket and licked my lips at all the choices.

"Hey," he said, wide-eyed. "I scrolled through my phone, mumbling about what to order, and she wasn't having it. The whirlwind flew around the kitchen, and the next thing I knew…" He pointed to the basket.

He handed me a turkey, BLT, and avocado on some kind of special bun. *Who has all this in their kitchen?* I took a bite, and it was yum. We both leaned back facing the house and ate in silence. In between bites of the sandwich, he fed me forkfuls of salad. I was stuffed long before he was. "I don't have room for that cookie, but I'm calling dibs. It's coming home with me."

He laughed. "If my brothers were here, you'd have to have claimed it first or go without. All of us are known for eating our cookies before the meal, and it never cuts down on how much we eat."

"It would be fun to meet everyone."

"It's a loud, raucous affair when we all show for a meal. We tease Mom with our latest antics, taming them down a lot, but they still make her laugh. And I doubt that she's fooled."

"Sounds fun. Too bad we couldn't hook Rosa and Pops up for real. And the new boyfriend?"

"He's a nice guy, and you can see that they enjoy being together. Mom made me pinky swear that I wouldn't threaten him. I asked her a couple of times before we got together if she'd changed her mind and got the *behave* glare." He mimicked her, narrowing his eyes. "Any updates for me?"

I told him about getting the phone call from the deceased's daughter and the lawyer showing up. He growled when I told him I went outside to talk to him. "Better than inviting him inside. How about if there's a next time, I crack open the door and stick the muzzle of the gun out?"

"Not funny."

"Kind of is." I smiled. "But I'll agree if it gets you to stop growling."

"I reserve the right… Based on experience, and factoring in the house and car, the dead guy had some cash, and the family isn't interested in sharing. Now that they know there's a paternity case, they'll be waiting to see what happens next."

"I'm thinking that lawyer dude could've gotten any information he needed without knocking on my door."

"That tells me he doesn't have anyone in his office or on speed dial with the ability to pull up that information on the computer for him. If he's only got basic skills, he'd have to go through the records county by county, and even then, he'd have to have the right software." Floyd cleaned everything up and set the basket on the backseat. He held up a soda and a water, and I chose the water. "If you have to a… uhm… pee, I can take you to a gas station."

He smirked as my cheeks caught fire. "I'm good," I mumbled. I did wonder if he usually used a tree but wasn't about to ask.

We sat there for the next couple of hours, sharing details of our lives and laughing, one or the other of us taking notes as the lights went on and off in various rooms of the house. After dusk had fallen, Floyd nudged me. The front door opened, and a middle-aged man came out, his arm around a blonde about the same age. "That's Fisher."

He walked the woman to one of the Mercedes parked in the driveway and opened the door. Turning the woman toward him, he laid on a long kiss, followed by another.

"Surprised she's not spending the night," I said.

Floyd chuckled.

Fisher gripped the woman's elbow, helped her into the car, and shut the door. She rolled down the window, he bent down, and they kissed again. With a wave, she backed out of the driveway, and he headed back to the house. As he stepped up on the porch, another car pulled up, blocking the driveway. The driver rolled down the window and honked, waving over Fisher, who turned and stared but didn't move. Seconds later, the driver took several shots, Fisher dropped to the ground, and the car squealed down the street.

"You stay here. That way, you won't be involved except as a witness." Floyd jumped out of the truck and sprinted across the street. He knelt next to Fisher, whipped out his phone, and wedged it between his ear and shoulder as he checked the man over.

"What made Pops think I was cut out for this business?" I mumbled to myself, scooting across the seat and keeping my eyes on Floyd.

Within minutes, I caught sight of the flashing lights of two cop cars as they came around the corner, stopping in front of the house. It was impressive how fast they'd gotten there. Seconds later, an ambulance pulled up behind them. Two medics jumped out, bags in hand, grabbed a stretcher, and booked it up the driveway. Their arrival cut off my view of what was happening.

It didn't take long before the paramedics were back, Fisher on the stretcher. They loaded it in the back of the ambulance and took off, siren blaring.

Floyd and the two cops moved to the middle of the driveway. Floyd talked to one for a while, and when the second one started to question him, the first made his way over to me. I rolled down the window and leaned my head out.

The officer introduced himself, and I did the same.

"Is Mr. Fisher going to be okay?" I asked.

"Based on the number of shots your friend reported, Fisher's lucky he wasn't killed outright. He needs that same luck to stick with him, as he's in critical condition. But he's headed to the local hospital and couldn't be in better hands."

I replayed it in my mind. "At least four shots."

The officer nodded. "Hear that you're the

backup on this stakeout?"

"More like relief from boredom. I've never been happier that this isn't my regular gig. Floyd and I are friends, and what with the offer of a sandwich, here I am. Hard to pass up his mom's cooking."

The cop asked me what I did, and I told him. He asked a couple of questions, and my answers garnered a couple of nods. He then asked me to relay what I witnessed.

"Fisher's woman friend had barely gotten out of the driveway when a black sedan with dark-tinted windows pulled up, and shots rang out. Floyd hopped out of the truck as the car took off, and I watched it turn left at the stop sign."

The cop took my contact information. "Should I have any more questions, I'll know how to get ahold of you." He thanked me and went back to join the other two men.

Not long after that, Floyd returned to the truck. "At least Fisher's not dead. The paramedics think he has a decent chance of survival."

"Let's hope. Do you think this has anything to do with your client?"

"I didn't hold back any information. When something goes south on a job, and the cops get called, it's always helpful when one of them knows Grey. Got the boss on the phone and handed it over, and I could hear that Grey was giving the same background on the case that I had, which helped to show I could be trusted. He also gave them our client's contact information."

"I'd think she'd be a top suspect until proven otherwise."

"I did learn that the black sedan doesn't match what Rita was driving when she came to the office." Floyd's phone rang, and from the conversation, I guessed it was Grey.

I didn't know the client but did know that people sometimes let their anger control them and took matters into their own hands. Good way to end up in jail. If Fisher died, the shooter would never get out. I listened as the guys rehashed everything that had happened.

Floyd finally hung up and pulled away from the curb. "Grey and I agree that there could be several suspects, based on how many people we know Fisher screwed, and those are only the ones we know about. But we agree with you that Rita's at the top of the list."

"Do you think this was her plan all along, and she used you as cover?" I asked.

"If that turns out to be the case, it was an illogical plan on her part, as it guaranteed there were witnesses. Grey is now investigating her, as he wants to make sure he wasn't being used, and nothing gets past the man. He's not going to let her, or any other client, ruin the reputation of the company he's built."

"This has certainly been... fun's not the right word." I guessed that his snort meant he agreed. "Good food, though. Never a dull moment on one of your jobs."

"Need I remind you that the last job was your client?" he said with a hint of humor.

# Chapter Twenty-Nine

Floyd spent the night, and I felt bad for sending him off to the office with just a cup of coffee. "If you can think of something I can whip up for breakfast in the microwave, I'll go to the store."

"Don't worry, I won't starve for long." On his way out, he stopped to talk to the construction crew, which had just arrived.

I took a cup of coffee and went to my office, happy that I didn't have any shootings to show up for. My phone rang, and I flipped it over. Pops' face stared back at me. Irked with all his shenanigans, I didn't answer. He called back, and the third time I answered, saying nothing and only breathing heavily into the phone.

"You sound like some old man that's on his last leg," Pops crabbed.

"You're lucky I didn't shut off my phone and ignore you altogether."

"You're hurting this old man's heart. What could I have possibly done to irk you off? Am I the one that ambushed you at lunch? How did that work out?" He made his favorite choking sound, showing he was still irritated with me over what went down.

"I'm going to opt for politeness and not get started with the guys you've sicced on me and how dreadful they were. Not to be rude, but what are you up to now?" It was getting to the point where I was afraid to ask the question.

"Six feet or so. A little taller if my hair's standing on end."

"Ha-ha."

"Your Pops needs some help, and who better than his favorite granddaughter?"

"That sounds fun." More like a setup. "My day is booked. I've got stacks of work on my desk that I need to get to in order to keep my clients happy." One file anyway, but he didn't need to know that.

"Do you remember that you promised, if the occasion arose, that you would go on a job with me? Well, that day is here, and it's an opportunity for you to learn from the best. Jeans would be perfect attire, and put your tennis shoes on; I'm on my way to your house."

"Maybe the next time."

"If I drop like a fly, you'll be consumed with guilt about having bailed on me. You don't want to be standing at my grave with regret."

"You know how to lay it on," I said with a shake of my head.

"So that's a yes. Be there in five, maybe ten." He hung up.

I double-checked the screen, then called him back, and he'd turned off the phone. What a conniving old man. I grumbled all the way to my bedroom to get changed, knowing that he'd beat on the door until I answered and not budge until he got me out of the house. I swapped out my sundress for a t-shirt and pair of sweat shorts, far comfier than jeans, and whipped my hair up into a ponytail, ready for whatever drama he was about to serve up… I hoped. Pocketing my phone, I grabbed a cold tea and my purse and walked out the door as he pulled into the driveway.

His smirk when I slid into the passenger side let me know he'd been certain I'd show. He nodded at the construction truck. "About time."

"Before you back out of the driveway, let's hear what this so-called job is about, since you didn't ante up a single detail when you called demanding my help."

"I object to your description." Pops hit the door locks and roared out in reverse, barely looking where he was going as he cleared the driveway. "Lesson one: you shouldn't have gotten in the truck if you weren't coming. Whatever the rest of your questions are, they can wait."

"Damn, slow down. There are ducks at the corner, and one just had babies—seven of them. They have a tendency to jaywalk." I was happy when he slowed and appeared to have an eye out for errant wildlife. "I'm waiting." I reached out and drummed my fingers on the dash.

"Stop that." He attempted to smack my hand down, but I was faster. At the corner, he gave me a side-eye. "Next job, jeans would be better than a sloppy look."

"I'll get the designer's number, and you can call and tell him his line of shorts isn't up to your standards. But guess what? He won't care, as he's making bank off his name."

He snorted with a shake of his head. "You made your Pops happy, getting off your high horse and coming along. Although it did force me to exercise my best negotiation skills."

"Negotiation! You've been drinking!" He glared at the highway, which I took as a maybe. "If you think I'm going to stop asking for details on this supposed job of yours, I'm not. In fact, I'll be a broken record on the subject. Next red light, I'm jumping out."

"Got this female friend. Nothing… you know."

"How old are you?" I rolled my eyes.

"Just didn't want there to be a question. Anyway, she's in trouble with the county—and though I didn't get a lot of details, I do know that if it's not taken care of, fines can be leveled and add up pretty quickly. They don't like their edicts to be ignored, so they get your attention by hitting you in the wallet."

"And without one question, you just hopped on your white horse? In your case, your black truck."

"Just honoring my word. 'If you ever need anything…'"

"All this drama, and you wonder how I ended

up working for Hollywood."

"Happy you're not out in Los Angeles," Pops grumbled.

"What you're telling me is that you didn't bother to find out what we're walking into, just ordered me to get my butt in gear. I'm willing to bet that you came up with the idea of involving me when you were already on the road."

"That about sums it up." He shot me a toothy smile, hitting the gas through a yellow light. "Got to stop and fill up. You want something to drink? Better to take our own."

"Since you're paying, a giganto bottle of water and another tea, and make sure they're both cold."

Pops parked at a pump, ran into the convenience store, and came back out before long, plastic bags in hand. Back on the road, he headed west and exited the Interstate, turning into a neighborhood of small block homes with attached garages. He parked behind another truck in front of the pink corner house. Fencing ran down both sides of the property, and the only difference between this one and the neighbors was that it had two garages, one detached.

I grabbed Pops' arm before he got out. "Still not sure what you expect me to do. Once you find out what the problem is, which I expect will be your first question, then what?"

He jerked his arm back. "A lot of this business is figuring it out as you go."

"If you'd asked at the get-go, you could've lined up any necessary resources and had everything ready to go."

"This is our first job together." Pops shot me a toothy smile, then jumped out and shut the door before I could ask any more questions.

*The biggest thing I've learned thus far is how to avoid answering questions.*

I hopped out and stayed a foot behind as I followed Pops up the driveway. Two twenty-something twins came out of the house and acknowledged him. It appeared they knew one another, and the three laughed about something.

Now I was wishing I'd been right behind him, as I couldn't hear what they were talking about. As I walked up to the three, the conversation stopped, and all eyes turned to me.

"Alexander and Nicholas, or vice versa—they pretty much answer to anything." Pops chuckled as he introduced the three of us.

*Good luck telling those two apart.*

"The twins are the grandsons of Livia, the woman I was telling you about."

So, he did have help lined up? I managed a smile as the twins checked me out. Pops skated away and beat on the front door, which left the three of us staring at each other. Who was going to speak first?

A blond woman—Pops' age, in an apricot tent dress and matching flip-flops—threw open the door and was all smiles, kissing his cheek. She linked her arm through his and dragged him into the house.

I turned to the twins and pasted on a tired smile. "My Pops was less than candid as to why we're here, so maybe one of you could fill me in."

The two looked at each other and laughed. "There's several issues, but the most important is finding a solution to Gran's immediate problem," one said.

I nodded, with a smile like I understood.

The other one's phone rang, and he pulled it out of his pocket, flashed the screen at his brother, and the two stepped away.

Feeling awkward standing in the middle of the driveway, I decided to check out the property and give the neighborhood a quick glance, so I walked to the corner. With the houses all looking the same, if you came home drunk, you better at least remember the color of your house, as it was practically the only difference. It was quiet, and I didn't catch sight of any of the neighbors.

The twins finished their call and met me at the end of the driveway. "Out of curiosity, since we figured you'd be a..." The first one apparently did all the talking. "Why is it you can't get a date?"

"What are you talking about?" I couldn't keep the coldness out of my tone.

"There are a few issues with Gran's house, but before they can be addressed, the issue of her hoarding needs to be tackled. We plan to have a talk with her about it, so it doesn't become a problem again."

"That has nothing to do with your snide comment about me dating."

"Calm down. Women." An eyeroll in his tone. "I could've phrased it a little better."

The other one nodded as though in agreement—but on which part? My guess was *Calm down*—and finally spoke up. "Your grandfather thought it a great idea to hook one of us up with you. And before we could tell him we both have girlfriends, here you are."

*Could I be more embarrassed?* Hoping my red cheeks looked more like windburn, I forcibly closed my mouth. "I have a boyfriend. Sorry, this was a waste of time all around." I found their smirks irritating. "Not sure what kind of help your grandmother needs, but I'm willing to lend a hand while I'm here." This was the last of these kinds of scenes that would ever play out, as I planned to kill Pops. He must be thinking my career wasn't a money-maker and needed to take a look at what I'd accomplished.

"Here's the deal: we've got a quick job," the first one said. "We'll get back as soon as we can... If you could just keep Gran calm and assure her that everything can easily be taken care of and impending doom won't be happening. She won't listen to either of us, thinking we want to protect her from the truth." The other one nodded. Without waiting for a response, they got in their truck and pulled away, turning at the corner.

Pops skirted by me with an absent wave that I took to mean he was grabbing something out of his truck and would be right back. I was wrong, as he climbed in and drove off in the same direction as the other truck, which had already disappeared.

Though I couldn't believe it, it sank in fairly quickly that everyone had disappeared and left me standing here. For how long? I whipped out my phone and called Pops. "You're a dead man," I roared when he answered. "You forget something? Like me?" I didn't notice Livia standing beside me until she giggled.

"Calm your shorts. Picking up an order for Livia and coming right back." He hung up.

I glared at the phone, took a couple of deep breaths, and managed to calm a scintilla before I turned and introduced myself.

## Chapter Thirty

"Men can be irritating," Livia said with a big smile. "I can promise you that Max is going to be back, and if you have somewhere to be, I'm more than happy to drive you. I hope you're not in too big a hurry, as Max has had great things to say about you, so it's fun to finally meet you."

"I'd love to hear any funny stories I can use against him." If I'd let him, Pops would snoop into every facet of my life, but he rarely shared anything about his own.

She laughed. "Max and I are part of a group that tosses down a beer or two at a local watering hole. We all shoot pool, and some darts. We've never…" She tapped her fingers together. "In case you wondered."

One of these days, I was going to be immune to embarrassment, and I hoped it happened before my cheeks suffered burn damage. "I don't want to, ah… hear about that." I shook my head. "Why don't you tell me how I can help?"

Livia linked her arm through mine and steered me back up the driveway. "One of my neighbors—and I have a hunch which one; that house over there…" She pointed to the house that sat diagonally from hers. "The owner, Robbie, has her nose in everyone's business. Anyway, whoever it was called the code department and reported me as a hoarder. The man who showed up was nice enough and pointed out that there were several issues that needed to be addressed for my safety. But none of the work could be done when I had so much "clutter," as he called it."

"You wouldn't know from the outside." I took a second look. "Surprised it was legal for him to go inside."

"I didn't ask what his authority was," Livia said, shaking her head. "Besides, as soon as I opened the door, he knew that I'm quite the collector. Then he went on about how living the way I did could affect my health. When he got to hoarding being a mental illness, I got scared and assured him I'd get it organized. Thought that was the end of it, but then a woman from Social Services showed up to check on me. The second time she came, I didn't answer the door." She paused, hand on the knob, and turned to me. "Are you easily shocked?"

"That depends." I chuckled nervously. "Is there a dead body or two inside?" I would know the second she opened the door—because who forgets that smell?—and wouldn't hesitate to walk home.

Livia looked shocked. "I have my oddities but can promise you that I don't have anything that's dead."

"Then I'm sure I'll be fine." Just the same, I

steeled myself as she opened the door.

It was difficult to determine the size of the entry based on the placement of the outside windows, and I surmised that the narrow path took us into the living room. It was difficult to take in the assortment of items that were lined up on both sides. On one side, the boxes were stacked to the ceiling, with none appearing to be marked. The other side was a hodgepodge of things, from clothing to household items, that were thrown on top of one another.

Where had she found all this stuff? I continued my survey, turning my head side-to-side as she led me down another path. Books, dishes, small pieces of furniture, and on and on. "I'm surprised you allowed the inspector to come inside."

"He said he had the legal right, and I only found out afterward that he lied. I can't be too mad, as he spotted a leak in the guest bathroom and turned the valve off."

The path ended at the far wall and led off in two directions. The one to the right went into the dining room, which I surmised from the table piled with a variety of dishware and linen, with other kitchen items stacked on top and stuff shoved underneath. Along one wall were chairs of various sizes haphazardly piled on top of one another.

The small kitchen didn't show the same degree of clutter. One counter was completely cleaned off and held a place setting, a stool within arm's reach. I surmised it was where she ate. I'd have to have something to read, as I couldn't stand to eat and stare at the cupboards. The other counters held an assortment of dishes, glassware, and silverware.

Livia turned to me. "You haven't said anything."

"Just taking it all in. Trying to think of ways you'll be able to get the county to go away and ensure it's the last you'll hear from them." I had no clue, but saying that out loud wouldn't be helpful. I found it hard to believe Pops would have any easy solutions either... and that's if he showed back up.

"That would be ambitious." She chuckled and turned, going back the way we came.

"Did you buy all this?" I asked.

"I wouldn't have two cents left, doing that." Livia shook her head. "Love a good yard sale, and the best time for a deal is the end of the day when they're boxing up. Depending on how many hours they've been sitting around and the money they've made, oftentimes, they're open to just getting rid of everything. I always come home with a full car. At first, I intended to sell it myself, but I hate to get rid of anything. No one will take care of it like I will."

Livia needed an anonymous hoarder group, but since a nice way to suggest it eluded me, and it was something that she'd need to discover on her own.

The first room on the right was the bathroom, which was clean and clutter-free. The bedroom on the left was crammed so tight that the door opened just enough to stick my head inside. There wasn't an inch of open space. At the end of the hall was another bedroom, which had a path around the queen-size bed. Clothes, shoes, and purses were piled high all along the walls. The closet doors stood open, and the rack was crammed with an assortment of clothing.

"What is it that you'd like to see happen?" I asked. "I'm assuming all this boxed up, and then—"

"But then what will happen to it all?" Livia cried.

"I noticed you have a two-car garage—that could be a start. And then there's the second garage. Once you have everything organized and boxed, it'll be easy to find anything you need." I'd bet that she couldn't guess at the extent of what she'd stockpiled.

"The single garage is a bigger problem," Livia confided in a hushed tone.

What did that mean? I envisioned opening the door, unleashing an avalanche, and running to get out of the way.

"I realize that we've just met, but can I trust you?" She eyed me as though trying to decide for herself. Before I could answer, she continued. "You can't tell anyone. I probably shouldn't tell you, but I can't keep it to myself any longer. And I wouldn't say anything if Max didn't speak so highly of you."

"I can keep a secret. I can assure you that if it turns out to be something we need help with, I'd get your permission before telling anyone else."

"That makes sense." Livia nodded, then grabbed my hand and steered us back to the front door. Once outside, I realized how stale and musty the air inside had been. She led the way to the detached building on the opposite side of the driveway from the main garage.

"Did you add this on?" I asked.

"Heck no, it came with the property. In the closing, I had to sign off that I knew it lacked proper permits, but nothing's ever come of it. The previous owner used it for his boat. I thought that when the youngster showed up from the code department, this was going to be the issue, but he barely gave it a glance."

I turned to look at the house that Livia had pointed out, where the possible snitcher lived. "How did nosey know that you were a collector?"

"She's been over here a couple of times, but I never invited her inside. I'm guessing that she got a look when I opened the door. Any friends that come over, I invite them to sit over there, and they know to bring their own drinks." Livia pointed to a line of dingy beach chairs in a variety of colors. "Now remember your promise." She raised the roll-up door.

Expecting another accumulation of stuff, I was

surprised to see only a large pile of bicycles. "That's quite a collection." At a quick count, there were eight. I started to inch forward, but she stopped me with a hand on my arm.

"Don't think it's a good idea to go looking around, since I don't know how they got here or even how long they've been here." Livia tugged on my arm. "Do I even want to know? I don't think anyone would believe that I had nothing to do with their showing up. I do know, since I check every once in a while, that bikes come and go, and there have been as many as a dozen. It's not often that something makes me nauseous, but this does." She held her stomach.

As she reached up to lower the door, I whipped out my phone and took a couple of pictures. "You know what I'm thinking?"

"Stolen? Me too. And if the police get wind… They won't believe that I don't know who's using my garage for whatever's going on." Livia sighed. "Didn't think about getting a lock, as I never used it, and all this time, I thought it was empty. I promised myself that I wouldn't fill it up like I did the other one."

"I'm thinking that since Max used to be a private investigator, he'd know what to do."

"I'm embarrassed to tell him," Livia said with a shake of her head. "I was thinking that maybe you could come back after dark and help me haul everything out and dump it. Then I'll lock it up like I should've done from the start."

"That's a bad idea, as we might get caught. How would we explain dumping bicycles that don't belong to either one of us? No one would believe we weren't the thieves. A couple of other things... Stop creeping around in the dark. Don't try to deny it." I waved her off.

"Okay," she squeaked.

"And stay away from this garage until we figure out what the next step is," I admonished. "The last thing you want is to get caught by whoever is doing this. Once it gets cleaned out, we'll get you a lock that takes a chainsaw to get off."

"I knew you were the one to trust." Livia beamed.

"One more thing: do you swear that you had nothing to do with the bicycles ending up in your garage? And have no clue who *is* involved?"

"I swear." Her right hand shot in the air.

"Come on." This time, *I* grabbed *her* arm and led her over to the chairs. Before we sat down, I eyed the other garage, noting the lock and wondering what condition it was in. The chairs looked far sturdier up close than they did at a distance. My mind was spinning. If she was telling the truth, and I did believe her, I feared for her safety. "Any clue where Pops was going when he flew out of here? Claimed to be picking up something—do you know if that's true?"

"Max claims to have a connection for used boxes who can get them for a song, so he went to pick some up."

"Appears that the plan is to pack everything up, and then what?" I asked. "Did Pops agree to help with this project? Do the heavy lifting?"

"Somehow, I need to get it all into boxes and not lollygag about it. The code fellow said that the leak in the bathroom is back behind the walls, and there might be rot or mold, but would need a professional to address the issue." Livia sighed. "Max didn't ask for the details, just offered to come and check it out, after which he'd know what to suggest next. I know it's a lot to ask, but I don't want the woman coming back. The talk about my mental health scared me. But I didn't get started on it—too busy wasting time, fretting over what to do instead of making calls and getting answers. I finally called Max because he's an old friend, and he assured me that he would get it figured out. Have to admit that I was happy he didn't hang up on me."

And I'd just bet in Pops' mind, figuring it out meant get Maren to do it. "Here's my honest assessment… I'm certain that with the three of us working, we can get everything boxed up, but how long it will take…" I shook my head. "Faster with the twins' help. Do you know when they're coming back?"

"Not until the weekend." Livia made a face. "Sorry if you were embarrassed by Max's attempt at matchmaking. If I'd known what he was going to ask, I'd have told him that they have girlfriends. To be honest, they're not ready to settle down—they always have someone new on their arms."

"You'd think I would be used to his matchmaking attempts by now. One of these days, I'm going to find a way to pay him back. My first attempt backfired." I told her about introducing him to Rosa and finding out she had a boyfriend, and Livia laughed. "Hear me out on this… I've got a friend and would like to share the garage bike thing with him. Since he's a PI, I know he'll have a good suggestion for what to do next. I can promise with no hesitation that he won't hang you out to dry. And just maybe he'll offer to lend some muscle packing up."

"What are you going to have to put out?" Livia made a face. "You know, nothing for free and all."

"Wait until you see him." I winked. "He's what's known as a looker."

She clapped. "You sweet on him?" I nodded. "Knew from the first hello that I could trust you."

"Promise that I'm not going to let you down. And just so you know that I'm not scamming you or full of it, you sit right there and listen in while I call him. It'll be one-sided, but you'll get the gist and know that I'm not putting something over on you." I pulled out my phone and called Floyd. Voicemail. What the heck? I tried again.

"No answer." Livia gave me a pouty frown.

"Not giving up just yet." It was a longshot to call him at the office. I hadn't done it before and hoped he wouldn't be annoyed. Not having the number in my phone, I had to look it up.

"WD Consulting," a deep male voice answered.

"May I speak with Floyd James?" I asked in my most professional voice.

"You could if he were here, but since he's not, how can I help you? I'm Grey Walker, and you are?"

One of the partners! I really wanted to hang up. "This is his girlfriend, some think his wife, and I'm trying to track him down." I'd meant to be funny and decided too late that maybe it wasn't.

"Maren North. I've heard a lot about you. We all have, and we're looking forward to meeting you."

"'Poor Floyd, hooked up with a lunatic'—is that how the story went?"

Grey chuckled. "Floyd's the half-crazy one. Dixon, on the other hand—everyone listens to him. Been after Floyd to bring you to the office so we can all meet you and make up our minds."

"Can't tell you how helpful Floyd and Dixon have both been. Floyd signing on for whatever's about to blow up in my face has saved me more than once."

"That's because whatever the two of you get up to has been more fun than work for him. I'm pretty certain it's the reason he's been showing up to work a lot less grouchy." Grey laughed. "Something tells me that the reason you're calling him at work is that you need his help.

Unfortunately, he's on assignment. But you've got me."

"I have this friend…" I patted Livia's hand, and she smiled at me. "I planned to ask Floyd if he could hit up his cop friend for a favor, with the stipulation that he keep my friend out of legal trouble. If the latter's not possible, then I'll come up with something else."

Grey chuckled again. "All of us here at WD have cop connections. We never mind giving one of them a call as long as we're not asking anything illegal."

"Well… I'm, hmm—"

"Just tell me, and we'll figure it out."

"It's illegal alright. At least, I'm fairly certain it is. Not sure how it couldn't be." Grey cleared his throat—guessing he wanted me to move the story along. I told him about Livia's second garage, and that she swore she had no idea who was using it, and I believed her. "It needs to stop before something bad happens. I took a couple of pictures if that would be helpful."

"Once Floyd gets back to the office, we'll come up with a plan of action, and he'll call you. In the meantime, tell Livia to stay away from the garage, as you don't know who's got eyes on the property. As for the pics, I'll text my cell number to you. You're calling me from your cell, right?"

"Yes. I really appreciate what you're doing, and Livia feels the same." She nodded enthusiastically.

"Is there anything else?"

I laughed, which came out more like a groan. "You shouldn't ask that question." He chuckled. I told him about the hoarding complaint and the county showing up, and that it scared her enough that she wanted to get everything packed up and stop the house calls. It was a big enough job that we could use a couple more hands, and I asked if he knew anyone I could call. I ignored Livia shaking her head, patting her leg to reassure her. "It's quite an interesting accumulation."

"Good news on that front. There's a company on the first floor of this building—Hugo's—and he cleans up anything and does a damn good job. I'll give him your number and can promise you'll get an immediate call."

Assuring Grey there was nothing else, I thanked him, and we hung up. I relayed the conversation to Livia, who hadn't stopped shaking her head, having hung on every word on my side of the call.

"I just..." She worried her bottom lip. "I can't afford this Hugo fellow."

"We're not going to worry about that until we get an estimate—"

"We can't waste the man's time," Livia said, wide-eyed.

"If you're worried about it, trading services is a popular option." I'd thrown out the first thing I could think of, though I was pretty sure the man would want cash. If so, Pops could damn well step up. Now that he'd involved me, I wasn't ditching the woman to fend for herself. In the short time I'd spent with her, I'd found her to be genuine and liked her.

"I'm an excellent cook." She clapped.

"You're not to worry about it," I lightly admonished. "What you're going to do is leave it to me to trot out my negotiation skills and get something worked out." Livia looked skeptical and would be more so if she knew it would be my first time trying to dicker with someone. I was still holding my phone, and we both stared when it began to ring. I glanced down at the screen and didn't have a clue who was calling. I'd promised myself I wouldn't answer any more calls from unknown numbers… but did it anyway.

"Hugo here," a man introduced himself in a gruff voice. "Grey tells me you need a clean-up job done stat. Why don't you run the details by me?"

I gave it to him straight and didn't paint a pretty picture. Livia looked down, shaking her head.

"This sounds like a job I need to check out. How about I stop by within the hour?"

I repeated the offer to Livia, who shook her finger at me, her eyes wide. I took that as "Heck no." I jumped up and didn't stop until I reached the end of the driveway, far enough that she couldn't hear me. "I want you to give Livia a dirt-cheap price. I'll cover the rest, and she's not to know."

Hugo chuckled. "Got it."

I gave him the address, and we hung up. Making my way back to the beach chairs, I reclaimed my chair. "Hugo assured me he was open to bargaining. Another plus is that he comes recommended, which is way better than some dude off the street." I reached out and covered her hands, which she was busy wringing. "Trust me. We're going to get this done."

## Chapter Thirty-One

"I'll admit that we've hit it off and have an easy rapport." Livia eyed me with a nod. "But face it, you don't know me from Adam… whoever he is. You always this helpful?"

"Normally, I'm holed up in my house, busy at work." I told her a little about my business. "These last few weeks…" I sighed and told her what Pops had been up to, which had her gasping and laughing. "Honestly, I was reluctant at first, but now that I'm involved, I'm determined to see it through until you don't have problem one." I smiled at her.

"I consider myself lucky that you showed up." Livia glanced at the street and pointed with her chin. "Look who's here."

Pops turned the corner and backed into the driveway.

Grabbing boxes took this long? I shot up and was standing in the driveway when he got out. "Nice of you to show back up," I grumbled. "Next time you decide to ditch me without a heads up, at least toss my purse out the window; I might've needed cash."

"You don't look like you suffered any." He dropped the tailgate.

"That's it?" I came close to a shriek as I counted the measly stack—twelve. "That's hardly going to make a dent in packing up Livia's collections."

"You mean piles of…" Pops managed to catch himself as Livia joined us. "Hope Maren hasn't been driving you nuts like she does me."

Two testosterone pickups pulled into the driveway, cutting off any response as the three of us turned to stare. An older grey-haired man climbed out of the first one and a younger version of him out of the other.

"Hugo." The older man waved and handed out his business card.

"I'm Maren." I stepped forward and shook hands, then introduced everyone else. "Thank you for coming so quickly."

Hugo, who'd been eyeing Livia, held out his arm to her. "Why don't you show me around, and we can discuss the job?"

The younger guy's phone rang, and he hung back, leaning against his bumper as he took the call.

"Don't even think about trying to run off again." I looped my arm in Pops' and pointed to the row of chairs. "Don't make me drag you."

He snorted and eyed the chairs suspiciously. "Will one of these hold my big butt?"

"Guess you're going to find out. Now sit."

The other guy had finished his call and walked over. "Maren?" I nodded. "I'm Brawn. This truck is courtesy of Grey. He said to leave it parked, blocking the garage until he can get someone out to deal with the problem. He promises it shouldn't be longer than a day, and if something comes up, he'll call. The man always keeps his word."

"I'll call and thank him."

"Anything else, waylay me on my way out of the house. Got to catch up to the other two and see what the job entails." Brawn took off into the house.

I turned on Pops with a fierce stare. "Okay, old man, you and I need to come to a very simple understanding — no more meddling."

"That's rude."

"There's more to discuss, but not in someone else's driveway. Thinking we do dinner and negotiate. Just the two of us in someplace nice… we should both be able to behave."

Pops held up his hands in a conciliatory gesture. "You know I only want the best for you."

I groaned and squinted at him, hoping another surprise wasn't going to hop out of the bushes.

"Pretty sure that Livia can't afford some highfalutin service to clean this place up. Thinking it should be bulldozed, but I'm guessing she won't go along with that idea."

"There's nothing wrong with the structure of the house." I unleashed a dramatic eyeroll. "Considering the work it will take to get it cleaned up and organized, hopefully she'll keep it that way. Since you brought it up…" I said, cutting off whatever he was about to say. "Instead of Livia worrying about how to pay, why don't you go behind her back and get it figured out? She never needs to know. I promised that we'd get the job done, and you're going to help me keep that promise."

"Had no clue what I was getting into when I agreed to come over—just helping a friend and all that. Called you, thinking what a great bonding moment."

"You're such a slickster," I said with a shake of my head. Pops made a face but barely contained a smile. "Have Hugo bill North and take it as a tax deduction. If not Hugo's crew, then who? You better get on the phone and strongarm everyone you know into getting their behinds over here. And while you're at it, hustle up a hundred more boxes, and that's for starters."

Pops got sidetracked from the hundred questions I knew he had, since thus far he hadn't asked enough to know what was truly going on. Livia, Hugo, and Brawn returned, and Livia opened the door to the two-car garage, and it was filled to the brim.

Pops groaned and leaned over to whisper, "Where did all this junk come from?"

I covered my lips with my finger. *Be nice*, I mouthed.

Hugo closed and locked the door for Livia, and the threesome came over to stand in front of us. "We'll be here tomorrow early to get this job knocked out. Two days, tops," Hugo announced. "The plan is to start with the garage, get it cleaned out, and then move to the house. The next visit some well-meaning sort pays will be the last."

The two men nodded. Livia walked Hugo to his truck, and he and Brawn took off. I jumped up and kept her out of earshot of Pops as I explained why the other truck was staying behind. I also gave her my number, assured her the bike problem would be dealt with, and told her not to worry. Then we joined Pops, who wasn't happy with me for leaving him out of the conversation.

"Can I depend on you to get me home, or will you be dumping me somewhere?" I shot at him.

"Drama Queen," he mumbled.

Livia threw her arms around me and gave me a hard hug. "You're the best," she whispered in my ear. "Can't thank you enough." She turned to Pops. "You did a good job with this one."

Typical Pops—he nodded and took all the credit.

"I'm off to the store. I promised muffins, coffee, and drinks for when they arrived in the morning. Mulling over some ideas for lunch. Since I'm betting on the boys being healthy eaters, I'm going to make sure there's plenty. And also cookies."

I almost licked my lips. "They're going to love working here."

## Chapter Thirty-Two

Pops dropped me off without any further drama. Happy to be home, I planned to work for a couple of hours but instead, lay on the couch. I'd opened the sliders for a breeze, and Gato jumped up and laid next to me, and we both fell asleep. A knock on my front door woke me up. I was slow to get up, and whoever it was knocked again. I made my way over to the window and peeked out the blinds. Floyd waved. I opened the door, and he held up the same picnic basket from the other night. "Hungry?"

"Yum." I licked my lips. "What if I'd had a date?"

"I would have kicked his ass." He set the basket on a side table and pulled me into a hug and a kiss. "I knew food would get me in the door. I have news."

"You know, you could take a chance on my cooking; it might surprise you. I swear no one's ever gotten sick."

Floyd laughed and twirled me around, setting me on my feet. "How was your day, dear?"

"Your smirk tells me that you got most of the deets from your boss, who was amazingly helpful. He sent Hugo, who didn't even flinch at the amount of accumulated... junk seems rude, knowing that Livia's attached, but it's everywhere."

"Hugo's a great guy. I worked for him for a while, and that's how I met Grey and Seven. Trust me when I tell you that Hugo never turns down a job; he always figures out a way to get it done."

"Let's sit outside." I grabbed dishes and silverware from a side cabinet and followed him, cleaning and setting the table. "What do you want to drink?"

"Got that covered; all we need is wine glasses." He pulled a bottle of red wine and an opener out of the basket.

I was back in a flash with the glasses. We sat side by side, facing the water. All was quiet for now, not a boat in sight and just a couple of seagulls floating by.

Floyd soon had the bottle open and filled the glasses. "Salute," he toasted, and we clinked glasses. "Hope you like Italian." He pulled out several containers, removing the lids and setting them in front of us.

"Looks and smells delicious," I said.

He dished up a serving of ravioli, some salad, and a slice of garlic bread on each. "It's great out here. I like how quiet it is and that you're not sitting outside staring at your neighbor. The builder got it right when he designed the houses to maintain everyone's privacy."

"It's turned out to be a great neighborhood all

around." Every bite of the food was great. I recognized the name on one of the lids as a local place and made a mental note to eat there sometime soon. "How was your day?"

"Filled in last minute on a bodyguarding job, as the wife of the guy assigned to the job went into labor. The client was an older man who spent the day in one meeting after another. I just sat there and looked pretty. And was happy when my replacement showed up, and I think the client was happy as well, as he knew the man."

"I take it that the client likes to see a familiar face."

"They get comfortable and like knowing what to expect," Floyd said, nodding. "Then I got back to the office and found out you were having adventures without me." He made a sad face. "Grey was amused by your job and wants me to find out how you got roped into it."

"Pops called and thought it would be fun for the two of us to go on a job together." I rolled my eyes, and Floyd laughed. "Looking back, he didn't really know what to expect, as he hadn't asked any questions, but I'm thinking his plan was to fluff everything off on me, though that plan changed when he saw all the heavy lifting involved. Not a job I could've done without help. Then there were the twins." I shook my head. "Good luck telling those two apart."

"Another ambush setup?"

"Don't know if he had it planned all along, or

the opportunity presented itself, and he ran with it. Can you imagine my embarrassment when they wanted to know why I couldn't get my own date?" I huffed a laugh. "Then what does Pops do? He splits. Last time I go anywhere with him driving." Floyd growled, which had me smiling. I then launched into how the rest of the day had unfolded.

"Hard to believe a homeowner could miss the fact that someone's storing probably stolen bicycles in their garage." He arched his eyebrows.

"I believed that Livia had no clue, and she was clearly frightened about the whole thing. I think the only reason she told me was that she was stressing about the possibility of the bikes being discovered and didn't have anyone else to confide in."

"Grey forwarded the pics to Lucas, and it didn't take him long to call back to say that a number of bikes had been reported stolen in the area, and they'd yet to get a break. Tonight, there's going to be eyes on the house to see if there's any activity."

"Pretty nervy and stupid to use someone else's garage for illegal activities and hope you're not discovered. Just so you know, I told Livia no more skulking around."

"You think she'll listen?" Floyd asked.

"She assured me she would."

"Grey and I came to the same conclusion about whoever's using the garage. We figure it's someone who knew that it wasn't being used and that they have eyes on the property."

"A neighbor?" I asked, surprised, but it made sense. "Livia thinks that the woman across from her reported her for the hoarding—you'd think if she saw unusual activity around the garage, she'd be asking questions, not caring that it's none of her business. Neighbor relations with her are already shaky."

"Once they bust the theft ring, and they will, it'll be interesting to see what else they uncover. We were also in agreement that if the thieves had seen all the activity currently going on at the house, they're going to want to get the garage cleaned out as soon as possible."

"You sit; I've got this." I picked up the dishes and took them into the house. While I did that, he packed the food containers back into the basket. "You have an update for me on the guy we staked out?" We took our glasses and moved out to the end of the deck, where we shared the same chaise.

"Fisher got lucky and is going to survive. Cops questioned the woman that hired us, but so far, no arrests. She did fire us, livid that we gave her name to the cops."

"She had to know that you'd have an obligation to hand it over."

"Grey let her go off until he got the gist of her issue and then cut her off, and she hung up. It was disclosed to us that there were several other women on the suspect list. Fisher's been living with one woman while smooching it up with the one we saw."

"I'd want to kick him out, but you can't take his stuff to the hospital."

"She rented a storage unit, packed his stuff into it, and had someone else deliver the key and his car to the hospital. My guess is that he was threatened with bodily harm if he ever went back to the house. If it were me, I'd have given him a detailed description of all the bones I would break if I ever saw his face again."

"Thinking this current woman is lucky that she wasn't cleaned out."

"Fishers got a track record of moving on to the next woman quickly, so I'm guessing he's got someone to call. Possibly the one he was kissing."

"The shooting was on the news. They showed the exterior of the house and a shot of his car, so it's possible she already knows."

"If she's smart, she'll change her number and stay as far away as possible. But there are some that don't want to hear the truth, and if they do accept it, they think they can 'fix' the man. I haven't heard of a case where that's worked."

"Enough about business. We should enjoy the rest of our evening. Movie perhaps?" I arched my brow.

"Just one more item. Grey would like me to bring you to the office and introduce you around. He's got a few questions about North Investigations."

"It would be fun to see where you work. Does the offer include where you live too?" I asked.

"I'd love to show you around, but fair warning, my place is a work in progress. Dixon invested my money, and I was able to buy a mixed-use property and live on the second floor. Some of the renovations I've done myself, and others have been hired out. I readily admit when I don't have the necessary skills. Hiring an electrician to rewire the building is a good example."

I shuddered at the reminder of a couple of projects I'd seen that were clearly done by someone not qualified. "Grey wants to talk about North?"

Floyd laughed. "You've made every effort to please your Pops. But I can tell by the way you talk that you love the business you've already built. I say go with the one that excites you. You don't want to mark time with some job that you couldn't care less about. Hard on the soul."

"Agreed. I just need to sit Pops down and make sure he's listening. Has the business portion of this evening concluded?"

"One more update." He held up a finger. "Just heard this yesterday about your friend Catnip…"

I scrunched my nose. "Almost forgot about that woman and had hoped it would stay that way."

"This is more about her ex, Herbie."

"Hope he's still among the living." Because otherwise… I didn't want to think about it.

"As you're aware, Herbie's been staying with

friends on the Gulf Coast. Doubt he'll be coming back anytime soon once he gets the news that someone broke into his apartment and set it on fire."

I gasped.

"The good news is that the fire alarm went off, and the neighbors on both sides heard it and called 911, knowing Herbie was out of town. The sprinklers in his unit helped to keep the fire from spreading as fast it otherwise could have, and the firefighters put it out before there was any damage to the neighboring units. Though they did have to evacuate."

"Sounds like the person who vandalized his car came back."

"Comparing the pictures captured by the security cameras, it certainly seems so—they were similar in build and dressed the same. Both times, the person knew just what to do to keep their face hidden."

"I imagine the neighbors would like him to move."

## Chapter Thirty-Three

Floyd left early for work, and I went back to sleep. When I finally got up, I made myself a pot of coffee, needing the caffeine jolt to get some work done. My thoughts wandered to Livia, and I wondered how she was faring. I called to check in, and it went to voicemail, so I left a message. "If you need anything, don't forget to call."

My phone rang almost immediately, and I was surprised to see WD on the caller ID. I'd entered the number after the first time I called them. Assuming it was Floyd, I answered, "Good morning," sexing it up.

A male voice chuckled. Not Floyd. "This is Grey Walker."

I let out an embarrassed laugh. "You're sounding cheery, so hoping this won't be bad news."

"Did Floyd happen to mention that I'd like to have a meeting with you?"

"Something about business… looking for a new PI? I'm thinking I'm not your girl."

"For someone new to the business, you've handled everything that's been thrown at you."

"Just barely," I mumbled.

"How about if you come to the office and I

wow you with a presentation?"

I made a face at the phone; happy Grey couldn't see. "As my Pops would say, 'Just spit it out.'"

"Heard quite a bit about him." He laughed. "I know that Floyd would like to show you around the office and the area in general."

"It would be fun to stop in and say hello to Dixon and thank him again for everything he did… it only took him a second to realize I was in over my head." I chuckled.

"How does day after tomorrow work for you?" Grey asked.

"Looking forward to meeting everyone. Do I at least get a hint before we hang up?"

"What fun would that be?"

We hung up, and I stared at the phone, thinking Floyd would have more details.

I tackled the work on my desk, also getting several texts from Floyd that made me laugh. In response to the first one, I had to assure him that another whacky client hadn't been sent my way.

He called at the end of the day, while on a break from his client. "I'm driving you to Biscayne Bay for the meeting with the guys," he insisted. "If I promise to take the scenic route, that should seal the deal." He ended by saying cryptically, "We have a few things to discuss."

Hanging up, I made a note to coffee up that morning.

My phone beeped right after that, and I

expected it to be another text from Floyd, but it was from Livia—a picture of the two-car garage, boxes neatly stacked and marked. "We're almost done." She added a happy face. One thing about Hugo's men, they didn't drag their size fifteens.

\* \* \*

"This is a business meeting," I told myself as I scanned my closet. I chose a simple black sleeveless dress with a fitted top and full skirt. Ignoring the stilettos staring at me, I opted for a more comfortable pair of wedge heels. I managed to secure my messy hair in a bun and was ready when Floyd arrived.

He whistled when I opened the door. He held out his hand and twirled me around, then laid a big kiss on me, and we walked out to his truck.

Once inside, I straightened my dress and caught him eyeing my legs. I grinned at him.

"I've got an interesting update on your hoarder friend."

"I wanted to reiterate to Grey that he not sell Livia out on the bicycle issue and forgot." I nibbled my lip.

"No worries about that one. Besides, Livia now has Hugo in her corner. The two hit it off over extreme packing, and apparently, she's a good cook. Hugo noticed she was stressed about something and talked her into confiding in him, and she spilled the whole bicycle story. By that time, the local cops were involved, and they showed up shortly afterward and interviewed her. Now she's on edge, wondering how it's all going to end."

"I should've stayed in better touch but got caught up in a client wanting something last-minute."

"Well... Hugo talked her into coming home with him. He offered up his guest room and suggested that she stay until they got her house completely cleaned out and the bicycle issue was resolved. He assured her that it wouldn't be a problem driving her back and forth every day, that she was an integral part of the cleaning crew."

"Livia sent me a pic, and it looked like they were making amazing progress," I said.

"Hugo's not without his persuasive talents—he got her to promise that she would sort through everything, some now and then more later, making the hard decision, for her anyway, of whether to keep, donate, or trash."

I made a face, shaking my head. "Hugo seems like a nice enough man, but they don't know one another. I know that Livia's overwhelmed, as it poured off her when we met, but I'm hoping she doesn't feel pressured in any way."

"Sensing everything you just said, Hugo brought her to the office and introduced her to Grey and Seven, who both vouched for his character and told her that they were all friends.

They assured her that, as far as the business went, there have been no customer complaints they've heard about. Grey gave her his business card and told her not to hesitate to call if an issue came up."

"Not that I expect her to need anything, but I'll send a reminder text that I'm available anytime."

"Hugo then took Livia downstairs to his business and introduced her to the guys, and it's quite the motley crew. They entertained her with stories about working for him, and most were very funny. That turned out to be a big icebreaker and eased her concerns."

"I'm happy for her." I noticed that we'd turned off the interstate. "How about a hint as to what to expect from the meeting this morning?" I wanted to tell him a chuckle was not an answer. "Just so you know, I looked up the address and know that I can get an Uber if you ditch me." It would take me weeks to walk home.

"Really wanted to kick Pops' ass but figured I should ask you first," Floyd growled. "Just give me the okay."

"If it had played out any other way, Livia wouldn't have gotten the help she needed. Pops took one look and was overwhelmed. He told me that he involved me on a whim and didn't know what he was getting into, and when he did figure it out, didn't want to flake on her. The other added bonus from his point of view… I'd have time to choose between the twins."

Another growl from Floyd. "And Livia and

Hugo wouldn't have met and teamed up and now be sweet on one another, as Mom would say, each waiting for the other to be the first to admit it." Floyd reached over and squeezed my hand. "We need to discuss our relationship, so we're on the same page."

"We have an option or two," I said to his raised eyebrows. "Admit that we're together, enjoying each other's time, and you've spent a lot of time at my house. Or go right to the phony marriage. I still have the ring." I held out my hand. "Forgot to give it back and don't want to lose it."

"Know that WD is one gossipy office, and nothing is a secret. There have been questions, which I've evaded for the most part, but they do enjoy their matchmaking antics. And so you know, no twins to pick from." Floyd looked at me, and we laughed. "What I would like is for us to come out as a couple."

"Like going steady? I'd like that."

"We're official then?" He stuck out his pinkie, and I linked mine in his. He leaned over and gave me a quick kiss. At the next red light, he pulled me in for a much longer kiss. "*Now* we're official."

"For our first official act, you come to dinner with Pops and me, and together, we tell him to knock off the dating setups." I laughed, picturing a growly showdown.

"I've got a few things to say to the man."

"Remember that he's an old man, and my love for him is boundless, even when he's meddling."

Floyd took the next exit and weaved through traffic, taking a few more turns onto a series of side streets. He passed towering high-rises, and once under the overpass, the buildings and warehouses got a lot older. The commercial neighborhood on this side of the freeway didn't get any traffic, all of it flying by overhead. He turned into the parking lot of a square four-story white stucco building. The billboard that graced the top advertised some brewery I'd never heard of. I was happy I wasn't the one that had to navigate the drive, since getting to the building wedged under a freeway with no off-ramps took knowledge of the area.

There were already a half-dozen other trucks and cars when Floyd backed into one of the available spaces. "There's a garage around the back." He pointed. "Most bypass it and park out here."

I peered out the windshield. "What's the story on the building? Appears to have quite a lot of character."

"Grey's father-in-law owned it for a number of years before Grey bought it. They haggled long and hard, and Grey swears it's because the man was enjoying himself, not that he was attached. You'd have thought he'd have hopped on the offer, which was generous, since he never sets foot in the place. But he did get it written into the sale agreement that he could come and go as he sees fit. Thus far, I've only seen him once, and he didn't stay long."

"Maybe he stopped by to test the waters — see if he'd be thrown out."

"Nothing would surprise me with that man." Floyd chuckled. "Heard he has an interesting background. No one talks particulars, as it's silently implied that if you do, you might disappear."

"Rethinking my idea of introducing the man to Pops. I was thinking the two men might have a lot in common, but if anything should go south, I don't want to get blamed."

Floyd pulled me into his arms and laid a big kiss on me. "In case you need a reminder of our new status."

"If I had a choice, I'd rather sit here and make out in the truck." I winked.

"If we fail to show, one of the guys will check the security monitor, if they haven't already, and then send someone down to check on us." Floyd hopped out of the truck and slid me across the seat, lifting me down and setting me on my feet. "First floor belongs to Hugo's maintenance service, and their entrance is around the front. All these trucks belong to his guys. Want your car washed, park it around the back and it'll get done."

"No signs?" I scanned the building.

"They're overrated. As for the billboard, that winery's been out of business for a number of years, but Harper's father liked the sign, and so does Grey." Floyd entered a code on the security pad at the side entrance of the building, and once inside, he hit the button for the elevator. "There are stairs if you're in a hurry." He pointed to a closed door. "The other door is another entrance to Hugo's." The elevator doors opened, we stepped inside, and he pressed the button for the third floor. "Second floor is AE Financial, which is Avery and Dixon."

"I'd like to stop on the way back down and say hello."

"This floor is WD Investigations," he said as the elevator door opened. We crossed to another door, directly across the hall, which opened into a wide-open space with three desks scattered around and plenty of room for more despite the conference table that took up a lot of space in the middle of the room. The two men seated there stood, both well-built and well over six feet, with dark hair.

"Grey Walker." The first man extended his hand. "Nice to meet you after all we've heard."

"Seven Donnelly." He also shook hands.

The door flew open. "If we missed anything, you have to start over." I recognized the red-haired woman who blew in like a full-force hurricane as Avery, the friend of Rella's I'd met a few weeks ago. "Dixon—" I grinned at the man behind her. "—great to see you."

Avery screwed up her nose. "You even think about luring Dixon away, and I'll beat you the hell up." She air-boxed.

For all her drama, I wouldn't put it past her. "Snatch him to do what? More PI work?" Dixon and I both laughed at that. "Thank goodness you were there that day."

"Floyd keeps me updated on Catnip, as he likes to call her, despite the many times I've reminded him it's Caturday." He turned an amused look on the man.

"Calm down, wife." Seven looped his arm around Avery and pulled a chair out for her at the table. The rest of us took a seat.

The door blew open again. "So much traffic, thought I'd never get here." Harper flew in, much the same as Avery had. She headed straight to her husband and dropped a kiss on Grey's cheek, then sat next to him. "Don't tell me—no refreshments?" She eyed the two lone laptops on the table.

"First one hurricane and then another, and I haven't had the chance to make the offer." Grey shook his head at his wife, who grinned at him.

Floyd, who was still standing, took drink orders. I passed.

I eyed the door, waiting for Rella to make her entrance. I'd heard they were a tight threesome, having been friends since college.

Reading my mind, Harper said, "Rella couldn't get out of her meeting. Made me promise to repeat everything that's said."

I nodded with a half-laugh.

"You do remember this is a business meeting, right?" Grey asked his wife.

Harper shot him a shifty smile, and the two engaged in a brief stare-down. Hard to tell who won. As for Avery, she ignored her husband's "Do you?" look, even after he nudged her.

"I'm bringing this meeting to order and would appreciate everyone keeping their opinions to themselves until after it's over. Anyone who disagrees can take it outside." Grey eyed Harper and Avery, who weren't the least bit intimidated, then turned to me. "The purpose of this get-together is to talk to you about buying North Investigations."

I tried to keep my face neutral but knew it had surprise written all over it. "Although my Pops did sign the business over to me, I wouldn't feel comfortable making a decision like this without talking to him. Even though he was running a con on me—handing down the company business was his line, when he was really matchmaking."

Grey chuckled. "How's that working out?"

Floyd reached out and grabbed my hand. "We're official," he said in a "dare you to say otherwise" tone.

Harper and Avery squealed and clapped.

I winked at Dixon, and he grinned, giving me a thumbs up.

Floyd pulled me sideways into a hard hug.

"Since you're running the company, I wanted to approach you first and see if you have any reservations. Figuring you'd want to include your grandfather in any discussions, I also wanted to ask if you think he'd entertain the idea, and if yes, that you introduce us." Grey didn't break eye contact the whole time.

"Honestly, North doesn't generate a lot of business, as Pops hasn't been active in more than a year, though I didn't know that at the time he was hustling me. It was Dixon who was able to figure it out from the disorganized records Pops left me and an investigation of his own." I smiled at the man, thankful he liked a puzzle.

"It was really the laptop that answered a lot of my questions. Although antiquated, it held a wealth of information," Dixon said. "When I learned that the guys were interested in opening an office in Fort Lauderdale, it was my suggestion that they talk to you. I want to assure you that I didn't disclose any financial details, other than that at one time, North had an impressive client list."

I smiled at him. "I'm more than happy to talk to Pops and see if he's open to an offer. Since he closed the office down some time ago, I feel fairly certain that he has no intention of going back," I said. "Are you wanting to rent? Buy the whole building?" The latter made the most sense to me.

"Very much interested in the building," Grey said and looked at Seven, who nodded.

"Are you familiar with the agreements with the current tenants?" Seven asked.

"The first and second floor are half leased, and none appear to be doing a booming business. The third floor is empty," I told them.

"I searched every file on the laptop," Dixon said. "There was a file of all the leases, and they all reverted to month-to-month long ago. Digging into the businesses that are still there, I found out that the two second-floor tenants will be giving their notices, as one is going out of business and the other plans to move out of state."

Dixon never failed to amaze me.

"It was never our plan to take over the building with the idea of kicking anyone out," Seven assured me. "We'd work out an agreement that incentivizes them to leave with no hard feelings."

"Or send a few of Hugo's guys to lurk around, and they might just pack up and run," I suggested. Grey and Seven laughed. "I'm happy to talk to Pops. The only reason I can think of that he'd be resistant is that it doesn't seem to bug him that the building's been standing empty, so he doesn't seem in a hurry to sell. You being an investigation company is in your favor and may well ramp up his enthusiasm. Knowing him, he'd like to see the building continue in the same industry."

"The introduction would be appreciated," Grey said.

"I'll set up a meeting at this great restaurant, I know—good food, and if you get in a fight, the staff doesn't say anything. Just leave a big tip."

Everyone laughed, and Floyd squeezed my thigh.

"If your numbers expert hasn't already put together a financial report, you should get him on it and have one available for Pops." I cast a glance at Dixon, taking his nod to mean he'd already done it.

"The reason Seven and I called you in is, that before approaching your grandfather about a sale, we wanted to make sure it was all right with you. If you're remotely interested in running the business, we'll step back."

I laughed. Then looked at Floyd and laughed again, and then the two of us laughed. "Not sure if you've heard, but I'm in over my head. In my defense, I did come in knowing nothing and found out quickly that there's lots to learn, some of which I've found appalling." The dead body smell came to mind. "I'm already very happy with the business I've built."

"Just wanted to be certain that you had no desire to carry on the family business," Seven said.

"I already planned to sit Pops down and tell him that, besides not being cut out for the job, I really do love what I do and would miss it too much."

Grey and Seven talked about their plans for expanding. They already knew a few men local to the area that they'd like to have come work for them.

"Any more questions?" Floyd asked.

He'd been tapping his foot, so I knew he was ready to leave.

"What are your intentions towards Floyd?" Harper asked me, her eyes full of amusement.

"Use him and then… use him some more." I grinned at him.

"I'm a big boy and can take care of myself," Floyd said with a shake of his head.

"If you weren't like family, we wouldn't care who you dated." Harper and he engaged in a glare-down, and she finally laughed.

"Speaking of dating, heard you tried to set your grandfather up with the feisty Rosa?" Grey laughed, as did the others.

"A little payback that backfired," I said, embarrassed.

"After the heated exchange, it all worked out. Swell of you two to bring it up." Floyd glared at his bosses.

"You know…"

"No matchmaking," Grey cut Harper off. "I know who you're thinking about, and that's more drama than anyone can handle."

"Okay, dear."

Avery and I exchanged amused glances.

## Chapter Thirty-Four

On the way downstairs, Floyd and I stopped at the second floor to check out Avery and Dixon's office. Once outside, we walked around to the front and into Hugo's business, where we found Hugo and Livia seated at a desk. The two appeared to be arguing. Livia jumped up and ran over to hug me.

"You okay?" I asked.

"Hugo and his guys have been amazing. Can you believe that we've almost got everything boxed up?"

It was hard to believe, and I wondered what it looked like.

She continued. "I'm the one being a pain, wanting to hang onto everything. Though I'm finding that I care a little less as each day goes by."

"You're going to be so happy when the job's done, and there are no more surprise visits," I said with a smile.

"So happy."

I slung my arm around her to walk her back to the table. "Hugo's cute, don't you think?"

"You stop," she whispered, her cheeks flaming.

"Livia was just singing your praises," I said to

Hugo. "Complimenting the great job you and your guys have been doing."

"Best client ever." He grinned and winked at her.

"I promised my girl lunch, and we're on our way out," Floyd told them. He took my hand, and with a wave, we left. Once back in the truck, he announced, "We're taking a slight detour."

I looked at him expectantly, unable to imagine where.

"You wanted to see where I live, and it's not far. Just know there's lots of construction material everywhere."

"You've put up with the work going on in my kitchen and not a complaint. Happy to say that with the tear-down already completed, the rebuild has gone faster than I expected. Yesterday, they unboxed the appliances, which are ready to be installed."

"I knew when I recommended Todd that he would do good work and you'd be happy."

"Todd also knew you'd hunt him down if he didn't."

Floyd nodded. "You betcha."

He cruised a few blocks from the office to a several-block shopping district. "I live here." He pointed to a brick building with an awning. He went around the corner and turned into the alley, hitting a button that caused a chain link fence to open into a parking lot with about a dozen spaces, half of them taken. "From the front, it looks like one property that's a block long, but it's actually made up of four properties that are individually owned. Each owner has space for three retailers, and most have been here for years."

I craned my neck. "You live on the second floor?"

"I do. And to avoid causing issues for the businesses below, I keep any construction to when they're closed, which is why renovating the place has been a slow project."

We got out, he unlocked the door on the far end, and we hiked up the stairs. "My grandfather left all of us boys a little money that he expected us to spend wisely. I gave it to Dixon to invest, and it's grown exponentially. When I found this place, he helped me secure the financing." Floyd threw open the door into a wide-open space that was further along in upgrades than he'd let on. It had been painted, the floors refinished, and it looked ready for a kitchen to be installed on one end. On the other end, a king-size bed was shoved into the corner. He opened the door to the bathroom, which he'd built out with a walk-in shower that could hold a party of six.

"Just got a case of bathroom envy." I eyed all the finishes.

"Did the work myself. There were times I didn't think it would be worth the effort, but it has been. The kitchen will soon be finished, but the rest… keep changing my mind."

I walked over to the wall of metal-shuttered

windows that overlooked the boulevard below and its steady stream of traffic. "Pretty quiet up here, considering all the cars below."

"This little shopping area closes at six, so it's really quiet at night."

"Love what you've done and the choices you've made." I turned to a table that held samples. "I've got no doubt that it's going to be amazing."

"Happy you like it." He engulfed me in a hug. "Ready for lunch?"

"You pulling out a picnic basket?"

"Got something better in mind." He pulled me to the door and locked up. "I promised you the scenic view, so we'll cut down to the water and cruise the coast."

"This was a great find. I never thought about living over a business, but since you can't hear a sound, you'd never know it was a booming shopping district. And you don't have to go far if you need something." I eyed the corner grocery store. Once outside, I took a last look at the building from the back side and noted that the whole block had its own fenced-off parking areas.

"Dixon not only invests my money himself, but he's always nudging me toward one investment or another. Having always been cautious, I'm slow to look at some of his ideas, but he's always patient and gives me all the time I need to come around."

Back in the truck, Floyd maneuvered the side

streets down to Ocean Drive, which was busy, but the cars were moving. "How do you feel about the guys being interested in buying your Pops' building?"

"The fact that it would be another investigation firm is a plus for me and just might be a selling point for Pops. He should at least think about the offer, as leaving it almost empty is certain to attract problems he won't want to deal with." I stared out the window, wishing I was sinking my toes into the sand. "If you haven't decided on a place for lunch, I vote for a dumpy little dive that serves tacos."

"The best kind of restaurant." Floyd chuckled. "There's a couple of places a little farther north. You'd think they'd have been run off by the increasing value of the real estate surrounding the area. I admire them for standing their ground and fending off some rather public attempts at buyouts. It helped that the locals banded behind them."

A few miles up the highway, he turned into a rock-filled parking lot containing a rundown blue-and-red building advertising "tacos" in bold letters on one side and "beer" on the other wall. "This place was recommended by Rella."

"Outside dining." I pointed to a row of tables and umbrellas off to one side.

"I'm aware that the place doesn't show well but promise you it has good food. All of us at the office have eaten here, and we all agree." Floyd scooped me out of the truck.

"I'm game," I said after a hesitant stare at the building.

He looped his arm through mine and led me over to a small opening in the fence. We were about to claim a table when we heard our names being yelled. Rella waved us over to her table, where she sat with a man, their hands joined.

"This is my husband, Pryce Thornton." Rella introduced me, and it was obvious that Pryce and Floyd already knew one another. "Come sit with us." She motioned over the server. "You have to have the taco platter; it's the best."

"Make it two more of what they're having," Floyd said to the server, then mouthed *margarita* to me, knowing they're a favorite. I nodded. He ordered one for me and a beer for himself.

Rella told Pryce and Floyd how we'd become fast friends in high school and how, though we went to different colleges, we'd surprisingly managed to stay in touch, however sporadically, over the years.

"Heard you were summoned to a meeting with the two Kings," Pryce said with amusement.

"Be nice." Rella nudged him.

At my raised eyebrows, he chuckled. "First thing you need to know about this group is that there are no secrets. My advice is to wring a good deal out of them. The guys love to dicker, so don't take the first offer."

"I'm not the sole decision-maker in this whole

transaction. My Pops will have the most input, and I'll be interested to see his reaction when I break the news. If it gets to negotiations, I'll be sitting in to watch him take the Kings on a ride."

Everyone laughed.

"Get yourself one of those cams that you pin on your clothes; that way, we can all see how it goes down," Pryce said with a chuckle.

I had no intention of telling him that I'd had a field day ordering all kinds of fun stuff, most of which I'd yet to use.

"As though Grey and Seven wouldn't notice that in a hot second." An eyeroll in Rella's tone.

Our drinks were delivered, and Floyd lifted his beer and touched it to the rim of my glass. I took a long drink and had a hard time not licking my lips.

"So… what's going on with you and Floyd?" Rella raised her eyebrows.

"We've been… and then we… and now it's official — we're dating," I said.

Floyd leaned over and brushed my lips with a kiss. "What's official is that we're exclusive."

"When I heard there was a chance…" Rella clapped. "You don't know how proud Dixon is of his matchmaking skills. He insisted from the beginning that you two were a sure bet."

"It's been an adventure from the start." I smiled at Floyd.

A woman plopped herself down on the bench next to me. "Imagine meeting you here. Didn't peg you for one to leave the neighborhood."

I felt Floyd stiffen as I got a better look at the woman. Caturday! "This isn't a good time to talk," I told her.

It was clear that didn't register, as she stared at me, her hard eyes assessing. "You never got back to me, and I thought we had a deal," she whined.

"I tried on several occasions to contact you, and not once did you answer your phone or return my messages." Catching Rella and Pryce watching, wide-eyed, I attempted to tone down my annoyance. "My number is still the same, so why don't you give me a call, and we'll schedule a meeting?"

Not one to take two hints, Caturday continued to blabber. "Just tell me, did you find Herbie?"

"That's something that we should sit down and discuss *privately*."

Just then, the server arrived, setting down two large plates and silverware.

"If this tastes as good as it smells…" Everything on the plate looked and smelled delicious.

"Well, doesn't that look good." Caturday licked her lips. "I'll have a vodka tonic," she told the server.

"Not to be rude, but you need to leave and make an appointment," Floyd told her in a stern tone.

"Who are you?" She eyed him as though he were a delectable morsel, and she'd like a nibble.

"The food's getting cold." Floyd stood, walked around to her side, and held out his hand. "Would you like me to walk you to your car?"

She brushed off his hand and shot to her feet, slamming into him. He grabbed her shoulders to keep her from falling. Without a word, she stomped over to the restaurant. At the door, she turned and yelled, "Expect a phone call."

"What was that all about?" Rella asked, wide-eyed. "I get that its none of my business but would still love to hear. And I know Pryce feels the same, but he's too gentlemanly to ask."

I lowered my voice. "Caturday—phony name by the way, though she insists it isn't—wanted to hire me to locate her ex and then, when I found him, send someone to kill him." Escalating shock on Rella and Pryce's faces. "Catnip—Floyd's nickname for her—wasn't happy that the ex was still breathing and wanted him gone but didn't want any blood on her hands."

"Maren and I paid Herbie, the ex, a visit. He couldn't get out of town fast enough, and thank goodness he did," Floyd told them. "Someone was after him then, and still is, and all evidence points to Catnip. We called in the cops, and since then, she's been elusive and impossible to locate. My cop connection will be happy to hear that she's turned up again. I'm thinking they're going to want you to set up another meeting with her." He nudged me.

I groaned inwardly.

"We're not that far from Lauderdale, but it's still interesting that she showed up here at the same time as you two," Pryce said.

"I'd have noticed her following us," Floyd said, his gaze distant, as if he was replaying the drive down here.

"You need to be careful of that one. Her eyes were dark, soulless pits." Rella shivered.

"I don't want to have any interactions with Caturday but feel compelled to do what the police need, as I don't want to find out later that she located Herbie, and he ended up dead." I'd feel responsible if I did nothing.

We tabled all talk of Caturday and her criminal activities and focused on the food. We did promise to keep Rella and Pryce updated on how the case turned out. All of us agreed that the woman needed to be arrested before anyone got hurt.

The food disappeared quickly, as it did, in fact, taste as good as it smelled.

"This restaurant was a good find," I said.

"The locals lobbied hard for them not to close up shop and move elsewhere," Rella told us. "The battle with the developer who wanted the property only increased their business and made it profitable for them to stay."

The server came back to take away the plates, and we all turned down another round of drinks. Pryce handed his card to the server, and Floyd objected but got shot down. "We're happy to be the first to lunch with the new couple."

The server was back quickly with the check, and Pryce was about to sign when he glanced at the bill and stopped, then called the server back. "What are these extra charges?"

"The woman who was sitting with you finished her drink at the bar and took her lunch to-go. Is that a problem?" He looked worried.

Pryce scratched his name and handed it back. "No problem."

"That took some nerve." Rella's mouth dropped open.

"More reason that I should be the one—"

Pryce cut Floyd off. "Too late. The check's already taken care of. If you do see her out anywhere, make sure you stick her with the bill."

\* \* \*

Floyd grumbled about Caturday's brass all the way back to my house. "That woman," he grouched as we walked in the front door. "Would you object to me putting a tracker on your phone?"

I fished my phone out of my purse, handed it over, and sat down next to him on the couch. "That was a sleezy trick she played, having her food charged to our bill. Bet it wasn't the first time she's done that."

Floyd shook his head. "What bothers me is that she showed up at the restaurant the same time we did. Coincidence? Maybe. But I'd have to be convinced." He got on his phone and made a call, and whoever he was talking to walked him through setting up my phone.

It didn't take long before he hung up. "If there's an emergency…" He showed me which button to press. "If I'm not close by, I'll get someone else to come to your rescue."

"What if I hit it by mistake?" I asked.

"No problem. Call me, and I'll call off the dogs."

"Probably not going to be needed, but it makes me feel safer, and I appreciate that you set it up for me."

Floyd hooked his arm around me and pulled me to his side. "When we're done making out, I'll show you how to use the app and also how to use it to track me."

## Chapter Thirty-Five

I'd sent Floyd off with a kiss and assured him I'd be talking to Pops and would give him a play-by-play.

To my extreme frustration, Pops ignored every one of my calls. I wasn't sure if he was up to something or embarrassed by his recent actions. Time to ambush him at his house. When I saw his truck in the driveway, I thought I had him. But banging on the door got me nothing, and when I used my key, I found he was nowhere in sight. He'd either ducked out the back or built a hideout that I knew nothing about.

Hanging out there wasn't going to do me any good, so I headed home, fuming. By the time I walked in the door, I had a plan. If the message I was about to leave didn't get me a return call, then maybe something bad *had* happened. I refused to think about that. "Pops, if I don't hear from you in the next half-hour, I'm calling the cops and requesting that they do a welfare check. If you're found watching television or twiddling your thumbs, I'm having you committed. I'm certain you know it's not that hard to do in Florida. And to make certain you end up in the looney bin, I'm prepared to go buy signed statements that you're a fruit loop from strangers on the corner."

Pops called back in a huff in twenty. "What does a man have to do to get a little peace? Thought you might like some of the same."

"That's malarkey — one of Gran's favorite words, in case you don't remember." I ignored his growl. "This is how you're going to make it up to me for ignoring my calls and causing me needless worry."

"I'd suggest a drink to calm down, but it's a little early. I imagine drunken Maren would then burn up the phone." He mimicked an explosion.

"I've got great news for you — something you've been wanting to hear for a while now."

"Uh-huh." His tone was skeptical.

"Pick a night, the sooner the better, and dinner is on me. I'll be introducing you to my boyfriend."

"For real or some scam to stop me from harping on your love life?"

"I guess you're going to find out. Tomorrow night, then? I'm choosing the Beach House because I know it's one of your favorites. Heads up: I have something else to discuss with you besides my love life."

"Make it early, since the place is always packed. That way, we can get a table without waiting and have a couple of drinks before the dinner crowd flocks in." We agreed on a time.

"Warning: if you're a no-show, I'm going to stir up a family stink by embellishing everything you've been up to lately. Not that I'd have to exaggerate, but that would be damn fun."

"Not only will I be there, I'll be packing in case this so-called boyfriend is a dip-you-know-what."

"So, we're agreed — you'll be on your best behavior." He snorted. "When I cruise into your driveway to pick you up, I expect you to be ready and in a perky mood."

He snorted again. "Thanks for the offer, but no thanks." His tone dripped with sarcasm. "Taking my truck in case I need to cut out early."

\* \* \*

When the doorbell rang, I threw open the front door, knowing it was Floyd, as he was right on time. "Hey babes." I gave him a leisurely once-over, getting an eyeful of him in jeans and a white button-down shirt. With a big smirk, he stepped inside, picked me up, and twirled me around, laying on a big kiss before setting me back on my feet.

He gave me the same perusal I'd given him as I smoothed down the front of my floral sundress, stepping off to the side to slip into a pair of sandals and grab my purse. "I'm thinking that with a little effort, this dinner won't end in a yell-fest… or with shots fired." I told him about Pops packing. "Think he was kidding though." I locked up, and we went out to his truck.

"Can't remember what kind of impression I

made the first time I met him. I should've held it together better when Mom announced that she had a boyfriend. Boy, did I get an earful—she said my poor behavior was why she hadn't brought it up sooner. Almost forgot I was a grown man and not six, considering all the trouble I was in."

"How did last night's dinner go?" I asked, knowing that Rosa had invited her new friend to a family dinner. "Did you threaten to rearrange his face if he stepped out of line?"

"I got a lecture about controlling my neanderthal ways." Floyd chuckled. "Dinner went off without a hitch—we sat around and talked, and he's not a bad guy. It's obvious that the two of them are happy, and that's all that matters." He maneuvered through the side streets, driving with one hand on my knee. "Anything else I should know about your Pops before we get to the restaurant?"

"Even though I told him he'd be meeting the new man in my life, I still think he'll be surprised when we show up together."

The restaurant was close by, and it didn't take long before we arrived. The parking lot was already half-full, so Pops' suggestion that we arrive early was a good one. I slid out of the truck and into Floyd's arms, and he kissed me before hooking his arm around me and heading into the restaurant. It was easy to spot Pops at one of the window tables, drink in hand. I reintroduced Floyd as we sat down.

"I remember him," Pops grouched.

"It's because of you that Maren and I met. She needed someone to show her the ropes of the business you wanted her to take over. After all, you weren't going to do it." Floyd eyed him sternly.

"You get to take all the credit for getting us together," I said. The credit belonged to Dixon, but if it would please Pops any, I'd give it to him.

"Yeah, well…"

"It didn't take us long to figure out that we liked each other." Floyd returned Pops' stare-down.

Pops ended it by scrunching up his nose. "Would be low of you two to be running a con on an old man."

The server came over, delivered the drinks we ordered on the way in, and took our food order.

"As for putting one over on you, *old man*," I said after he left, "as much fun as it would be, that's not what's happening."

Pre-dinner small talk centered on Pops and Floyd getting to know one another. Pops sneaked in a couple of stories about me rarely doing what I was told growing up, and I rolled my eyes while the two men laughed.

"I'm told I take after you." I winked at him.

"Never, ever have I been disappointed in you, starting with your career in the entertainment business, which I knew was going to be hard. But you built it up and made me very proud." Pops smiled at me. "This is where I fess up that I only meant to meddle a little… Granted, it wasn't well thought out. How hard could it be to give my Maren a happy ever after and me some grandkids?"

"I knew it." I faux-glared. "Just took me a while to get you to admit it."

"Grandkids, huh?" Floyd arched his brow. "How soon are we talking?"

"Pops wants them next week, but he's going to have to wait." I barely refrained from shaking my finger at him.

"Not getting any younger. My advice is that if one of you decides the other doesn't float your boat, then move along. No hard feelings." He nodded in agreement with himself. "Riper fruit on the trees and all that."

"That last bit doesn't make any sense," I said. Pops shrugged.

"Now that you're going to take a rest from managing Maren's love life, you got any prospects for yourself?" Floyd tipped his glass at Pops.

I brought my glass to my lips to cover my laugh.

After Pops got over his shock, he laughed, though it sounded fake. "That ride has passed me by, and I've got no energy to track one down. Don't you go stirring up anything," he said in a stern tone.

*Who me?* I gave him an innocent look, which earned me a double take.

The food was delivered, and we ordered another round of drinks. Talk slowed while we ate, as it took most of our attention.

Once the plates were cleared, I said, "Besides giving you the honor of renewing your acquaintance with Floyd, I did have another reason for corralling you to go out to dinner."

"I don't know what you're up to now, but I'm thinking we should take this party back to my house. That way, I can have another drink or six and not have to worry about driving." Pops flagged over the server and requested the check.

"I want you sober to hear what I have to say. And so you know, *no*, *hell no*, and *not interested* are all acceptable responses to what I'm about to pitch."

The server was back with the check, and Pops grabbed it before Floyd could beat him to it. "Don't give him the check, or I'll fight him right here in the restaurant," he practically yelled.

"I made it very clear that this was my treat." I tapped his arm. "We like the food here, so try not to get us kicked out and labeled persona non grata."

"Makes me happy, so you should indulge me, and besides, it's a good excuse to do it again," Pops grumped and handed over his credit card. "We'll take one more round of drinks."

Deciding that one more drink was a good idea, I waited for them to arrive and for everyone to take a sip. "While mismanaging North, I met quite a few people, several of whom work for WD Consulting, an investigation firm in Miami Beach," I said. "They approached me about wanting to buy your client list, along with the building, as it's their intention to expand into this area. I told the two honchos that you'd be the one to make the decision, and they asked that I set up a meeting to go over the particulars of the offer if you're interested."

"I'm currently one of their investigators and have worked for them for a while," Floyd told Pops. "Besides being great to work for, they've been successful building their business and have a great reputation."

"The property, hmm…" Pops mused, thinking that one over.

"It's ideal, since it's centrally located and on one of the most trafficked streets," Floyd told him, and I nodded.

"They'd take over all the floors?" Pops asked. Floyd nodded. "Like the idea of it being an investigation firm. Must be hot snot if they're going to take over the whole building. You know, a good portion of the building is empty, and that's my fault. I had a realtor that managed the other spaces for me, and then he died. I should've replaced him but never did, thinking I'd deal with it. Never got around to it."

I reached out and patted his hand.

"I didn't want to just lock the doors, but when business slowed, I just never got off my duff and drummed up more. Got lazy, not being at someone's beck and call, and found I liked it." He shot me a look that said, *What do you think?*

"Time for me to finally fess up. Much as I love you and don't want to disappoint you, I love my voiceover work. Investigation work, dead people, the craziness…" I wrinkled my nose.

"Sorry." Pops frowned. "I should've thought the idea out a little better. Instead, I got overly excited and just made it up as I went along, and that seldom works out. But…" He grinned and pointed at Floyd and me. "Here you two sit, holding hands most of the time."

"If I were you, I'd retire my matchmaking skills," I said.

"Good idea." He chuckled. "Before agreeing to a meeting, I'm going to need some information about the buyers so I can do some research of my own. That will give me time to think on the idea."

"If you agree to a sit-down, insist that Grey and Seven get their butts up here for the meeting. Know that whichever way you decide, no one is going to pressure you," Floyd told him.

"The only North business I still need to wrap up is the situation with the Caturday woman." I reminded Pops about that particular can of worms and told him about her crashing our lunch. "Even though I'm not wild about the idea, I may be the only one that can set up a meeting with her."

Floyd told him about calling in a couple of his

cop friends and how they wanted to get Caturday on tape and arrest her for attempted murder.

"Where did this woman get the idea that North was available to carry out murder for hire?" Pops asked. "I can assure you that I never had that kind of reputation. I can also tell you that I never had a client by that name. It's not one you'd forget."

"How about Mildred Bellwether?" Floyd asked.

"Maren mentioned the name, and I did date a Mildred a number of years back, but her last name was Smithson or something close. Don't recognize Bellwether at all. How did she end up in the office, asking you to commit a crime? There's no sign on the outside of the building."

"This Mildred woman called you Maxi, does that ring a bell?" I asked. Pops shook his head. "She also mentioned that you talked a lot about me."

"As you know, when I occupied the office, I had lots of family pictures up and a ready story for anyone willing to listen."

"Did you and this Mildred Smithson, or whatever, end the relationship on amicable terms?" I asked. "Or was it a free-for-all?"

"Only went out a few times. Then, without a word, she brought over a couple of boxes, and when I asked her what she was doing, she said something about being fated to be together." Pops rolled his eyes. "When I told her it wasn't happening, we got into a big row, and she stomped out. I drove her boxes to her house so she wouldn't come back. I caught her lurking around after that and confronted her—told her I had security cameras and if she came back, I was calling the cops. Never saw her again."

"You're lucky that was the end of it." Floyd and I exchanged a look, both of us thinking, *Could this be the same woman?*

"Did Maren fill you in on her dog case?" Floyd asked Pops, then went on to share the details. "She didn't take any guff off that woman, who was once friendly with my mom, but not after Maren blackmailed her into not snatching the dog back."

Pops grinned. "That's my girl."

"Got an update for you on that case," Floyd continued, looking at me. "Mrs. Hart wants another dog to keep Frito company but is running into the same age restriction everywhere."

"For pity's sake. Even a young person can croak."

"When I heard that Rella backs an animal rescue, I gave her a call, and she said no problem, she'd take care of it. Her rescue will call Mrs. Hart and arrange to meet her and Frito, then have her come to the kennel for a look around."

"Hell yes." Pops held out his knuckles for a bump, and the two men laughed.

I leaned over and kissed Pops' cheek. "Don't feel obligated about sitting down with WD. If you want me to tell them to scram, I will." I caught Floyd's grin.

"If nothing else, it would be fun to talk it over," Pops mused.

# Chapter Thirty-Six

I'd begun to hope that I'd never hear from Caturday again. Two days passed, and then a call came in from a number I didn't recognize.

"Do you have anything new for me?"

I recognized Caturday's growly tone, which was more brusque than usual, with a sinking feeling. "I do have a couple of addresses for you," I said and made sure that she could hear me rustling papers.

Floyd had given me a couple of addresses to pass along to keep her busy. He'd also installed another app on my phone, and I hit the record button on it.

Having a few questions of my own, I decided to see if she'd actually answer me. "Do you know the owner of North Investigations?"

"No, no..." she said breezily, apparently forgetting she'd admitted to knowing Pops when she first waltzed into the office. "Remember seeing the sign a time or two and, on a whim, decided to stop and check it out. Fortunate for me, catching you in the office that day."

"You really need to come to the office to talk about the case and discuss strategy. I have nothing for you beyond a couple of potential addresses. Lucas is the investigator on the case, and you need to have a meeting with him."

"That sounds like a waste of my time." Caturday snickered. "Just give me what you've got. If this is about you getting cash out of me… you owe me as a courtesy for how long you've dragged your feet." When I didn't have an immediate answer, she said, "If you insist on being paid, I've got a credit card but will have to call you back with the number. Hope you're not going to gouge me."

"Just know that I haven't had time to check either of these addresses out." I rattled them off. The first one was a vacant field in Miami that belonged to a client of WD's. The man had planned to use it for mail delivery and installed a mailbox for that purpose, and thus far, the only thing he'd gotten was a notice from the post office that they wouldn't make any deliveries there. They sent back the envelope he'd mailed to himself as undeliverable. The second one was a large apartment building with no unit number — good luck.

"If one of these turns out to be paydirt, this is the last you'll be hearing from me."

"If I get anything else, can I contact you at this number?"

"Sure," Caturday grunted and hung up.

I stared at the phone. If she somehow managed to find Herbie, did she have someone on standby to off him? Did she plan to do it herself? I called Floyd and had to leave a message. I had time to grab an iced tea and get back to my desk before he called back.

"You-know-who called, and not much to relay," I told him. "I'll forward the recording." He asked for the number she called in on, and I gave it to him.

"Let you know what I find out about this number. I'm expecting it to be a burner she bought five minutes ago," Floyd griped. "That woman creeps me out. You need to be alert—when she makes the drive to Miami and finds a lot filled with weeds, she's going to be irked."

"Just swell. But it may be the one thing that forces her into a face-to-face meeting."

He groaned. "How about I bring dinner, and we sit out on the patio and watch the seagulls make out again?"

"Sounds good."

\* \* \*

Floyd came through the door, loaded down with pizza and salad. "Hey, looks like they're damn near finished." He walked around the kitchen inspecting the work, nodding as he went.

"No complaints here. They show up every day, and it's coming together faster than I expected." I linked my arm in his and led him out to the patio, where I'd set the table.

We'd just finished and gathered up all the trash when my phone rang. I looked at the screen and recognized the number from earlier. "It's her. Didn't expect two calls in one day."

"Hit the record and speaker buttons."

I nodded. Over dinner, he'd told me he forwarded the first conversation to Lucas.

Caturday didn't wait for a hello. "Did you even check out either of these addresses before sending me chasing across town?" Livid, she was practically spitting.

"I believe I told you when I gave them to you that I hadn't had time. Giving you the addresses was a courtesy."

"Isn't that your job?" Caturday snapped.

Done with her snootiness, I reminded her, "It was a freebie. Sorry if it was a waste of your time, but sometimes these leads turn out that way." I stopped short of matching her irritated tone but barely.

Floyd nodded encouragement and motioned to keep her talking. He'd gotten up, took out his phone, and moved to the other side of the slider.

"Do you have anything else? Something that's been verified?" Caturday snapped.

"I'm sorry," I said in a sickeningly sweet tone.

Floyd grinned as he joined me at the table.

"How long will it take you to get something? And by that, I mean information that's not a complete waste."

"If I should get something, I'd be more than

happy to call you, but we will need to meet at the office."

"It's all about money. Fine. But it better be good or expect to give me a refund," Caturday bit out. "Another thing, stopped by that office of yours and was surprised that the third floor was not accessible. How do your clients reach you?"

*None of your business.* But I did find it interesting that she'd stopped by after evading my attempts at a meeting. I'd already asked this question but thought I'd try again, see if I got another lie. "Well, you know what Max is like."

After a long pause, she said, "Name's familiar. But I've met a lot of people in my life, and names aren't a priority for me."

"I'll do some more digging on Herbie and, of course, let you know should I find anything."

"One would think you'd be eager for more work. Your blasé get-around-to-it attitude isn't working for you. I asked one of your tenants, and they knew you'd taken over but couldn't remember the last time they'd seen you. A slacker work ethic doesn't get you ahead."

*Thanks for the tip.* I shook my head. "Like I said, if I find anything, I'll call."

"Before you do, check it out this time." Caturday grunted and hung up.

Floyd wrapped his arms around me and hugged me. "You had way more patience than I'd have managed."

"Barely. If she were a normal client—though

I'm thinking those don't exist in this field—I'd have told her to take the fast train to hell."

Floyd chuckled. "Talked to Lucas, and do you have time first thing in the morning for a video call?" I nodded. "We're going to come up with something and call her back in a couple of days, and this time, she comes to the office. Hopefully she shows, and we can be done with this case."

"But if she's careful and doesn't talk about killing Herbie, won't it be a waste of time?"

"Pretty much," Floyd said, sounding aggravated.

\* \* \*

We got up early the next morning, and I made coffee for us. I felt bad that I had nothing for breakfast, but Floyd knew a local place that had the best food, and we'd be headed there once we were done talking to Lucas.

We settled on the couch, and Gato jumped up on the footrest. I scratched him behind the ears, and he stretched out. It surprised me that he spent most of his time indoors and showed no interest in going out unless I was on the patio. Made me happy, as I didn't have to worry.

Floyd had his laptop open. "Ready to get this chat over with?"

"What I'm really wanting is to get Caturday out of our lives and stop having to worry about what she might do next."

"Agreed." He made the call and, after some friendly banter, shared the screen.

"Was going to suggest a face-to-face meeting, but this works out better," said Lucas, whose face had appeared on screen. "Beats trooping down to police headquarters. Do I have your permission to record the call?" We both agreed. "Let's go over how you met this woman again."

I rested my head against Floyd's shoulder.

"You and Floyd…" He raised an eyebrow.

"We're official," Floyd confirmed.

Lucas shot us a thumbs up.

Floyd started with where he came into the story. "Caturday showed up before we met, and thankfully Dixon was there for her felonious request and can confirm that Maren made it very clear she wasn't getting her hands dirty."

"In addition to a long arrest record, there have been several reports of her making threats towards other people. But before any investigation could be completed, those people changed their minds and were adamant about not pressing charges," Lucas said, disgusted. "Caturday probably thinks she's off the hook if she gets someone else to commit the crime for her, but she's wrong. Been putting together a couple of plans of action, and which one I go with depends on whether we can arrange a sit-down. Getting her to come to your office and then out herself on tape would be ideal. If not, then we'll let her walk out, and one of my men will follow her, as we haven't been able to locate a current address for the woman."

"She sounded more desperate for information," I said. "I think she's been getting information from someone else, but they haven't gotten the job done, and she's expecting me to come through. Wonder what happened to whoever the previous investigator was? Caturday has to be desperate to come back to me, as you can hear in her voice that she's leery of me."

"Plan A is getting her to come to the office. I'll be there, and you introduce me as your new partner," Lucas told us. "Not sure who she'd be expecting, Floyd or Dixon, but either way, there's no need to offer up a reason for the switch."

"In the last call, I mentioned you by name and told her that you'd been assigned the case," I told him. "Also told her that I didn't have anything else for her and she needed to meet with you. She wasn't happy to hear that, so don't be surprised if she gets suspicious and I can't get her to agree to a meeting."

Lucas waved a piece of paper at the screen. "Plan B. When Floyd told me how cagey she's been about even answering your calls, I knew we couldn't rely on being able to get her into a meeting. We've got a small house in Miami set up to look like Herbie lives there. An officer similar in looks and height has already moved in and introduced himself to the neighbors as Herbie. Then we left a couple of pieces of mail addressed to the man in the mailbox on the porch." He read off the address, which I scrambled to write down.

"What if Caturday sends someone else to do her dirty work?" I asked, wide-eyed.

"Arrest him or her. Chances are high they'll turn on her, and that would be two criminals off the streets," Lucas said. "I'd like a chance to question her about the fire at the condos. A lot of people could've been hurt, or worse, and if it was her, she needs to be off the streets. Either way, actually."

"How about I make the call now?" Both men agreed. I pulled out my phone, put it on speaker, and hit the record button. "This is Maren North," I said when Caturday answered. "I worked most of the night and have an address for you. I thought you could come by the office and bring your credit card."

Floyd poked me with a smirk.

"Just give it to me now."

I could hear her moving around in the background.

When I didn't respond, she said, "Considering all the time I wasted running down your previous bogus info, you owe me."

"How about paying me first? Last time, you forgot to call me back with your credit card number." I'd asked that without running it by Lucas first, but when I looked at him, he nodded.

Caturday called out the number, which surprised me. She didn't even know how much she was paying. Probably meant the number was bogus.

"Here's the address…" After I finished giving it to her, I said, "So we're agreed—no matter whether this address turns out to be good or bad, you won't call me again?"

"I can't believe all the snootiness I've had to put up with from you just to get you to do your job. You might want to think about that. Probably why you don't have any business." She hung up.

"She's been like a dog with a bone, trying to find Herbie," Floyd told Lucas. "If she's the one that shows up at the property, who knows what she'll have planned. Tell your officer to be on high alert."

"No worries. Hopefully, with her record, this time she stays in jail."

# Chapter Thirty-Seven

A week went by, and nothing from Caturday. She hadn't shown up at the house in Miami, and neither had anyone else. Floyd wasn't happy and wondered if she'd somehow found out that it was a setup. He became even more worried for my safety. I assured him that she didn't have my address and wouldn't get it with any kind of a search, as I'd taken steps to keep it private when I first moved in.

I was holed up in my office when my phone rang. It was Pops. "You behaving?" I asked upon answering.

"You know me…" He sounded stressed. "Don't do anything she says— Ouch!"

"What's going on?"

"Mildred—"

It sounded like there was a struggle. Pops yelled again. Then a woman's voice came over the line. "Stupid man can't do a damn thing he's told. Now you better listen up if you want him to stay alive."

"Who is this?" I demanded.

"You hurt my feelings, not recognizing the voice of the client you screwed over."

I managed to take a breath and firm up my

voice to keep it from shaking, channeling Floyd and adopting a tough-sounding façade. "What do you want now, Caturday? Whatever it is, you hurt my Pops more than it sounds like you already have, and you won't get anything from me." I broke out in a cold sweat, knowing the woman was crazy and terrified for Pops.

"You're not the one holding all the cards. I am. Now listen up. Get your butt to Maxi's house. Don't think about calling anyone. You do, and I'll know and…" Caturday made a noise like she was slitting a throat. "I've got eyes on you, and they'll be following you here. Anyone tags along, and he's dead."

"Put him on the phone. I want to hear for myself that he's okay."

"You do what I say, not the other way around."

"I need to hear his voice, or I'm calling the police."

"That would damn stupid. Hold on. I'll see if I can rouse him."

I heard shuffling and Pops grumbling, which I took as a good sign. He finally got on the line. "Love you, baby. Whatever she says, do the opposite."

He yelled again, and Caturday was back on the phone. "Listen to him, and I'll blow both of us up. Kaboom."

"You listen to me. I'm certain we can reach a mutual agreement, but for me to live up to my end, Max needs to be alive."

"It's your fault that I had to force you, and whatever happens is on you. Remember: I've got eyes on you. You've got a half-hour. Tick-tock. One foot out of line, and the old man's death is on you."

"On my way."

She disconnected without another word. I stared at the phone.

I jumped up and raced to the bedroom, taking my handgun out of the safe and checking to ensure it was loaded. Floyd had bought me a holster, which I strapped around my waist. I changed into sweats and a t-shirt, pulled the latter down over my gun, and slid into tennis shoes.

I went back to my desk and inserted a nude earpiece that fit completely inside my ear—another gift from Floyd—grabbed my phone, purse, and a black bag from Floyd that I prayed tipped the scales in our favor, then raced out to my SUV. Backing out of the driveway, I scanned the street in both directions and didn't see another car. There was no way Caturday could have found out my address, I was sure of it... but I couldn't take the chance. I edged to the corner, and a car zoomed by, not another one in sight.

I called Floyd, and after ringing several times, it went to voicemail. I left a detailed message, repeating all the threats that Caturday had made. "I'm headed to my Pops' and *really* need help." I hung up and pushed the button on the app Floyd had set up, sending an alert that I was in trouble.

It seemed like an hour but it was only minutes before my phone rang, Floyd's number popping up. "Lucas is on the line. Got your message and relayed everything to him."

Lucas and I exchanged hellos. "I don't know what to do," I said, fighting to keep my voice from shaking.

"I want you to turn around and go home," Floyd ordered.

"Caturday's expecting me, and I've got fifteen minutes before I'm late. Not only that, but she's having me watched. If I'm late or a no-show, who knows what she'll do. Same goes if the cops surround the place," I said.

"Backups on the way," Lucas assured me. "Give me the layout of your grandfather's house and yard. How easy would it be for us to come in through the back?"

"He shares the property line with the blue house on the right, and the gate is never locked. Since that side backs up to the garage, you wouldn't be seen from the house." I went on to give him as many details as I could remember.

"Have you been on the lookout for a tail?" Floyd asked.

"I've kept my eyes peeled since I walked out the door, and so far, nothing. I've been careful to keep to the speed limit, so most of the cars have passed me, a few honking to let me know I should get off the road."

"I want you to hold back and wait for me and

my guys to show up," Lucas ordered.

"Can't do that." I heard Floyd's groan. "I'm running out of time, and Pops' life is on the line. My showing up buys time, as Caturday wants something from me and knows she won't get it if she hurts him." I tried not to think that this was my fault, the woman wanting revenge because I hadn't delivered Herbie to her.

"What you *can* damn well do is slow down," Floyd barked. "I'm thinking there's a chance we'll all arrive at the same time."

"You need to back off and let us do our job," Lucas reprimanded him.

"Fat chance." Floyd snorted. "You have the microphone pin on you?" he asked me.

"I grabbed the bag of fun stuff you gave me on the way out the door."

"Pin it on yourself in an inconspicuous place," Floyd instructed.

I fished it out of the bag one-handed and got it attached to my sweats' waistband with surprisingly little fumbling.

"Don't arrive a second sooner than you have to. By that time, we should be nearly there," Lucas said, his tone commanding.

"Okay… I'm coming up to his street."

"We're a couple of blocks away in unmarked cars. Floyd, you need to stand down," Lucas ordered.

"Got it," Floyd snapped.

"Pulling into the driveway." I parked and got

out of my SUV. When I made it to the front door, it stood open, Caturday beckoning me inside with the muzzle of her gun.

I held up my hands. "No need for violence. Put down the gun and tell me what you want." A groan that sounded a lot like Floyd came over the earpiece. Standing in the entryway, I spotted Pops in the dining room, sitting in a chair with paper towels in his mouth and one wrist tied to the arm of the chair. He was working on freeing it while Caturday had her back turned.

"You think you can get away with running me around on one goose chase after another? The last one was a setup, and for what? To get me arrested? The man living there wasn't Herbie. Just by luck, I caught him leaving, followed him to the store, and got a good look at the man."

"I gave you information based on searches of public records and then hit up a hacker friend, who found that particular address. If you recall, I told you I hadn't checked it out."

"I think you're a big fat liar and are protecting Herbie for whatever reason. Did he pay you more to withhold the information?"

"You never paid anything—the card you gave me was bogus." Something Lucas verified after our call.

Caturday snorted. "Why would I fork over cash to get nothing in return? Not how it works. Herbie's got to be around—he's not smart enough to stay hidden."

"I told you that I was working with a partner on your case. He's adamant about not giving out any information without meeting with you—*he* doesn't do freebies."

She scrutinized me with a scowl, clearly not sure whether to believe me or not. "You have one option here—get the information out of your partner or else." She waved her gun.

"Does Herbie have any out-of-town friends he could have gone to stay with?" I asked. "Maybe I can figure this out on my own with some more information from you," I said to buy time.

"He always claimed to know this person or that, although I never met a single one of them."

I moved to the table and jerked the paper towels out of Pops' mouth.

He spit. "Thank you."

"He starts mouthing off, and they're going back in," Caturday warned.

I turned to Pops and put my finger over my lips. I turned back to Caturday, taking a surreptitious step away from the table, as I didn't want to be trapped behind it with her waving a gun around.

"We're in the backyard; keep her talking," Lucas said in my ear.

"A setup," Caturday hissed, staring out the back window. She turned and leveled her gun at Pops. I leaped towards him, shoving him out of the way, and the shot went wild. I stumbled, and Caturday jerked on my top, twisting me around while I tried to grab my gun and using me as a shield when the cops threw open the door and burst inside.

"Drop it," Lucas yelled. Two officers came in behind him, and then Floyd.

"*You* drop it, or she's dead." Caturday stuck her gun in my side.

I'd had enough of her, and without thinking about what I was doing, I put all my weight into elbowing her in the gut. She stumbled back, somehow managing to stay on her feet while I went down.

In a screaming rage, she pointed her gun. Not sure if she'd decided who she was aiming at, but the cops shot her, so we'd never know.

I jumped up, ran to Pops, who'd just managed to untie himself, threw my arms around him, and buried my face in his chest. I never wanted to see another corpse in my life.

"Did you miss the part where I told you not to do a damn thing?" Pops yelled. "That woman was a damn looney." He gave me a crushing hug.

"You squeeze any harder, and I'm going to vomit on you." I faked the sound.

Pops hugged me again but less intensely this time.

Floyd came up behind me and pulled me away from Pops and into his arms for a hug.

"How could you let Maren give herself up to Caturday, knowing she had a screw loose?" Pops grouched at Floyd as the color returned to his cheeks.

"Stop. It was my decision. You owe Floyd a big thanks. We both do. He got the cops involved and tricked me out with some handy stuff." I pointed to the earpiece and mic, then pulled up my shirt to show the gun. "He showed me how to load it; we just hadn't gotten to shooting lessons yet."

Pops leaned forward for a closer look. "That's mine."

"Possession is the law, or something like that — it's mine now," I said.

Lucas, who'd walked up in time to hear me, laughed. "Coroner's wagon and ambulance are on the way."

I didn't want to turn around but took a peek anyway, and Caturday had been covered with a beach towel.

"Let's take this outside," Lucas directed. "Medics will check you out when they get here." He eyed Pops closely, particularly the big bruise on the side of his head that was gradually darkening.

The four of us walked out the front door, Pops limping badly, and stood in the driveway. The other two cops stayed inside.

"That woman wiggled her way in the door and cracked me on the side of the head with the butt of her gun. Damn, that hurt. And she did it not once, but twice." Pops gently patted the side of his head.

"Mildred happen to tell you what she wanted and why?" Lucas asked him. I didn't blame him; I also wanted to know more about the lunatic's plans.

"Crazy broad had a jones for her ex. She needed his money to support her lifestyle and wouldn't get any if they divorced, so she thought murdering him was the next best option; that way, she'd inherit it all," Pops told him. "Tried to tell her that if he had any family, they'd fight her tooth and nail, even if they were still married when he died. Nothing like splitting up money to get people to fighting. She didn't want to hear it — she'd cooked up a plan in that pea brain of hers and couldn't be made to listen." He turned to me. "She had a real jones on for you too, certain that you'd found the ex and were holding out. I insisted you wouldn't do such a thing, but she wasn't listening. The woman never did."

Floyd shot him a sharp glance at that last. "I take it that this is indeed the same Mildred you used to know?"

"Yeah, can you believe it?" Pops nodded. "Should have known she was nuts when she wanted to leap straight to marriage. There was only one woman for me, and I had no intention of marrying again after my wife died."

I stepped over to him and hugged him. "I knew Caturday showing up at your office wasn't a fluke, as it didn't make any sense."

The ambulance pulled up, and two paramedics

got out and came up the driveway with their bags and a stretcher. Lucas met them, and after a short conversation, they had Pops sit and checked him out. The next thing I knew, they were helping him lie down on the stretcher, strapping him down, and rolling him to the ambulance.

I ran after them. "Where are you taking him?"

"Holy Cross—he needs a couple of x-rays," one told me.

"I'm right behind you." I kissed Pops' cheek. "Behave yourself."

He winked before they loaded him into the ambulance and took off.

I went back to Lucas. Before I could ask anything, he spoke up. "Floyd will drive you to the hospital. I know where to find you if I have any questions, but I don't think that will be necessary. Thank you for helping stop that woman, even though it didn't end quite how we wanted."

I ran to my SUV and grabbed my purse. Then Floyd helped me into his truck, and we were off to the hospital.

"Do you think—"

Floyd cut me off. "Whatever you're worrying about, you can stop. When we get to the hospital, you're going to find out that your Pops has a hard head."

# Chapter Thirty-Eight

A month had gone by, and I'd gone back to my old routine. Pops had decided to sell North Investigations to WD, and a party was planned to celebrate the deal. Not some bash at the office—no, it was going to be held on a yacht docked in Miami. Seven's family was in the yacht-selling business, and in addition, they had several they rented out for parties and special occasions. What did one wear to a party on a yacht? The question plagued me until I finally gave up, went online, and just bought a spaghetti-strap linen dress I thought was the right amount of casual and dressy, which I paired with sandals.

Floyd and I had become almost inseparable, always finding time for something fun in between his assignments. Our favorite thing to do was ride bicycles on the beach.

On the day of the party, Floyd was late finishing up a job and came to my house to shower and change. We got on the road and headed south and, once off the freeway, could see the sun flickering off the waters of Biscayne Bay in the distance. It looked like a busy day for boats cruising around.

Floyd turned into a large parking lot and easily

found a space, and we made our way down the dock to the end, where a white two-story yacht was parked. There were a number of people gathered on the top deck, and a couple of the men catcalled and waved to Floyd.

"Looking forward to meeting your friends." I snuggled closer to him.

"Every one of them thinks they're a comedian." Floyd waved back. "Called Max a couple of times to offer him a ride, but the stubborn goat insisted he'd drive himself."

I chuckled. "He must've been frustrated, as I also called and suggested the same thing."

Floyd grabbed my hand as we climbed onboard, and after a brief tour of the main floor, we went up the stairs to the second level, where the unobstructed view of the water was breathtaking. Along with a pool and plenty of seating, this level also had a bar and bartender, who was busy mixing drinks. More people yelled and called our names as Floyd led us to where Pops sat at a large table with Grey, Seven, Pryce, and their wives, Harper, Avery, and Rella.

"Have you been behaving?" I kissed Pops' cheek and returned his flinty stare.

"That doesn't sound like a bit of fun," he grumped.

A server came and took our drink order, noting everyone who needed refills.

Soon, Lucas showed up with two officers I recognized, and the three took a seat.

I smiled and waved. "Can't thank you guys enough for stopping Caturday. Happy that none of you got hurt."

"We're all good," Lucas assured me. "Old Cat got the last laugh, sort of. Since she was still married to Herbie Brogan, he got the call to claim the body. I'd had a conversation with him after her death, so he had my number and called me, totally peeved. I suggested an inexpensive send-off and be done with it."

"I thought he asked if it was legal to feed her remains to local wildlife," Seven said with a smirk.

"I told him to check with the county, as you damn well know," Lucas reminded him, humor in his eyes.

"Now there's an option," Avery said, appearing to mull the idea over. "Can you imagine being the employee to get that call?"

"Hold on while I look that up," I said, mimicking an older female phone operator's voice, which garnered laughs.

Our drinks arrived. When my margarita was set down in front of me, I eyed it with a smile. "Whatever happened with the stolen bicycles?" I asked Lucas.

"Sorry about that; forgot to update you," Floyd whispered.

I squeezed his hand.

"That was a cluster. Couple of my guys staked it out, and nothing. It wasn't enough of a priority for the stake-out to go on indefinitely, so we went in and cleaned it out. None of the bikes had registration numbers, so pics were posted on our social media, but we didn't get a single call. After the holding period expires, they'll get sold. Livia got Hugo's guys to go in and check out the building, and they discovered two cameras. Based on that, we figured the thieves knew we were onto them and weren't coming back. Due to the lack of sophistication, I'd figured it was some neighborhood kids, but the cameras made me rethink that assumption."

The guys threw questions at Lucas, which he answered with a shrug.

*Another round or… maybe I should slow down.*

Grey stood and got everyone's attention. "Thank you for coming." He raised his glass, and everyone else followed suit. "As you all know, Maxwell North sold me his building in Ft. Lauderdale, and within the next couple of months, we'll be expanding WD." Everyone toasted and gave Grey a round of applause.

"I sold off all but a small portion, which I'm leaving to you, so know that it's not too late for you to become a licensed PI," Pops said, staring at me.

I gave him a dramatic eyeroll, which resulted in a couple of chuckles, but several people were clearly waiting to see what I'd say.

"Maren's happy with her voiceover work, which she's damn good at." Floyd flung his arm around me. "She's going to be one of the voices in a children's cartoon coming out soon." He glared at Pops, who laughed at him.

"So, this means I get to show up at the office and tell everyone what to do?" I asked. "I'm thinking I should bring donuts or key lime pie."

"Both." Seven licked his lips and raised his glass to me. "You'll be the most popular person in the office."

"Appreciate the plaque you had made for me," Pops said to me. "When Grey walked me around and talked about the changes he'd be making, he showed me where he planned to hang it. It's going to be fancy."

"I'm happy this deal worked out." I lifted my glass, ready for a refill. "Just know that if you need someone to answer the phone or… I'm only a phone call away. Seriously, the best part will be staying in touch with all of you."

"Thank you for paving the way," Grey said, and Seven nodded.

"Maxwell North," a female voice shrieked.

"I thought you'd been behaving," I whispered to Pops, who shrugged. It was clear he didn't know who the woman was or what was going on.

Harper beckoned the older woman over and introduced Pops to Jean Winters.

"I prefer to be called Gram; don't care if we're not relations."

"Heard you like fix-ups—" Harper patted Pops' cheek. "—so, I thought you might like one of your own."

His cheeks turned bright red.

I laughed, eager to see what happened next, and everyone around the table had stopped talking, also waiting.

"Buy me a drink." Gram tugged on Pops' arm. "Easier to talk without all these gawkers." He rose, and the two walked off.

"Surprised he went with her." I stared after them. "Did you outfit your Gram with a camera?" I asked Harper.

"I tried…" She sighed. "Told me I was too snoopy for my own good, as if there is such a thing."

I struggled not to laugh.

Avery and Rella groaned. "Gram is a force to be reckoned with, and based on her shifty smile, she's up to something," Rella said, and it was clear she'd been in the woman's sights in the past.

"Gram's always up to something." Avery winced. "Try telling her no. She never listens."

"She looks sweet to me," I said.

They all laughed, conveying, *you'll find out the hard way.*

"Is someone going to go rescue his butt?" Floyd asked.

"Not as long as Harper can promise that nothing bad will happen…" I pointed to Harper, including Avery and Rella.

"No worries. Gram's not crazy… She is, but not out of her mind," Harper said.

"You know that if anything goes south, I'll get the blame." I grinned. "And while Pops is going off in that blustery way of his, I'm just going to laugh."

*~*

## PARADISE SERIES

Crazy in Paradise
Deception in Paradise
Trouble in Paradise
Murder in Paradise
Greed in Paradise
Revenge in Paradise
Kidnapped in Paradise
Swindled in Paradise
Executed in Paradise
Hurricane in Paradise
Lottery in Paradise
Ambushed in Paradise
Christmas in Paradise
Blownup in Paradise
Psycho in Paradise
Overdose in Paradise
Initiation in Paradise
Jealous in Paradise
Wronged in Paradise
Vanished in Paradise
Fraud in Paradise
Naïve in Paradise
Bodies in Paradise
Accused in Paradise
Deceit in Paradise
Escaped in Paradise
Fear in Paradise

Available on Amazon
amazon.com/dp/B074CDKKKZ

## BISCAYNE BAY SERIES

Hired Killer
Not guilty
Jilted


Available on Amazon

amazon.com/dp/B09BRFYYYN

## About the Author

Deborah Brown is an Amazon bestselling author of the Paradise series. She lives on the Gulf of Mexico, with her ungrateful animals, where Mother Nature takes out her bad attitude in the form of hurricanes.

For a free short story, sign up for my newsletter.
It will also keep you up-to-date with
new releases and special promotions:
www.deborahbrownbooks.com

Follow on FaceBook:
facebook.com/DeborahBrownAuthor

Join private Facebook group:
Deborah Brown's Paradise Fan Club:
facebook.com/groups/1580456012034195

You can contact her at Wildcurls@hotmail.com

Deborah's books are available on Amazon

amazon.com/Deborah-Brown/e/B0059MAIKQ

Made in the USA
Monee, IL
15 December 2022